SOMETHING

TO

REMEMBER

ME

BY

_____

ALSO BY SAUL BELLOW

The Bellarosa Connection
A Theft
More Die of Heartbreak
Him with His Foot in His Mouth and Other Stories
The Dean's December
To Jerusalem and Back: A Personal Account
Humboldt's Gift
Mr. Sammler's Planet
Mosby's Memoirs and Other Stories
Herzog
Henderson the Rain King
Seize the Day
The Adventures of Augie March
The Victim
Dangling Man

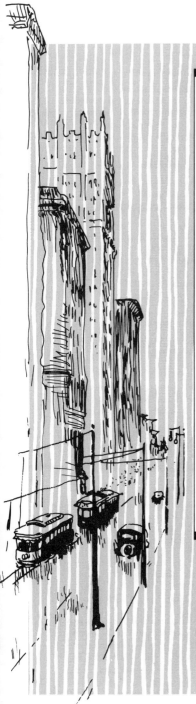

SOMETHING

TO

REMEMBER

ME

BY

THREE TALES BY
SAUL BELLOW

VIKING

VIKING
Published by the Penguin Group
Viking Penguin, a division of Penguin Books USA Inc.,
375 Hudson Street, New York, New York 10014, U.S.A.
Penguin Books Ltd, 27 Wrights Lane, London W8 5TZ, England
Penguin Books Australia Ltd, Ringwood, Victoria, Australia
Penguin Books Canada Ltd, 2801 John Street, Markham, Ontario, Canada L3R 1B4
Penguin Books (N.Z.) Ltd, 182–190 Wairau Road, Auckland 10, New Zealand

Penguin Books Ltd, Registered Offices: Harmondsworth, Middlesex, England

This volume first published in 1991 by Viking Penguin,
a division of Penguin Books USA Inc.
Published simultaneously in an NAL /Signet edition

1 3 5 7 9 10 8 6 4 2

A Theft first published in Penguin Books 1989
Copyright © Saul Bellow, 1989

The Bellarosa Connection first published in Penguin Books 1989
Copyright © Saul Bellow, 1989

Something to Remember Me By first published in *Esquire* magazine 1990
Copyright © Saul Bellow, 1990

PUBLISHER'S NOTE
These are works of fiction. Names, characters, places, and incidents either
are the product of the author's imagination or are used fictitiously, and
resemblance to actual persons, living or dead, events, or locales is entirely
coincidental.

LIBRARY OF CONGRESS CATALOGING-IN-PUBLICATION DATA
Bellow, Saul.
Something to remember me by: three tales / by Saul Bellow.
p. cm.
Includes bibliographical references.
Contents: The Bellarosa connection—A theft—Something to remember me by.
ISBN 0-670-84216-8
I. Title.
PS3503.E4488S66 1991
813'.52—dc20   91-51059

Printed in the United States of America
Set in Bembo
Designed by Fritz Metsch

FOREWORD

A Japanese sage—I forget his name—told his disciples, "Write as short as you can." Sydney Smith, an English clergyman and wit of the last century, also spoke out for brevity: "Short views, for God's sake, short views!" he said. And Miss Ferguson, the lively spinster who was my composition teacher in Chicago some sixty years ago, would dance before the class, clap her hands, and chant (her music borrowed from Handel's "Hallelujah" Chorus):

> Be
> speci—
> fic!

Miss Ferguson would not put up with redundancy, prolixity, periphrasis, or bombast. She taught us to stick to the necessary and avoid the superfluous. Did I heed her warnings, follow her teaching? Not absolutely, I'm afraid, for in my early years I wrote more than one fat book. It's difficult for me now to read those early novels, not because they lack interest but because I find myself editing them, slimming down my sentences and cutting whole paragraphs.

Men who loved stout women used to say (how long ago *that* was!), "You can't have too much of a good thing."

Everyone does understand, however, that a good thing can be overdone. Those devoted men, it should be added, didn't invent the obese ladies whom they loved; they discovered them.

Some of our greatest novels are very thick. Fiction is a loose popular art, and many of the classic novelists get their effects by heaping up masses of words. Decades ago, Somerset Maugham was inspired to publish pared-down versions of some of the very best. His experiment didn't succeed. Something went out of the books when their bulk was reduced. It would be mad to edit a novel like *Little Dorrit*. That sea of words *is* a sea, a force of nature. We want it that way, ample, capable of breeding life. When its amplitude tires us we readily forgive it. We wouldn't want it any other way.

Yet we respond with approval when Chekhov tells us, "Odd, I have now a mania for shortness. Whatever I read— my own or other people's works—it all seems to me not short enough." I find myself emphatically agreeing with this. There is a modern taste for brevity and condensation. Kafka, Beckett, and Borges wrote short. People of course do write long, and write successfully, but to write short is felt by a growing public to be a very good thing—perhaps the best. At once a multitude of possible reasons for this feeling comes to mind: This is the end of the millennium. We have heard it all. We have no time. We have more significant fish to fry. We require a wider understanding, new terms, a deeper penetration.

Of course, to obtain attention is harder than it used to be. The more leisure we have, the stiffer the competition for eyes and ears and mental space. On the front page of this morning's national edition of *The New York Times*, Michael Jackson, with hundreds of millions of fans worldwide, has signed a new contract worth a billion with Sony Software "to create feature films, theatrical shorts, television programming and a new record label for the Japanese conglomerate's American entertainment subsidiaries." Writers do not have such expectations and are not directly affected by the entertainment world. What is of interest to us here is that these are facts involving multitudes, that the news is commented upon by a leading "communications analyst," and that the article is continued in the Living Arts section of the paper, where the Trump divorce is also prominently featured, together with the usual television stuff, bridge, gardening, and Paris fashions. A new novel is reviewed on page B2.

I don't want to be understood as saying that writers should be concerned about the existence of these other publics.

There is a wonderful Daumier caricature of a bluestocking, a severe lady stormily looking through the newspaper at a café table. "Nothing but sports, snipe-hunting. And not a single word about my novel!" she complains.

What I do say is that we (we writers, I mean) must cope with a plethora of attractions and excitements—world crises, hot and cold wars, threats to survival, famines, unspeakable crimes. To conceive of these as "rivals" would be absurd—even monstrous. I say no more than that these crises produce states of mind and attitudes toward existence that artists must take into account.

The subject is not an easy one. I shall try to make a new beginning: Years ago Robert Frost and I exchanged signed copies. I gave him a novel respectfully dedicated. He signed a copy of his collected poems for me, adding, "To read if I will read him." A great tease, Frost. He couldn't promise to read my novel. I already knew his poems. You couldn't get a high school certificate in Chicago without memorizing "Mending Wall." What Frost hinted, perhaps, was that my novel might not stand high on his list of priorities. Why should he read mine, why not another? And why should I read *his* poems? I had my choice of dozens of other poets.

It's perfectly plain that we are astray in forests of printed matter. The daily papers are thick. Giant newsstands are virtually thatched with magazines. As for books—well, the English scholar F. L. Lucas wrote in the fifties: "With nearly twenty thousand volumes published yearly in Britain alone, there is a danger of good books, both new and old, being buried under the bad. If the process went on indefinitely we should finally be pushed into the sea by our libraries. Yet there are few of these books that might not at least be shorter, and all the better for being shorter; and most of them could, I believe, be most effectively shortened, not by cutting out whole chapters but by purging their sentences of useless words and paragraphs of their useless sentences." Answer the problem of quantity with improved quality— a touching idea, but Utopian. Too late, thirty years ago we had already been pushed into the sea.

The modern reader (or viewer, or listener: let's include everybody) is perilously overloaded. His attention is, to use the latest lingo, "targeted" by powerful forces. I hate to make lists of these forces, but I suppose that some of them had better be mentioned. Okay, then: automobile and pharmaceutical giants, cable TV, politicians, entertainers, academics, opinion makers, porn videos, Ninja Turtles, et cetera. The list is tedious because it is an inventory of what is put into our heads day in, day out. Our consciousness is a staging area, a field of operations for all kinds of enterprises, which make free use of it. True, we are at liberty to think our own thoughts, but our independent ideas, such as they may be, must live with thousands of ideas and notions inculcated by influential teachers or floated by "idea men," advertisers, communications people, columnists, anchormen, et cetera. Better-regulated (educated) minds are less easily overcome by these gas clouds of opinion. But no one can have an easy time of it. In all fields we are forced to seek special instruction, expert guidance to the interpretation of the seeming facts we are stuffed with. This is in itself a full-time occupation. A part of every mind, perhaps the major portion, is open to public matters. Without being actively conscious of it we somehow keep track of the Middle East, Japan, South Africa, reunified Germany, oil, munitions, the New York subways, the homeless, the markets, the banks, the major leagues, news from Washington; and also, pell-mell, films, trials, medical discoveries, rap groups, racial clashes, congressional scandals, the spread of AIDS, child murders—a crowd of horrors. Public life in the United States is a mass of distractions.

By some this is seen as a challenge to their ability to maintain internal order. Others have acquired a taste for distraction, and they freely consent to be addled. It may even seem to many that by being agitated they are satisfying the claims of society. The scope of the disorder can even be oddly flattering: "Just look—this tremendous noisy frantic monstrous agglomeration. There's never been anything like it. And we are *it*! This is *us*!"

Vast organizations exist to get our attention. They make cunning plans. They bite us with their ten-second bites. Our consciousness is their staple; they live on it. Think of consciousness as a territory just opening to settlement and exploitation, something like an Oklahoma land rush. Put it in color, set it to music, frame it in images—but even this fails to do justice to the vision. Obviously consciousness is infinitely bigger than Oklahoma.

Now what of writers? They materialize, somehow, and they ask the public (more accurately, *a* public) for its attention. Perhaps the writer has no actual public in mind. Often his only assumption is that he participates in a state of psychic unity with others not distinctly known to him. The mental condition of these others is understood by him, for it is his condition also. One way or another he understands, or intuits, what the effort, often a secret and hidden effort to put the distracted consciousness in order, is costing. These unidentified or partially identified others are his readers. They have been waiting for him. He must assure them immediately that reading him will be worth their while. They have many times been cheated by writers who promised good value but delivered nothing. Their attention has been abused. Nevertheless they long to give it. In his diaries Kafka says of a certain woman, "She holds herself by force below the level of her true human destiny and requires only . . . a tearing open of the door. . . ."

The reader will open his heart and mind to a writer who has understood this—has understood because in his person he has gone through it all, has experienced the same privations; who knows where the sore spots are; who has discerned the power of the need to come back to the level of one's true human destiny. Such a writer will trouble no one with his own vanities, will make no unnecessary gestures, indulge himself in no mannerisms, waste no reader's time. He will write as short as he can.

I offer this as a brief introduction to the stories in this volume.

THE

BELLAROSA

CONNECTION

———

TO MY DEAR FRIEND

JOHN AUERBACH

———————

As founder of the Mnemosyne Institute in Philadelphia, forty years in the trade, I trained many executives, politicians, and members of the defense establishment, and now that I am retired, with the Institute in the capable hands of my son, I would like to *forget* about remembering. Which is an Alice-in-Wonderland proposition. In your twilight years, having hung up your gloves (or sheathed your knife), you don't want to keep doing what you did throughout your life: a change, a change—your kingdom for a change! A lawyer will walk away from his clients, a doctor from his patients, a general will paint china, a diplomatist turn to fly-fishing. My case is different in that I owe my worldly success to the innate gift of memory—a tricky word, "innate," referring to the hidden sources of everything that really matters. As I used to say to clients, "Memory is life." That was a neat way to impress a member of the National Security Council whom I was coaching, but it puts me now in an uncomfortable position because if you have worked in memory, which is life itself, there is no retirement except in death.

There are other discomforts to reckon with: This gift of mine became the foundation of a commercial success—an income from X millions soundly invested and an antebellum house in Philadelphia furnished by my late wife, a woman who knew everything there was to know about eighteenth-century furniture. Since I am not one of your stubborn defensive rationalizers who deny that they misuse their talents and insist that they can face God with a clear conscience, I force myself to remember that I was not born in a Philadelphia house with twenty-foot ceilings but began life as the child of Russian Jews from New Jersey. A walking memory file like me can't trash his beginnings or distort his early history. Sure, in the universal process of self revision anybody can be carried away from the true facts. For instance, Europeanized Americans in Europe will assume a false English or French correctness and bring a disturbing edge of self-consciousness into their relations with their friends. I have observed this. It makes an unpleasant impression. So whenever I was tempted to fake it, I asked myself, "And how are things out in New Jersey?"

The matters that concern me now had their moving axis in New Jersey. These are not data from the memory bank of a computer. I am preoccupied with feelings and longings, and emotional memory is nothing like rocketry or gross national products. What we have before us are the late Harry Fonstein and his late wife, Sorella. My pictures of them are probably too clear and pleasing to be true. Therefore they have to be represented pictorially first and then *wiped out and reconstituted*. But these are technical considerations, having to do with the difference between literal and affective recollection.

If you were living in a house of such dimensions, among armoires, hangings, Persian rugs, sideboards, carved fireplaces, ornamented ceilings—with a closed garden and a bathtub on a marble dais fitted with a faucet that would not be out of place in the Trevi Fountain—you would better understand why the recollection of a refugee like Fonstein and his Newark wife might become significant.

No, he, Fonstein, wasn't a poor schlepp; he succeeded in business and made a fair amount of dough. Nothing like my Philadelphia millions, but not bad for a guy who arrived after the war via Cuba and got a late start in the heating business—and, moreover, a gimpy Galitzianer. Fonstein wore an orthopedic shoe, and there were other peculiarities: His hair looked thin, but it was anything but weak, it was a strong black growth, and although sparse it was vividly kinky. The head itself was heavy enough to topple a less determined man. His eyes were dark and they were warm, so perhaps it was their placement that made them look shrewd as well. Perhaps it was the expression of his mouth—not severe, not even unkind—which worked together with the dark eyes. You got a smart inspection from this immigrant.

We were not related by blood. Fonstein was the nephew of my stepmother, whom I called Aunt Mildred (a euphemistic courtesy—I was far too old for mothering when my widower father married her). Most of Fonstein's family were killed by the Germans. In Auschwitz he would have been gassed immediately, because of the orthopedic boot. Some Dr. Mengele would have pointed his swagger stick to the left, and Fonstein's boot might by now have been on view in the camp's exhibition hall—they have a hill of cripple boots there, and a hill of crutches and of back braces and one of human hair and one of eyeglasses. Objects that might have been useful in German hospitals or homes.

Harry Fonstein and his mother, Aunt Mildred's sister, had escaped from Poland. Somehow they had reached Italy. In Ravenna there were refugee relatives, who helped as well as they could. The heat was on Italian Jews too, since Mussolini had adopted the Nuremberg racial laws. Fonstein's mother, who was a diabetic, soon died, and Fonstein went on to Milan, traveling with phony papers while learning Italian as fast as he was able. My father, who had a passion for refugee stories, told me all this. He hoped it would straighten me out to hear what people had suffered in Europe, in the real world.

"I want you to see Mildred's nephew," my old man said to me in Lakewood, New Jersey, about forty years ago. "Just a young fellow, maybe younger than you. Got away from the Nazis, dragging one foot. He's just off the boat from Cuba. Not long married."

I was at the bar of paternal judgment again, charged with American puerility. When would I shape up, at last! At the age of thirty-two, I still behaved like a twelve-year-old, hanging out in Greenwich Village, immature, drifting, a layabout, shacking up with Bennington girls, a foolish intellectual gossip, nothing in his head but froth—the founder, said my father with comic bewilderment, of the Mnemosyne Institute, about as profitable as it was pronounceable.

As my Village pals liked to say, it cost no more than twelve hundred dollars a year to be poor—or to play at poverty, yet another American game.

Surviving-Fonstein, with all the furies of Europe at his back, made me look bad. But he wasn't to blame for that, and his presence actually made my visits easier. It was only on the odd Sunday that I paid my respects to the folks at home in green Lakewood, near Lakehurst, where in the thirties the Graf Hindenburg Zeppelin had gone up in flames as it approached its fatal mooring mast, and the screams of the dying could be heard on the ground.

Fonstein and I took turns at the chessboard with my father, who easily beat us both—listless competitors who had the architectural weight of Sunday on our caryatid heads. Sorella Fonstein sometimes sat on the sofa, which had a transparent zippered plastic cover. Sorella was a New Jersey girl—correction: lady. She was very heavy and she wore makeup. Her cheeks were downy. Her hair was done up in a beehive. A pince-nez, highly unusual, a deliberate disguise, gave her a theatrical air. She was still a novice then, trying on these props. Her aim was to achieve an authoritative, declarative manner. However, she was no fool.

Fonstein's place of origin was Lemberg, I think. I wish I had more patience with maps. I can visualize continents and the outlines of countries, but I'm antsy about exact locations. Lemberg is now Lvov, as Danzig is Gdansk. I never was strong in geography. My main investment was in memory. As an undergraduate showing off at parties, I would store up and reel off lists of words fired at me by a circle of twenty people. Hence I can tell you more than you will want to know about Fonstein. In 1938 his father, a jeweler, didn't survive the confiscation by the Germans of his investments (valuable property) in Vienna. When the war had broken out, with Nazi paratroopers dressed as nuns spilling from planes, Fonstein's sister and her husband hid in the countryside, and both were caught and ended in the camps. Fonstein and his mother escaped to Zagreb and eventually got to Ravenna. It was in the north of Italy that Mrs. Fonstein died, and she was buried in a Jewish cemetery, perhaps the Venetian one. Then and there Fonstein's adolescence came to an end. A refugee with an orthopedic boot, he had to consider his moves carefully. "He couldn't vault over walls like Douglas Fairbanks," said Sorella.

I could see why my father took to Fonstein. Fonstein had survived the greatest ordeal of Jewish history. He still looked as if the worst, even now, would not take him by surprise. The impression he gave was unusually firm. When he spoke to you he engaged your look and held it. This didn't encourage small talk. Still, there were hints of wit at the corners of his mouth and around the eyes. So you didn't want to play the fool with Fonstein. I sized him up as a Central European Jewish type. He saw me, probably, as an immature unstable Jewish American, humanly ignorant and loosely kind: in the history of civilization, something new in the way of human types, perhaps not so bad as it looked at first.

To survive in Milan he had to learn Italian pretty damn quick. So as not to waste time, he tried to arrange to speak it even in his dreams. Later, in Cuba, he acquired Spanish too. He was gifted that way. In New Jersey he soon was fluent in English, though to humor me he spoke Yiddish now and then; it was the right language for his European experiences. I had had a tame war myself—company clerk in the Aleutians. So I listened, stooped over him (like a bishop's crook; I had six or eight inches on him), for he was the one who had seen real action.

In Milan he did kitchen work, and in Turin he was a hall porter and shined shoes. By the time he got to Rome he was an assistant concierge. Before long he was working on the Via Veneto. The city was full of Germans, and as Fonstein's German was good, he was employed as an interpreter now and then. He was noticed by Count Ciano, Mussolini's son-in-law and foreign minister.

"So you knew him?"

"Yes, but he didn't know me, not by name. When he gave a party and needed extra translators, I was sent for. There was a reception for Hitler—"

"You mean you saw Hitler?"

"My little boy says it that way too: 'My daddy saw Adolf Hitler.' Hitler was at the far end of the *grande salle*."

"Did he give a speech?"

"Thank God I wasn't close by. Maybe he made a statement. He ate some pastry. He was in military uniform."

"Yes, I've seen pictures of him on company manners, acting sweet."

"One thing," said Fonstein. "There was no color in his face."

"He wasn't killing anybody that day."

"There was nobody he couldn't kill if he liked, but this was a reception. I was happy he didn't notice me."

"I think I would have been grateful too," I said. "You can even feel love for somebody who can kill you but doesn't. Horrible love, but it is a kind of love."

"He would have gotten around to me. My trouble began with this reception. A police check was run, my papers were fishy, and that's why I was arrested."

My father, absorbed in his knights and rooks, didn't look up, but Sorella Fonstein, sitting in state as obese ladies seem to do, took off her pince-nez (she had been copying a recipe) and said, probably because her husband needed help at this point in his story, "He was locked up."

"Yes, I see."

"You *can't* see," said my stepmother. "Nobody could guess who saved him."

Sorella, who had been a teacher in the Newark school system, made a teacherly gesture. She raised her arm as though to mark a check on the blackboard beside a student's sentence. "Here comes the strange element. This is where Billy Rose plays a part."

I said, "Billy Rose, in Rome? What would he be doing there? Are we talking about Broadway Billy Rose? You mean Damon Runyon's pal, the guy who married Fanny Brice?"

"He can't believe it," said my stepmother.

In Fascist Rome, the child of her sister, her own flesh and blood, had seen Hitler at a reception. He was put in prison. There was no hope for him. Roman Jews were then being trucked to caves outside the city and shot. But he was saved by a New York celebrity.

"You're telling me," I said, "that Billy was running an underground operation in Rome?"

"For a while, yes, he had an Italian organization," said

Sorella. Just then I needed an American intermediary. The range of Aunt Mildred's English was limited. Besides, she was a dull lady, slow in all her ways, totally unlike my hasty, vivid father. Mildred had a powdered look, like her own strudel. Her strudel was the best. But when she talked to you she lowered her head. She too had a heavy head. You saw her parted hair oftener than her face.

"Billy Rose did good things too," she said, nursing her fingers in her lap. On Sundays she wore a green, beaded dark dress.

"*That* character! I can't feature it. The Aquacade man? He saved you from the Roman cops?"

"From the Nazis." My stepmother again lowered her head when she spoke. It was her dyed and parted hair that I had to interpret.

"How did you find this out?" I asked Fonstein.

"I was in a cell by myself. Those years, every jail in Europe was full, I guess. Then one day, a stranger showed up and talked to me through the grille. You know what? I thought maybe Ciano sent him. It came in my mind because this Ciano could have asked for me at the hotel. Sure he dressed in fancy uniforms and walked around with his hand on a long knife he carried in his belt. He was a playactor, but I thought he was civilized. He was pleasant. So when the man stood by the grille and looked at me, I went over and said, 'Ciano?' He shook one finger back and forth and said, 'Billy Rose.' I had no idea what he meant. Was it one word or two? A man or a woman? The message from this Italianer was: 'Tomorrow night, same time, your door will be open. Go out in the corridor. Keep turning left. And nobody will stop you. A person will be waiting in a car, and he'll take you to the train for Genoa.' "

"Why, that little operator! Billy had an underground all to himself," I said. "He must've seen Leslie Howard in *The Scarlet Pimpernel*."

"Next night, the guard didn't lock my door after supper, and when the corridor was empty I came out. I felt as if I had whiskey in my legs, but I realized they were holding me for deportation, the SS was at work already, so I opened every door, walked upstairs, downstairs, and when I got to the street there was a car waiting and people leaning on it, speaking in normal voices. When I came up, the driver pushed me in the back and drove me to the Trastevere station. He gave me new identity papers. He said nobody would be looking for me, because my whole police file had been stolen. There was a hat and coat for me in the rear seat, and he gave me the name of a hotel in Genoa, by the waterfront. That's where I was contacted. I had passage on a Swedish ship to Lisbon."

Europe could go to hell without Fonstein.

My father looked at us sidelong with those keen eyes of his. He had heard the story many times.

I came to know it too. I got it in episodes, like a Hollywood serial—the Saturday thriller, featuring Harry Fonstein and Billy Rose, or Bellarosa. For Fonstein, in Genoa, while he was hiding in great fear in a waterfront hotel, had no other name for him. During the voyage, nobody on the refugee ship had ever heard of Bellarosa.

When the ladies were in the kitchen and my father was in the den, reading the Sunday paper, I would ask Fonstein for further details of his adventures (his torments). He couldn't have known what mental files they were going into or that they were being cross-referenced with Billy Rose— one of those insignificant-significant characters whose name will be recognized chiefly by show-biz historians. The late Billy, the business partner of Prohibition hoodlums, the sidekick of Arnold Rothstein; multimillionaire Billy, the protégé of Bernard Baruch, the young shorthand prodigy whom Woodrow Wilson, mad for shorthand, invited to the White House for a discussion of the rival systems of Pitman and Gregg; Billy the producer, the consort of Eleanor Holm, the mermaid queen of the New York World's Fair; Billy the collector of Matisse, Seurat, and so forth . . . nationally syndicated Billy, the gossip columnist. A Village pal of mine was a member of his ghostwriting team.

This was the Billy to whom Harry Fonstein owed his life.

I spoke of this ghostwriter—Wolfe was his name—and thereafter Fonstein may have considered me a possible channel to Billy himself. He never had met Billy, you see. Apparently Billy refused to be thanked by the Jews his Broadway underground had rescued.

The Italian agents who had moved Fonstein from place to place wouldn't talk. The Genoa man referred to Bellarosa but answered none of Fonstein's questions. I assume that Mafia people from Brooklyn had put together Billy's Italian operation. After the war, Sicilian gangsters were decorated by the British for their work in the Resistance. Fonstein said that with Italians, when they had secrets to keep, tiny muscles came out in the face that nobody otherwise saw. "The man lifted up his hands as if he was going to steal a shadow off the wall and stick it in his pocket." Yesterday a hit man, today working against the Nazis.

Fonstein's type was *edel*—well-bred—but he also was a tough Jew. Sometimes his look was that of a man holding the lead in the hundred-meter breast-stroke race. Unless you shot him, he was going to win. He had something in common with his Mafia saviors, whose secrets convulsed their faces.

During the crossing he thought a great deal about the person who had had him smuggled out of Italy, imagining various kinds of philanthropists and idealists ready to spend their last buck to rescue their people from Treblinka.

"How was I supposed to guess what kind of man—or maybe a committee, the Bellarosa Society—did it?"

No, it was Billy acting alone on a spurt of feeling for his fellow Jews and squaring himself to outwit Hitler and Himmler and cheat them of their victims. On another day he'd set his heart on a baked potato, a hot dog, a cruise around Manhattan on the Circle Line. There were, however, spots of deep feeling in flimsy Billy. The God of his fathers still mattered. Billy was as spattered as a Jackson Pollock painting, and among the main trickles was his Jewishness, with other streaks flowing toward secrecy—streaks of sexual weakness, sexual humiliation. At the same time, he had to have his name in the paper. As someone said, he had a buglike tropism for publicity. Yet his rescue operation in Europe remained secret.

Fonstein, one of the refugee crowd sailing to New York, wondered how many others among the passengers might have been saved by Billy. Nobody talked much. Experienced people begin at a certain point to keep their own counsel and refrain from telling their stories to one another. Fonstein was eaten alive by his fantasies of what he would do in New York. He said that at night when the ship rolled he was like a weighted rope, twisting and untwisting. He expected that Billy, if he had saved scads of people, would have laid plans for their future too. Fonstein didn't foresee that they would gather together and cry like Joseph and his brethren. Nothing like that. No, they would be put up in hotels or maybe in an old sanitarium, or boarded with charitable families. Some would want to go to Palestine; most would opt for the U.S.A. and study English, perhaps finding jobs in industry or going to technical schools.

But Fonstein was detained at Ellis Island. Refugees were not being admitted then. "They fed us well," he told me. "I slept in a wire bin, on an upper bunk. I could see Manhattan. They told me, though, that I'd have to go to Cuba. I still didn't know who Billy was, but I waited for his help.

"And after a few weeks a woman was sent by Rose Productions to talk to me. She dressed like a young girl—lipstick, high heels, earrings, a hat. She had legs like posts and looked like an actress from the Yiddish theater, about ready to begin to play older roles, disappointed and sad. She called herself a *dramatisten* and was in her fifties if not more. She said my case was being turned over to the Hebrew Immigrant Aid Society. They would take care of me. No more Billy Rose."

"You must have been shook up."

"Of course. But I was even more curious than dashed. I asked her about the man who rescued me. I said I would like to give Billy my thanks personally. She brushed this aside. Irrelevant. She said, 'After Cuba, maybe.' I saw that she doubted it would happen. I asked, did he help lots of people. She said, 'Sure he helps, but himself he helps first, and you should hear him scream over a dime.' He was very famous, he was rich, he owned the Ziegfeld building and was continually in the papers. What was he like? Tiny, greedy, smart. He underpaid the employees, and they were afraid of the boss. He dressed very well, and he was a Broadway character and sat all night in cafés. 'He can call up Governor Dewey and talk to him whenever he likes.'

"That was what she said. She said also, 'He pays me twenty-two bucks, and if I even hint a raise I'll be fired. So what then? Second Avenue is dead. For Yiddish radio there's a talent oversupply. If not for the boss, I'd fade away in the Bronx. Like this, at least I work on Broadway. But you're a greener, and to you it's all a blank.'

" 'If he hadn't saved me from deportation, I'd have ended like others in my family. I owe him my life.'

" 'Probably so,' she agreed.

" 'Wouldn't it be normal to be interested in a man you did that for? Or at least have a look, shake a hand, speak a word?'

" 'It would have *been* normal,' she said. 'Once.'

"I began to realize," said Fonstein, "that she was a sick person. I believe she had TB. It wasn't the face powder that made her so white. White was to her what yellow color is to a lemon. What I saw was not makeup—it was the Angel of Death. Tubercular people often are quick and nervous. Her name was Missus Hamet—*khomet* being the Yiddish word for a horse collar. She was from Galicia, like me. We had the same accent."

A Chinese singsong. Aunt Mildred had it too—comical to other Jews, uproarious in a Yiddish music hall.

" 'HIAS will get work for you in Cuba. They take terrific care of you fellas. Billy thinks the war is in a new stage. Roosevelt is for King Saud, and those Arabians hate Jews and keep the door to Palestine shut. That's why Rose changed his operations. He and his friends are now chartering ships for refugees. The Rumanian government will sell them to the Jews at fifty bucks a head, and there are seventy thousand of them. That's a lot of moola. Better hurry before the Nazis take over Rumania.' "

Fonstein said very reasonably, "I told her how useful I might be. I spoke four languages. But she was hardened to people pleading, ingratiating themselves with their lousy gratitude. Hey, it's an ancient routine," said Fonstein, standing on the four-inch sole of his laced boot. His hands were in his pockets and took no part in the eloquence of his shrug. His face was, briefly, like a notable face in a museum case, in a dark room, its pallor spotlighted so that the skin was stippled, a curious effect, like stony gooseflesh. Except that he was not on show for the brilliant deeds he had done. As men go, he was as plain as seltzer.

Billy didn't want his gratitude. First your suppliant takes you by the knees. Then he asks for a small loan. He wants a handout, a pair of pants, a pad to sleep in, a meal ticket, a bit of capital to go into business. One man's gratitude is poison to his benefactor. Besides, Billy was fastidious about persons. In principle they were welcome to his goodwill, but they drove him to hysteria when they put their moves on him.

"Never having set foot in Manhattan, I had no clue," said Fonstein. "Instead there were bizarre fantasies, but what good were those? New York is a collective fantasy of millions. There's just so much a single mind can do with it."

Mrs. Horsecollar (her people had had to be low-caste teamsters in the Old Country) warned Fonstein, "Billy doesn't want you to mention his name to HIAS."

"So how did I get to Ellis Island?"

"Make up what you like. Say that a married Italian woman loved you and stole money from her husband to buy papers for you. But no leaks on Billy."

Here my father told Fonstein, "I can mate you in five moves." My old man would have made a mathematician if he had been more withdrawn from human affairs. Only, his motive for concentrated thought was winning. My father wouldn't apply himself where there was no opponent to beat.

I have my own fashion of testing my powers. Memory is my field. But also my faculties are not what they once were. I haven't got Alzheimer's, *absit omen* or *nicht da gedacht*—no sticky matter on my recollection cells. But I am growing slower. Now who was the man that Fonstein had worked for in Havana? Once I had instant retrieval for such names. No electronic system was in it with me. Today I darken and grope occasionally. But thank God I get a reprieve—Fonstein's Cuban employer was Salkind, and Fonstein was his legman. All over South America there were Yiddish newspapers. In the Western Hemisphere, Jews were searching for surviving relatives and studying the published lists of names. Many DPs were dumped in the Caribbean and in Mexico. Fonstein quickly added Spanish and English to his Polish, German, Italian, and Yiddish. He took engineering courses in a night school instead of hanging out in bars or refugee cafés. To tourists, Havana was a holiday town for gambling, drinking, and whoring—an abortion center as well. Unhappy single girls came down from the States to end their love pregnancies. Others, more far-sighted, flew in to look among the refugees for husbands and wives. Find a spouse of a stable European background, a person schooled in suffering and endurance. Somebody who had escaped death. Women who found no takers in Baltimore, Kansas City, or Minneapolis, worthy girls to whom men never proposed, found husbands in Mexico, Honduras, and Cuba.

After five years, Fonstein's employer was prepared to vouch for him, and sent for Sorella, his niece. To imagine what Fonstein and Sorella saw in each other when they were introduced was in the early years beyond me. Whenever we met in Lakewood, Sorella was dressed in a suit. When she crossed her legs and he noted the volume of her underthighs, an American observer like me could, and would, picture the entire woman unclothed, and depending on his experience of life and his acquaintance with art, he might attribute her type to an appropriate painter. In my mental picture of Sorella I chose Rembrandt's Saskia over the nudes of Rubens. But then Fonstein, when he took off his surgical boot, was . . . well, he had imperfections too. So man and wife could forgive each other. I think my tastes would have been more like those of Billy Rose—water nymphs, Loreleis, or chorus girls. Eastern European men had more sober standards. In my father's place, I would have had to make the sign of the cross over Aunt Mildred's face while getting into bed with her—something exorcistic (farfetched) to take the curse off. But you see, I was not my father, I was his spoiled American son. Your stoical forebears took their lumps in bed. As for Billy, with his trousers and shorts at his ankles, chasing girls who had come to be auditioned, he would have done better with Mrs. Horsecollar. If he'd forgive her bagpipe udders and estuary leg veins, she'd forgive his unheroic privates, and they could pool their wretched mortalities and stand by each other for better or worse.

Sorella's obesity, her beehive coif, the preposterous pince-nez—a "lady" put-on—made me wonder: What *is* it with such people? Are they female impersonators, drag queens?

This was a false conclusion reached by a middle-class boy who considered himself an enlightened bohemian. I was steeped in the exciting sophistication of the Village.

I was altogether wrong, dead wrong about Sorella, but at the time my perverse theory found some support in Fonstein's story of his adventures. He told me how he had sailed from New York and gone to work for Salkind in Havana while learning Spanish together with English and studying refrigeration and heating in a night school. "Till I met an American girl, down there on a visit."

"You met Sorella. And you fell in love with her?"

He gave me a hard-edged Jewish look when I spoke of love. How do you distinguish among love, need, and prudence?

Deeply experienced people—this continually impresses me—will keep things to themselves. Which is all right for those who don't intend to go beyond experience. But Fonstein belonged to an even more advanced category, those who don't put such restraints on themselves and feel able to enter the next zone; in that next zone, their aim is to convert weaknesses and secrets into burnable energy. A first-class man subsists on the matter he destroys, just as the stars do. But I am going beyond Fonstein, needlessly digressing. Sorella wanted a husband, while Fonstein needed U.S. naturalization papers. *Mariage de convenance* was how I saw it.

It's always the falsest formulation that you're proudest of. Fonstein took a job in a New Jersey shop that subcontracted the manufacture of parts in the heating-equipment line. He did well there, a beaver for work, and made rapid progress in his sixth language. Before long he was driving a new Pontiac. Aunt Mildred said it was a wedding present from Sorella's family. "They are *so* relieved," Mildred told me. "A few years more, and Sorella would be too old for a baby." One child was what the Fonsteins had, a son, Gilbert. He was said to be a prodigy in mathematics and physics. Some years down the line, Fonstein consulted me about the boy's education. By then he had the money to send him to the best schools. Fonstein had improved and patented a thermostat, and with Sorella's indispensable help he became a rich man. She was a tiger wife. Without her, he was to tell me, there would have been no patent. "My company would have stolen me blind. I wouldn't be the man you're looking at today."

I then examined the Fonstein who stood before me. He was wearing an Italian shirt, a French necktie, and his orthopedic boot was British-made—bespoke on Jermyn Street. With that heel he might have danced the flamenco. How different from the crude Polish article, boorishly ill-made, in which he had hobbled across Europe and escaped from prison in Rome. *That* boot, as he dodged the Nazis, he had dreaded to take off, nights, for if it had been stolen he would have been caught and killed in his short-legged nakedness. The SS would not have bothered to drive him into a cattle car.

How pleased his rescuer, Billy Rose, should have been to see the Fonstein of today: the pink, white-collared Italian shirt, the Rue de Rivoli tie, knotted under Sorella's instruction, the easy hang of the imported suit, the good color of his face, which, no longer stone white, had the full planes and the color of a ripe pomegranate.

But Fonstein and Billy never actually met. Fonstein had made it his business to see Billy, but Billy was never to see Fonstein. Letters were returned. Sometimes there were accompanying messages, never once in Billy's own hand. Mr. Rose wished Harry Fonstein well but at the moment couldn't give him an appointment. When Fonstein sent Billy a check accompanied by a note of thanks and the request that the money be used for charitable purposes, it was returned without acknowledgment. Fonstein came to his office and was turned away. When he tried one day to approach Billy at Sardi's he was intercepted by one of the restaurant's personnel. You weren't allowed to molest celebrities here.

Finding his way blocked, Fonstein said to Billy in his Galician-Chinese singsong, "I came to tell you I'm one of the people you rescued in Italy." Billy turned toward the wall of his booth, and Fonstein was escorted to the street.

In the course of years, long letters were sent. "I want nothing from you, not even to shake hands, but to speak man to man for a minute."

It was Sorella, back in Lakewood, who told me this, while Fonstein and my father were sunk in a trance over the chessboard. "Rose, that special party, won't see Harry," said Sorella.

My comment was, "I break my head trying to understand why it's so important for Fonstein. He's been turned down? So he's been turned down."

"To express gratitude," said Sorella. "All he wants to say is 'Thanks.' "

"And this wild pygmy absolutely refuses."

"Behaves as if Harry Fonstein never existed."

"Why, do you suppose? Afraid of the emotions? Too Jewish a moment for him? Drags him down from his standing as a full-fledged American? What's your husband's opinion?"

"Harry thinks it's some kind of change in the descendants of immigrants in this country," said Sorella.

And I remember today what a pause this answer gave me. I myself had often wondered uncomfortably about the Americanization of the Jews. One could begin with physical differences. My father's height was five feet six inches, mine was six feet two inches. To my father, this seemed foolishly wasteful somehow. Perhaps the reason was Biblical, for King Saul, who stood head and shoulders above the others, was *verrucht*—demented and doomed. The prophet Samuel had warned Israel not to take a king, and Saul did not find favor in God's eyes. Therefore a Jew should not be unnecessarily large but rather finely made, strong but compact. The main thing was to be deft and quick-witted. That was how my father was and how he would have preferred me to be. My length was superfluous, I had too much chest and shoulders, big hands, a wide mouth, a band of black mustache, too much voice, excessive hair; the shirts that covered my trunk had too many red and gray stripes, idiotically flashy. Fools ought to come in smaller sizes. A big son was a threat, a parricide. Now Fonstein despite his short leg was a proper man, well arranged, trim, sensible, and clever. His development was hastened by Hitlerism. Losing your father at the age of fourteen brings your childhood to an end. Burying your mother in a foreign cemetery, no time to mourn, caught with false documents, doing time in the slammer ("sitting" is the Jewish term for it: "*Er hat gesessen*"). A man acquainted with grief. No time for froth or moronic laughter, for vanities and games, for climbing the walls, for effeminacies or infantile plaintiveness.

I didn't agree, of course, with my father. We were bigger in my generation because we had better nutrition. We were, moreover, less restricted, we had wider liberties. We grew up under a larger range of influences and thoughts—we were the children of a great democracy, bred to equality, living it up with no pales to confine us. Why, until the end of the last century, the Jews of Rome were still locked in for the night; the Pope ceremonially entered the ghetto once a year and spat ritually on the garments of the Chief Rabbi. Were we giddy here? No doubt about it. But there were no cattle cars waiting to take us to camps and gas chambers.

One can think of such things—and think and *think*—but nothing is resolved by these historical meditations. To *think* doesn't settle anything. No idea is more than an imaginary potency, a mushroom cloud (destroying nothing, making nothing) rising from blinding consciousness.

And Billy Rose wasn't big; he was about the size of Peter Lorre. But oh! he was American. There was a penny-arcade jingle about Billy, the popping of shooting galleries, the rattling of pinballs, the weak human cry of the Times Square geckos, the lizard gaze of sideshow freaks. To see him as he was, you have to place him against the whitewash glare of Broadway in the wee hours. But even such places have their grandees—people whose defects can be converted to seed money for enterprises. There's nothing in this country that you can't sell, nothing too weird to bring to market and found a fortune on. And once you got as much major real estate as Billy had, then it didn't matter that you were one of the human deer that came uptown from the Lower East Side to graze on greasy sandwich papers. Billy? Well, Billy had bluffed out mad giants like Robert Moses. He bought the Ziegfeld building for peanuts. He installed Eleanor Holm in a mansion and hung the walls with masterpieces. And he went on from there. They'd say in feudal Ireland that a proud man is a lovely man (Yeats's Parnell), but in glamorous New York he could be lovely because the columnists said he was—George Sokolsky, Walter Winchell, Leonard Lyons, the "Midnight Earl"—and also Hollywood pals and leaders of nightclub society. Billy was all over the place. Why, he was even a newspaper columnist, and syndicated. True, he had ghostwriters, but he was the mastermind who made all the basic decisions and vetted every word they printed.

Fonstein was soon familiar with Billy's doings, more familiar than I ever was or cared to be. But then Billy had saved the man: took him out of prison, paid his way to Genoa, installed him in a hotel, got him passage on a neutral ship. None of this could Fonstein have done for himself, and you'd never in the world hear him deny it.

"Of course," said Sorella, with gestures that only a two-hundred-pound woman can produce, because her delicacy rests on the mad overflow of her behind, "though my husband has given up on making contact, he hasn't stopped, and he can't stop being grateful. He's a dignified individual himself, but he's also a very smart man and has got to be conscious of the kind of person that saved him."

"Does it upset him? It could make him unhappy to be snatched from death by a kibitzer."

"It gets to him sometimes, yes."

She proved quite a talker, this Sorella. I began to look forward to our conversations as much for what came out of her as for the intrinsic interest of the subject. Also I had mentioned that I was a friend of Wolfe, one of Billy's ghosts, and maybe she was priming me. Wolfe might even take the matter up with Billy. I informed Sorella up front that Wolfe would never do it. "This Wolfe," I told her, "is a funny type, a little guy who seduces big girls. Very clever. He hangs out at Birdland and dotes on Broadway freaks. In addition, he's a Yale-trained intellectual heavy, or so he likes to picture himself; he treasures his kinks and loves being deep. For instance, his mother also is his cleaning lady. He told me recently as I watched a woman on her knees scrubbing out his pad, 'The old girl you're looking at is my mother.' "

"Her own dear boy?" said Sorella.

"An only child," I said.

"She must love him like anything."

"I don't doubt it for a minute. To him, that's what's deep. Although Wolfe is decent, under it all. He has to support her anyway. What harm is there in saving ten bucks a week on the cleaning? Besides which he builds up his reputation as a weirdo nihilist. He wants to become the Thomas Mann of science fiction. That's his real aim, he says, and he only dabbles in Broadway. It amuses him to write Billy's columns and break through in print with expressions like: 'I'm going to hit him on his pointy head. I'll give him such a *hit*!' "

Sorella listened and smiled, though she didn't wish to appear familiar with these underground characters and their language or habits, with Village sex or Broadway sleaze. She brought the conversation back to Fonstein's rescue and the history of the Jews.

She and I found each other congenial, and before long I was speaking as openly to her as I would in a Village conversation, let's say with Paul Goodman at the Casbah, not as though she were merely a square fat lady from the dark night of petty-bourgeois New Jersey—no more than a carrier or genetic relay to produce a science savant of the next generation. She had made a respectable ("contemptible") marriage. However, she was also a tiger wife, a tiger mother. It was no negligible person who had patented Fonstein's thermostat and rounded up the money for his little factory (it *was* little at first), meanwhile raising a boy who was a mathematical genius. She was a spirited woman, at home with ideas. This heavy tailored lady was extremely well informed. I wasn't inclined to discuss Jewish history with her—it put my teeth on edge at first—but she overcame my resistance. She was well up on the subject, and besides, damn it, you couldn't say no to Jewish history after what had happened in Nazi Germany. You had to listen. It turned out that as the wife of a refugee she had set herself to master the subject, and I heard a great deal from her about the technics of annihilation, the large-scale-industry aspect of it. What she occasionally talked about while Fonstein and my father stared at the chessboard, sealed in their trance, was the black humor, the slapstick side of certain camp operations. Being a French teacher, she was familiar with Jarry and *Ubu Roi,* Pataphysics, Absurdism, Dada, Surrealism. Some camps were run in a burlesque style that forced you to make these connections. Prisoners were sent naked into a swamp and had to croak and hop like frogs. Children were hanged while starved, freezing slave laborers lined up on parade in front of the gallows and a prison band played Viennese light opera waltzes.

I didn't want to hear this, and I said impatiently, "All right, Billy Rose wasn't the only one in show biz. So the Germans did it too, and what they staged in Nuremberg was bigger than Billy's rally in Madison Square Garden—the 'We Will Never Die' pageant."

I understood Sorella: the object of her researches was to assist her husband. He was alive today because a little Jewish promoter took it into his queer head to organize a Hollywood-style rescue. I was invited to meditate on themes like: Can Death Be Funny? or Who Gets the Last Laugh? I wouldn't do it, though. First those people murdered you, then they forced you to brood on their crimes. It suffocated me to do this. Hunting for causes was a horrible imposition added to the original "selection," gassing, cremation. I didn't want to think of the history and psychology of these abominations, death chambers and furnaces. Stars are nuclear furnaces too. Such things are utterly beyond me, a pointless exercise.

Also my advice to Fonstein—given mentally—was: Forget it. Go American. Work at your business. Market your thermostats. Leave the theory side of it to your wife. She has a taste for it, and she's a clever woman. If she enjoys collecting a Holocaust library and wants to ponder the subject, why not? Maybe she'll write a book herself, about the Nazis and the entertainment industry. Death and mass fantasy.

My own suspicion was that there was a degree of fantasy embodied in Sorella's obesity. She was biologically dramatized in waves and scrolls of tissue. Still, she was, at bottom, a serious woman fully devoted to her husband and child. Fonstein had his talents; Sorella, however, had the business brain. And Fonstein didn't have to be told to go American. Together this couple soon passed from decent prosperity to real money. They bought property east of Princeton, off toward the ocean, they educated the boy, and when they had sent him away to camp in the summer, they traveled. Sorella, the onetime French teacher, had a taste for Europe. She had had, moreover, the good luck to find a European husband.

Toward the close of the fifties they went to Israel, and as it happened, business had brought me to Jerusalem too. The Israelis, who culturally had one of everything in the world, invited me to open a memory institute.

So, in the lobby of the King David, I met the Fonsteins. "Haven't seen you in years!" said Fonstein.

True, I had moved to Philadelphia and married a Main Line lady. We lived in a brownstone mansion, which had a closed garden and an 1817 staircase photographed by *American Heritage* magazine. My father had died; his widow had gone to live with a niece. I seldom saw the old lady and had to ask the Fonsteins how she was. Over the last decade I had had only one contact with the Fonsteins, a telephone conversation about their gifted boy.

This year, they had sent him to a summer camp for little science prodigies.

Sorella was particularly happy to see me. She was sitting—at her weight I suppose one generally is more comfortable seated—and she was unaffectedly pleased to find me in Jerusalem. My thought about the two of them was that it was good for a DP to have ample ballast in his missus. Besides, I believe that he loved her. My own wife was something of a Twiggy. One never does strike it absolutely right. Sorella, calling me "Cousin," said in French that she was still a *femme bien en chair*. I wondered how a man found his way among so many creases. But that was none of my business. They looked happy enough.

The Fonsteins had rented a car. Harry had relations in Haifa, and they were going to tour the north of the country. Wasn't it an extraordinary place! said Sorella, dropping her voice to a theatrical whisper. (What was there to keep secret?) Jews who were electricians and bricklayers, Jewish policemen, engineers, and sea captains. Fonstein was a good walker. In Europe he had walked a thousand miles in his Polish boot. Sorella, however, was not built for sightseeing. "I should be carried in a litter," she said. "But that's not a trade for Israelis, is it?" She invited me to have tea with her while Fonstein looked up hometown people—neighbors from Lemberg.

Before our tea, I went up to my room to read the *Herald Tribune*—one of the distinct pleasures of being abroad—but I settled down with the paper in order to think about the Fonsteins (my two-in-one habit—like using music as a background for reflection). The Fonsteins were not your predictable, disposable distant family relations who labeled themselves by their clothes, their conversation, the cars they drove, their temple memberships, their party politics. Fonstein for all his Jermyn Street boots and Italianate suits was still the man who had buried his mother in Venice and waited in his cell for Ciano to rescue him. Though his face was silent and his manner "socially advanced"—this was the only term I could apply: far from the Jewish style acquired in New Jersey communities—I believe that he was thinking intensely about his European origin and his American transformation: Part I and Part II. Signs of a tenacious memory in others seldom escape me. I always ask, however, what people are doing with their recollections. Rote, mechanical storage, an unusual capacity for retaining facts, has a limited interest for me. Idiots can have that gift. Nor do I care much for nostalgia and its associated sentiments. In most cases, I dislike it. Fonstein was *doing* something with his past. This was the lively, the active element of his still look. But you no more discussed this with a man than you asked how he felt about his smooth boot with the four-inch sole.

Then there was Sorella. No ordinary woman, she broke with every sign of ordinariness. Her obesity, assuming she had some psychic choice in the matter, was a sign of this. She might have willed herself to be thinner, for she had the strength of character to do it. Instead she accepted the challenge of size as a Houdini might have asked for tighter knots, more locks on the trunk, deeper rivers to escape from. She was, as people nowadays say, "off the continuum"—her graph went beyond the chart and filled up the whole wall. In my King David reverie, I put it that she had had to wait for an uncle in Havana to find a husband for her—she had been a matrimonial defective, a reject. To come out of it gave her a revolutionary impulse. There was going to be no sign of her early humiliation, not in *any* form, no bitter residue. What you didn't want you would shut out decisively. You had been unhealthy, lumpish. Your fat had made you pale and clumsy. Nobody, not even a lout, had come to court you. What do you do now with this painful record of disgrace? You don't bury nor do you transform it; you *annihilate* it and then use the space to draw a more powerful design. You draw it in freedom because you can afford to, not because there's anything to hide. The new design, as I saw it, was not an invention. The Sorella I saw was not constructed but revealed.

I put aside the *Herald Tribune* and went down in the elevator. Sorella had settled herself on the terrace of the King David. She wore a dress of whitish beige. The bodice was ornamented with a large square of scalloped material. There was something military and also mystical about this. It made me think of the Knights of Malta—a curious thing to be associated with a Jewish lady from New Jersey. But then the medieval wall of the Old City was just across the valley. In 1959 the Israelis were still shut out of it; it was Indian country then. At the moment, I wasn't thinking of Jews and Jordanians, however. I was having a civilized tea with a huge lady who was also distinctly, authoritatively dainty. The beehive was gone. Her fair hair was cropped, she wore Turkish slippers on her small feet, which were innocently crossed under the beaten brass of the tray table. The Vale of Hinnom, once the Ottoman reservoir, was green and blossoming. What I have to say here is that I was aware of —I directly experienced—the beating of Sorella's heart as it faced the challenge of supply in so extensive an organism. This to me was a bold operation, bigger than the Turkish waterworks. I felt my own heart signifying admiration for hers—the extent of the project it had to face.

Sorella put me in a tranquil state.

"Far from Lakewood."

"That's the way travel is now," I said. "We've done something to distance. Some transformation, some bewilderment."

"And you've come here to set up a branch of your institute—do these people need one?"

"They think they do," I said. "They have a modified Noah's Ark idea. They don't want to miss out on anything from the advanced countries. They have to keep up with the world and be a complete microcosm."

"Do you mind if I give you a short, friendly test?"

"Go right ahead."

"Can you remember what I was wearing when we first met in your father's house?"

"You had on a gray tailored suit, not too dark, with a light stripe, and jet earrings."

"Can you tell me who built the Graf Zeppelin?"

"I can—Dr. Hugo Eckener."

"The name of your second-grade teacher, fifty years ago?"

"Miss Emma Cox."

Sorella sighed, less in admiration than in sorrow, in sympathy with the burden of so much useless information.

"That's pretty remarkable," she said. "At least your success with the Mnemosyne Institute has a legitimate basis— I wonder, do you recall the name of the woman Billy Rose sent to Ellis Island to talk to Harry?"

"That was Mrs. Hamet. Harry thought she was suffering from TB."

"Yes, that's correct."

"Why do you ask?"

"Over the years I had some contact with her. First she looked us up. Then I looked her up. I cultivated her. I liked the old lady, and she found me also sympathetic. We saw a lot of each other."

"You put it all in the past tense."

"That's where it belongs. A while back, she passed away in a sanitarium near White Plains. I used to visit her. You might say a bond formed between us. She had no family to speak of. . . ."

"A Yiddish actress, wasn't she?"

"True, and she was personally theatrical, but not only from nostalgia for a vanished art—the Vilna Troupe, or Second Avenue. It was also because she had a combative personality. There was lots of sophistication in that character, lots of purpose. Plenty of patience. Plus a hell of a lot of stealth."

"What did she need the stealth for?"

"For many years she kept an eye on Billy's doings. She put everything in a journal. As well as she could, she maintained a documented file—notes on comings and goings, dated records of telephone conversations, carbon copies of letters."

"Personal or business?"

"You couldn't draw a clear line."

"What's the good of all this material?"

"I can't say exactly."

"Did she hate the man? Was she trying to get him?"

"Actually, I don't believe she was. She was very tolerant—as much as she could be, leading a nickel-and-dime life and feeling mistreated. But I don't think she wanted to nail him by his iniquities. He was a celeb, to her—that was what she called him. She ate at the Automat; he was a celeb, so he took his meals at Sardi's, Dempsey's, or in Sherman Billingsley's joint. No hard feelings over it. The Automat gave good value for your nickels, and she used to say she had a healthier diet."

"I seem to recall she was badly treated."

"So was everybody else, and they all said they detested him. What did your friend Wolfe tell you?"

"He said that Billy had a short fuse. That he was a kind of botch. Still, it made Wolfe ecstatic to have a Broadway connection. There was glamour in the Village if you were one of Billy's ghosts. It gave Wolfe an edge with smart girls who came downtown from Vassar or Smith. He didn't have first-class intellectual credentials in the Village, he wasn't a big-time wit, but he was eager to go forward, meaning that he was prepared to take abuse—and they had plenty of it to give—from the top wise-guy theoreticians, the heavy-weight pundits, in order to get an education in modern life—which meant you could combine Kierkegaard and Birdland in the same breath. He was a big chaser. But he didn't abuse or sponge on girls. When he was seducing, he started the young lady off on a box of candy. The next stage, always the same, was a cashmere sweater—both candy and cash-mere from a guy who dealt in stolen goods. When the affair was over, the chicks were passed on to somebody more crude and lower on the totem pole. . . ."

Here I made a citizen's arrest, mentally—I checked my-self. It was the totem pole that did it. A Jew in Jerusalem, and one who was able to explain where we were at—how Moses had handed on the law to Joshua, and Joshua to the Judges, the Judges to the Prophets, the Prophets to the Rab-bis, so that at the end of the line, a Jew from secular America (a diaspora within a diaspora) could jive glibly about the swinging Village scene of the fifties and about totem poles, about Broadway lowlife and squalor. Especially if you bear in mind that this particular Jew couldn't say what place he held in this great historical procession. I had concluded long ago that the Chosen were chosen to read God's mind. Over the millennia, this turned out to be a zero-sum game.

I wasn't about to get into that.

"So old Mrs. Hamet died," I said, in a sad tone. I recalled her face as Fonstein had described it, whiter than confec-tioners' sugar. It was almost as though I had known her.

"She wasn't exactly a poor old thing," said Sorella. "Nobody asked her to participate, but she was a player nevertheless."

"She kept this record—why?"

"Billy obsessed her to a bizarre degree. She believed that they belonged together because they were similar—defective people. The unfit, the rejects, coming together to share each other's burden."

"Did she want to be Mrs. Rose?"

"No, no—that was out of the question. He only married celebs. She had no PR value—she was old, no figure, no complexion, no money, no status. Too late even for penicillin to save her. But she did make it her business to know everything about him. When she let herself go, she was extremely obscene. Obscenity was linked to everything. She certainly knew all the words. She could sound like a man."

"And she thought she should tell you? Share her research?"

"Me, yes. She approached us through Harry, but the friendship was with me. Those two seldom met, almost never."

"And she left you her files?"

"A journal plus supporting evidence."

"Ugh!" I said. The tea had steeped too long and was dark. Lemon lightened the color, and sugar was just what I needed late in the afternoon to pick me up. I said to Sorella, "Is this journal any good to you? You don't need any help from Billy."

"Certainly not. America, as they say, has been good to us. However, it's quite a document she left. I think you'd find it so."

"If I cared to read it."

"If you started, you'd go on, all right."

She was offering it. She had brought it with her to Jerusalem! And why had she done that? Not to show to me, certainly. She couldn't have known that she was going to meet me here. We had been out of touch for years. I was not on good terms with the family, you see. I had married a Wasp lady, and my father and I had quarreled. I was a Philadelphian now, without contacts in New Jersey. New Jersey to me was only a delay en route to New York or Boston. A psychic darkness. Whenever possible I omitted New Jersey. Anyway, I chose not to read the journal.

Sorella said, "You may be wondering what use I might make of it."

Well, I wondered, of course, why she hadn't left Mrs. Hamet's journal at home. Frankly, I didn't care to speculate on her motives. What I understood clearly was that she was oddly keen to have me read it. Maybe she wanted my advice. "Has your husband gone through it?" I said.

"He wouldn't understand the language."

"And it would embarrass you to translate it."

"That's more or less it," said Sorella.

"So it's pretty hairy in places? You said she knew the words. Clinical stuff didn't scare Mrs. Hamet, did it."

"In these days of scientific sex studies, there's not much that's new and shocking," said Sorella.

"The shock comes from the source. When it's someone in the public eye."

"Yes, I figured that."

Sorella was a proper person. She was not suggesting that I share any lewdnesses with her. Nothing was farther from her than evil communications. She had never in her life seduced anyone—I'd bet a year's income on that. She was as stable in character as she was immense in her person. The square on the bosom of her dress, with its scalloped design, was like a repudiation of all trivial mischief. The scallops themselves seemed to me to be a kind of message in cursive characters, warning against kinky interpretations, perverse attributions.

She was silent. She seemed to say: Do you doubt me?

Well, this was Jerusalem, and I am unusually susceptible to places. In a moment I had touched base with the Crusaders, with Caesar and Christ, the kings of Israel. There was also the heart beating in her (in me too) with the persistence of fidelity, a faith in the necessary continuation of a radical mystery—don't ask me to spell it out.

I wouldn't have felt this way in blue-collar Trenton.

Sorella was too big a person to play any kind of troublemaking games or to create minor mischief. Her eyes were like vents of atmospheric blue, and their backing (the camera obscura) referred you to the black of universal space, where there is no object to reflect the flow of invisible light.

Clarification came in a day or two, from an item in that rag the *Post*. Expected soon in Jerusalem were Billy Rose and the designer, artistic planner, and architectural sculptor Isamu Noguchi. Magnificent Rose, always a friend of Israel, was donating a sculpture garden here, filling it with his collection of masterpieces. He had persuaded Noguchi to lay it out for him—or, if that wasn't nifty enough, to preside over its creation, for Billy, as the reporter said, had the philanthropic impulses but was hopeless with the aesthetic requirements. Knew what he wanted; even more, he knew what he *didn't* want.

Any day now they would arrive. They would meet with Jerusalem planning officials, and the prime minister would invite them to dinner.

I couldn't talk to Sorella about this. The Fonsteins had gone to Haifa. Their driver would take them to Nazareth and the Galil, up to the Syrian border. Gennesaret, Capernaum, the Mount of the Beatitudes were on the itinerary. There was no need for questions; I now understood what Sorella was up to. From the poor old Hamet lady, possibly (that sapper, that mole, that dedicated researcher), she had had advance notice, and it wouldn't have been hard to learn the date of Billy's arrival with the eminent Noguchi. Sorella, if she liked, could read Billy the riot act, using Mrs. Hamet's journal as her prompt book. I wondered just how this would happen. The general intention was all I could make out. If Billy was ingenious in getting maximum attention (half magnificence, half baloney and smelling like it), if Noguchi was ingenious in the department of beautiful settings, it remained to be seen what Sorella could come up with in the way of ingenuity.

Technically, she was a housewife. On any questionnaire or application she would have put a check in the housewife box. None of what goes with that—home decoration, the choice of place mats, flatware, wallpapers, cooking utensils, the control of salt, cholesterol, carcinogens, preoccupation with hairdressers and nail care, cosmetics, shoes, dress lengths, the time devoted to shopping malls, department stores, health clubs, luncheons, cocktails—none of these things, or forces, or powers (for I see them also as powers, or even spirits), could keep a woman like Sorella in subjection. She was no more a housewife than Mrs. Hamet had been a secretary. Mrs. Hamet was a dramatic artist out of work, a tubercular, moribund, and finally demonic old woman. In leaving her dynamite journal to Sorella, she made a calculated choice, dazzlingly appropriate.

Since Billy and Noguchi arrived at the King David while Sorella and Fonstein were taking time off on the shore of Galilee, and although I was busy with Mnemosyne business, I nevertheless kept an eye on the newcomers as if I had been assigned by Sorella to watch and report. Predictably, Billy made a stir among the King David guests—mainly Jews from the United States. To some, it was a privilege to see a legendary personality in the lobby and the dining room, or on the terrace. For his part, he didn't encourage contacts, didn't particularly want to know anybody. He had the high color of people who are observed—the cynosure flush.

Immediately he made a scene in the pillared, carpeted lobby. El Al had lost his luggage. A messenger from the prime minister's office came to tell him that it was being traced. It might have gone on to Jakarta. Billy said, "You better fuckin' find it fast. I *order* you! All I got is this suit I traveled in, and how'm I supposed to shave, brush my teeth, change socks, underpants, and sleep without pajamas?" The government would take care of this, but the messenger was forced to hear that the shirts were made at Sulka's and the suits by the Fifth Avenue tailor who served Winchell, or Jack Dempsey, or top executives at RCA. The designer must have chosen a model from the bird family. The cut of Billy's jacket suggested the elegance of thrushes or robins, dazzling fast walkers, fat in the breast and folded wings upcurved. There the analogy stopped. The rest was complex vanity, peevish haughtiness, cold outrage—a proud-peewee performance, of which the premises were that he was a considerable figure, a Broadway personage requiring special consideration, and that he himself owed it to his high showbiz standing to stamp and scream and demand and threaten. Yet all the while, if you looked close at the pink, histrionic, Oriental little face, you saw a small but distinct private sector. It contained quite different data. Billy looked as if he, the *personal* Billy, had other concerns, arising from secret inner reckonings. He had come up from the gutter. That was okay, though, in America the land of opportunity. If he had some gutter in him still, he didn't have to hide it much. In the U.S.A. you could come from nowhere and still stand tall, especially if you had the cash. If you pushed Billy he'd retaliate, and if you can retaliate you've got your self-respect. He could even be a cheapie, it wasn't worth the trouble of covering up. He didn't give a shit who thought what. On the other hand, if he wanted a memorial in Jerusalem, a cultural beauty spot, *that* noble gift was a Billy Rose concept, and don't you forget it. Such components made Billy worth looking at. He combed his hair back like George Raft, or that earlier dude sweetheart Rudolph Valentino. (In the Valentino days, Billy had been a tune-smith in Tin Pan Alley—had composed a little, stolen a little, promoted a whole lot; he still held valuable copy-rights.) His look was simultaneously weak and strong. He could claim nothing classic that a well-bred Wasp might claim—a man, say, whose grandfather had gone to Groton, whose remoter ancestors had had the right to wear a breast-plate and carry a sword. Weapons were a no-no for Jews in those remoter times, as were blooded horses. Or the big wars. But the best you could do in the present age if you were of privileged descent was to dress in drab expensive good taste and bear yourself with what was left of the Brah-min or Knickerbocker style. By now that, too, was tired and hokey. For Billy, however, the tailored wardrobe was indispensable—like having an executive lavatory of your own. He couldn't present himself without his suits, and this was what fed his anger with El Al and also his despair. This, as he threw his weight around, was how I read him. No-guchi, in what I fancied to be a state of Zen calm, also watched silently as Billy went through his nerve-storm dis-play.

In quieter moments, when he was in the lounge drinking fruit juice and reading messages from New York, Billy looked as if he couldn't stop lamenting the long sufferings of the Jews and, in addition, his own defeats at the hands of fellow Jews. My guess was that his defeats by lady Jews were the most deeply wounding of all. He could win against men. Women, if I was correctly informed, were too much for him.

If he had been an old-time Eastern European Jew, he would have despised such sex defeats. His main connection being with his God, he would have granted no such power to a woman. The sexual misery you read in Billy's looks was an American torment—straight American. Broadway Billy was, moreover, in the pleasure business. Everything, on his New York premises, was resolved in play, in jokes, games, laughs, put-ons, cock teases. And his business efforts were crowned with money. Uneasy lies the head that has no money crown to wear. Billy didn't have to worry about *that*.

Combine these themes, and you can understand Billy's residual wistfulness, his resignation to forces he couldn't control. What he could control he controlled with great effectiveness. But there was so much that counted—how it counted! And how well he knew that he could do nothing about it.

The Fonsteins returned from Galilee sooner than expected. "Gorgeous, but more for the Christians," Sorella said to me. "For instance, the Mount of Beatitudes." She also said, "There wasn't a rowboat big enough for me to sit in. As for swimming, Harry went in, but I didn't bring a bathing suit."

Her comment on Billy's lost luggage was: "It must have embarrassed the hell out of the government. He came to build them a major tourist attraction. If he had kept on hollering, I could see Ben-Gurion himself sitting down at the sewing machine to make him a suit."

The missing bags by then had been recovered—fine-looking articles, like slim leather trunks, brass-bound, and monogrammed. Not from Tiffany, but from the Italian manufacturer who would have supplied Tiffany if Tiffany had sold luggage (obtained through contacts, like the candy and cashmeres of Wolfe the ghostwriter: why should you pay full retail price just because you're a multimillionaire?). Billy gave a press interview and complimented Israel on being part of the modern world. The peevish shadow left his face, and he and Noguchi went out every day to confer on the site of the sculpture garden. The atmosphere at the

King David became friendlier. Billy stopped hassling the desk clerks, and the clerks for their part stopped lousing him up. Billy on arrival had made the mistake of asking one of them how much to tip the porter who carried his briefcase to his suite. He said he was not yet at home with the Israeli currency. The clerk had flared up. It made him indignant that a man of such wealth should be miserly with nickels and dimes, and he let him have it. Billy saw to it that the clerk was disciplined by the management. When he heard of this, Fonstein said that in Rome a receptionist in a class hotel would never in the world have made a scene with one of the guests.

"Jewish assumptions," he said. "Not clerks and guests, but one Jew letting another Jew have it—plain talk."

I had expected Harry Fonstein to react strongly to Billy's presence—a guest in the same hotel at prices only the affluent could afford. Fonstein, whom Billy had saved from death, was no more than an undistinguished Jewish American, two tables away in the restaurant. And Fonstein was strong-willed. Under no circumstances would he have approached Billy to introduce himself or to confront him: "I am the man your organization smuggled out of Rome. You brought me to Ellis Island and washed your hands of me, never gave a damn about the future of this refugee. Cut me at Sardi's." No, no, not Harry Fonstein. He understood that there is such a thing as making too much of the destiny of an individual. Besides, it's not really in us nowadays to extend ourselves, to become involved in the fortunes of anyone who happens to approach us.

"Mr. Rose, I am the person you wouldn't see—couldn't fit into your schedule." A look of scalding irony on Fonstein's retributive face. "Now the two of us, in God's eye of terrible judgment, are standing here in this holy city . . ."

Impossible words, an impossible scenario. Nobody says

such things, nor would anyone seriously listen if they were said.

No, Fonstein contented himself with observation. You saw a curious light in his eyes when Billy passed, talking to Noguchi. I can't recall a moment when Noguchi replied. Not once did Fonstein discuss with me Billy's presence in the hotel. Again I was impressed with the importance of keeping your mouth shut, the kind of fertility it can induce, the hidden advantages of a buttoned lip.

I did ask Sorella how Fonstein felt at finding Billy here after their trip north.

"A complete surprise."

"Not to you, it wasn't."

"You figured that out, did you?"

"Well, it took no special shrewdness," I said. "I now feel what Dr. Watson must have felt when Sherlock Holmes complimented him on a deduction Holmes had made as soon as the case was outlined to him. Does your husband know about Mrs. Hamet's file?"

"I told him, but I haven't mentioned that I brought the notebook to Jerusalem. Harry is a sound sleeper, whereas I am an insomniac, so I've been up half the night reading the old woman's record, which damns the guy in the suite upstairs. If I didn't have insomnia, this would keep me awake."

"All about his deals, his vices? Damaging stuff?"

Sorella first shrugged and then nodded. I believe that she herself was perplexed, couldn't quite make up her mind about it.

"If he were thinking of running for president, he wouldn't like this information made public."

"Sure. But he isn't running. He's not a candidate. He's Broadway Billy, not the principal of a girls' school or pastor of the Riverside Church."

"That's the truth. Still, he is a public person."

I didn't pursue the subject. Certainly Billy was an oddity. On the physical side (and in her character too), Sorella also was genuinely odd. She was so much bigger than the bride I had first met in Lakewood that I couldn't keep from speculating on her expansion. She made you look twice at a doorway. When she came to it, she filled the space like a freighter in a canal lock. In its own right, consciousness— and here I refer to my own conscious mind—was yet another oddity. But the strangeness of souls is certainly no news in this day and age.

Fonstein loved her, that was a clear fact. He respected his wife, and I did too. I wasn't poking fun at either of them when I wondered at her size. I never lost sight of Fonstein's history, or of what it meant to be the survivor of such a destruction. Maybe Sorella was trying to incorporate in fatty tissue some portion of what he had lost—members of his family. There's no telling what she might have been up to. All I can say is that it (whatever it was at bottom) was accomplished with some class or style. Exquisite singers can make you forget what hillocks of suet their backsides are. Besides, Sorella did dead sober what delirious sopranos put over on us in a state of false Wagnerian intoxication.

Her approach to Billy, however, was anything but sober, and I doubt that any sober move would have had an effect on Billy. What she did was to send him several pages, three or four items copied from the journal of that poor consumptive the late Mrs. Hamet. Sorella made sure that the clerk put it in Billy's box, for the material was explosive, and in the wrong hands it might have been deadly.

When this was a *fait accompli,* she told me about it. Too late now to advise her not to do it. "I invited him to have a drink," she said to me.

"Not the three of you . . . ?"

"No. Harry hasn't forgotten the bouncer scene at Sardi's— you may remember—when Billy turned his face to the back of the booth. He'd never again force himself on Billy or any celebrity."

"Billy might still ignore you."

"Well, it's in the nature of an experiment, let's say."

I put aside for once the look of social acceptance so many of us have mastered perfectly and let her see what I thought of her "experiment." She might talk "Science" to her adolescent son, the future physicist. I was not a child you could easily fake out with a prestigious buzzword. Experiment? She was an ingenious and powerful woman who devised intricate, glittering, bristling, needling schemes. What she had in mind was confrontation, a hand-to-hand struggle. The laboratory word was a put-on. "Boldness," "Statecraft," "Passion," "Justice," were the real terms. Still, she may not herself have been clearly aware of this. And then, I later thought, the antagonist *was* Broadway Billy Rose. And she didn't expect him to meet her on the ground she had chosen, did she? What did he care for her big abstractions? He was completely free to say, "I don't know what the fuck you're talking about, and I couldn't care less, lady."

Most interesting—at least to an American mind.

I went about my Mnemosyne business in Jerusalem at a seminar table, unfolding my methods to the Israelis. In the end, Mnemosyne didn't take root in Tel Aviv. (It did thrive in Taiwan and Tokyo.)

On the terrace next day, Sorella, looking pleased and pleasant over her tea, said, "We're going to meet. But he wants me to come to his suite at five o'clock."

"Doesn't want to be seen in public, discussing this . . . ?"

"Exactly."

So she did have real clout, after all. I was sorry now that I hadn't taken the opportunity to read Mrs. Hamet's record. (So much zeal, malice, fury, and tenderness I missed out on.) And I didn't even feel free to ask why Sorella thought

Billy had agreed to talk to her. I was sure he wouldn't want to discuss moral theory upstairs. There weren't going to be any revelations, confessions, speculations. People like Billy didn't worry about their deeds, weren't in the habit of accounting to themselves. Very few of us, for that matter, bother about accountability or keep spread sheets of conscience.

What follows is based on Sorella's report and supplemented by my observations. I don't have to say, "If memory serves." In my case it serves, all right. Besides, I made tiny notes, while she was speaking, on the back pages of my appointment book (the yearly gift to depositors in my Philadelphia bank).

Billy's behavior throughout was austere-to-hostile. Mainly he was displeased. His conversation from the first was negative. The King David suite wasn't up to his standards. You had to rough it here in Jerusalem, he said. But the state was young. They'd catch up by and by. These comments were made when he opened the door. He didn't invite Sorella to sit, but at her weight, on her small feet, she wasn't going to be kept standing, and she settled her body in a striped chair, justifying herself by the human sound she made when she seated herself—exhaling as the cushions exhaled.

This was her first opportunity to look Billy over, and she had a few unforeseeable impressions: so this was Billy from the world of the stars. He was very well dressed, in the clothes he had made such a fuss about. At moments you had the feeling that his sleeves were stuffed with the paper tissue used by high-grade cleaners. I had mentioned that there was something birdlike about the cut of his coat, and she agreed with me, but where I saw a robin or a thrush, plump under the shirt, she said (through having installed a bird feeder in New Jersey) that he was more like a grosbeak; he even had some of the color. One eye was set a little closer to the nose than the other, giving a touch of Jewish pathos to his look. Actually, she said, he was a little like Mrs. Hamet, with the one sad eye in her consumptive theatrical death-white face. And though his hair was groomed, it wasn't absolutely in place. There was a grosbeak disorder about it.

"At first he thought I was here to put the arm on him," she said.

"Money?"

"Sure—probably money."

I kept her going, with nods and half words, as she described this meeting. Of course: blackmail. A man as deep as Billy could call on years of savvy; he had endless experience in handling the people who came to get something out of him—anglers, con artists, crazies.

Billy said, "I glanced over the pages. How much of it is there, and how upset am I supposed to be about it?"

"Deborah Hamet gave me a stack of material before she died."

"Dead, is she?"

"You know she is."

"I don't know anything," said Billy, meaning that this was information from a sector he cared nothing about.

"Yes, but you do," Sorella insisted. "That woman was mad for you."

"That didn't have to be my business, her emotional makeup. She was part of my office force and got her pay. Flowers were sent to White Plains when she got sick. If I had an idea how she was spying, I wouldn't have been so considerate—the dirt that wild old bag was piling up against me."

Sorella told me, and I entirely believed her, that she had come not to threaten but to discuss, to explore, to sound out. She refused to be drawn into a dispute. She could rely on her bulk to give an impression of the fullest calm. Billy had a quantitative cast of mind—businessmen do—and there was lots of woman here. He couldn't deal even with the slenderest of girls. The least of them had the power to put the sexual whammy (Indian sign) on him. Sorella herself saw this. "If he could change my gender, then he could fight me." This was a hint at the masculinity possibly implicit in her huge size. But she had tidy wrists, small feet, a feminine, lyrical voice. She was wearing perfume. She set her lady self before him, massively. . . . What a formidable, clever wife Fonstein had. The protection he lacked when he was in flight from Hitler he had found on our side of the Atlantic.

"Mr. Rose, you haven't called me by name," she said to him. "You read my letter, didn't you? I'm Mrs. Fonstein. Does that ring a bell?"

"And why should it . . . ?" he said, refusing recognition.

"I married Fonstein."

"And my neck size is fourteen. So what?"

"The man you saved in Rome—one of them. He wrote so many letters. I can't believe you don't remember."

"Remember, forget—what's the difference to me?"

"You sent Deborah Hamet to Ellis Island to talk to him."

"Lady, this is one of a trillion incidents in a life like mine. Why should I recollect it?"

Why, yes, I see his point. These details were like the scales of innumerable shoals of fish—the mackerel-crowded seas: like the particles of those light-annihilating masses, the dense matter of black holes.

"I sent Deborah to Ellis Island—so, okay. . . ."

"With instructions for my husband never to approach you."

"It's a blank to me. But so what?"

"No personal concern for a man you rescued?"

"I did all I could," said Billy. "And for that point of time, that's more than most can say. Go holler at Stephen Wise. Raise hell with Sam Rosenman. Guys were sitting on their

hands. They would call on Roosevelt and Cordell Hull, who
didn't care a damn for Jews, and they were so proud and
happy to be close enough to the White House, even getting
the runaround was such a delicious privilege. FDR snowed
those famous rabbis when they visited him. He blinded them
with his footwork, that genius cripple. Churchill also was
in on this with him. The goddam white paper. So? There
were refugees by the hundred thousands to ship to Palestine.
Or there wouldn't have been a state here today. That's why
I gave up the single-party rescue operation and started to
raise money to get through the British blockade in those
rusty Greek tramp ships. . . . Now what do you want from
me—that I didn't receive your husband! What's the matter?
I see you did all right. Now you have to have special recognition?"

The level, as Sorella was to say to me, being dragged
down, down, downward, the greatness of the events being
beyond anybody's personal scope . . . At times she would
make such remarks.

"Now," Billy asked her, "what do you want with this
lousy scandal stuff collected by that cracked old bitch? To
embarrass me in Jerusalem, when I came to start this major
project?"

Sorella said that she raised both her hands to slow him
down. She told him she had come to have a sensible discussion. Nothing threatening had been hinted. . . .

"No! Except that Hamet woman was collecting poison
in bottles, and you have the whole collection. Try and place
this material in the papers—you'd have to be crazy in the
head. If you did try, the stuff would come flying back on
you faster than shit through a tin whistle. Look at these
charges—that I bribed Robert Moses' people to put across
my patriotic Aquacade at the Fair. Or I hired an arsonist to
torch a storefront for revenge. Or I sabotaged Baby Snooks
because I was jealous of Fanny's big success, and I even

tried to poison her. Listen, we still have libel laws. That Hamet was one sick lady. And you—you should stop and think. If not for me, where would you be, a woman like you . . . ?" The meaning was, a woman deformed by obesity.

"Did he say *that?*" I interrupted. But what excited me was not what *he* said. Sorella stopped me in my tracks. I never knew a woman to be so candid about herself. What a demonstration this was of pure objectivity and self-realism. What it signified was that in a time when disguise and deception are practiced so extensively as to numb the powers of awareness, only a major force of personality could produce such admissions. "I *am* built like a Mack truck. My flesh *is* boundless. An Everest of lipoids," she told me. Together with this came, unspoken, an auxiliary admission: she confessed that she was guilty of self-indulgence. This deformity, my outrageous size, an imposition on Fonstein, the brave man who loves me. Who else would want me? All this was fully implicit in the plain, unforced style of her comment. Greatness is the word for such candor, for such an admission, made so naturally. In this world of liars and cowards, there *are* people like Sorella. One waits for them in the blind faith that they *do* exist.

"He was reminding me that he had saved Harry. For me."

Translation: The SS would have liquidated him pretty quick. So except for the magic intervention of this little Lower East Side rat, the starved child who had survived on pastrami trimmings and pushcart apples . . .

Sorella went on. "I explained to Billy: it took Deborah's journal to put me through to him. He had turned his back on us. His answer was, 'I don't need entanglements—what I did, I did. I have to keep down the number of relationships and contacts. What I did for you, take it and welcome, but spare me the relationship and all the rest of it.' "

"I can understand that," I said.

I can't tell you how much I relished Sorella's account of this meeting with Billy. These extraordinary revelations, and also the comments on them that were made. In what he said there was an echo of George Washington's Farewell Address. Avoid entanglements. Billy had to reserve himself for his deals, devote himself body and soul to his super-publicized bad marriages; together with the squalid, rich residences he furnished; plus his gossip columns, his chorus lines, and the awful pursuit of provocative, teasing chicks whom he couldn't do a thing with when they stopped and stripped and waited for him. He had to be free to work his curse out fully. And now he had arrived in Jerusalem to put a top dressing of Jewish grandeur on his chicken-scratch career, on this poor punished N.Y. soil of his. (I am thinking of the tiny prison enclosures—a few black palings—narrow slices of ground preserved at the heart of Manhattan for leaves and grass.) Here Noguchi would create for him a Rose Garden of Sculpture, an art corner within a few kilometers of the stunned desert sloping toward the Dead Sea.

"Tell me, Sorella, what were you after? The objective."

"Billy to meet with Fonstein."

"But Fonstein gave up on him long ago. They must pass each other at the King David every other day. What would be simpler than to stop and say, 'You're Rose? I'm Harry Fonstein. You led me out of Egypt *b'yad hazzakah.*"

"What is that?"

"With a mighty hand. So the Lord God described the rescue of Israel—part of my boyhood basic training. But Fonstein has backed away from this. While you . . ."

"I made up my mind that Billy was going to do right by him."

Yes, sure, of course; Roger; I read you. Something is due from every man to every man. But Billy hadn't heard and didn't want to hear about these generalities.

"If you lived with Fonstein's feelings as I have lived with

them," said Sorella, "you'd agree he should get a chance to complete them. To finish out."

In a spirit of high-level discussion, I said to her, "Well, it's a nice idea, only nobody expects to complete their feelings anymore. They have to give up on closure. It's just not available."

"For some it is."

So I was obliged to think again. Sure—what about the history of Sorella's own feelings? She had been an unwanted Newark French teacher until her Havana uncle had a lucky hunch about Fonstein. They were married, and thanks to him, she obtained her closure, she became the tiger wife, the tiger mother, grew into a biological monument and a victorious personality . . . a figure!

But Billy's reply was: "So what's it got to do with me?"

"Spend fifteen minutes alone with my husband," she said to him.

Billy refused her. "It's not the kind of thing I do."

"A handshake, and he'll say thanks."

"First of all, I warned you already about libel, and as for the rest, what do you think you're holding over me anyway? I wouldn't do this. You haven't convinced me that I must. I don't like things from the past being laid on me. This happened one time, years ago. What's it got to do with now—1959? If your husband has a nice story, that's his good luck. Let him tell it to people who go for stories. I don't care for them. I don't care for my own story. If I had to listen to it, I'd break out in a cold sweat. And I wouldn't go around and shake everybody's hand unless I was running for mayor. That's why I never would run. I shake when I close a deal. Otherwise, my hands stay in my pockets."

Sorella said, "Since Deborah Hamet had given me the goods on him and the worst could be assumed, he stood up to me on the worst basis, with all the bruises on his reputation, under every curse—grungy, weak, cheap, perverted. He made me take him for what he was—a kinky little kike finagler whose life history was one disgrace after another. Take this man: He never flew a single mission, never hunted big game, never played football or went down in the Pacific. Never even tried suicide. And this reject was a celeb! . . . You know, Deborah had a hundred ways to say celeb. Mostly she cut him down, but a celeb is still a celeb—you can't take that away. When American Jews decided to make a statement about the War Against the Jews, they had to fill Madison Square Garden with big-name celebs singing Hebrew and 'America the Beautiful.' Hollywood stars blowing the *shofar*. The man to produce this spectacular and arrange the press coverage was Billy. They turned to him, and he took total charge. . . . How many people does the Garden hold? Well, it was full, and everybody was in mourning. I suppose the whole place was in tears. The *Times* covered it, which is the paper of record, so the record shows that the American Jewish way was to assemble twenty-five thousand people, Hollywood style, and weep publicly for what had happened."

Continuing her report on her interview with Billy, Sorella said that he adopted what negotiators call a bargaining posture. He behaved as though he had reason to be proud of his record, of the deals he had made, and I suppose that he was standing his ground behind this front of pride. Sorella hadn't yet formulated her threat. Beside her on a chair that decorators would have called a love seat there lay (and he saw) a large manila envelope. It contained Deborah's papers—what else would she have brought to his suite? To make a grab for this envelope was out of the question. "I outreached him and outweighed him," said Sorella. "I could scratch him as well, and also shriek. And the very thought of a scene, a scandal, would have made him sick. Actually, the man was looking sick. His calculation in Jerusalem was to make a major gesture, to enter Jewish history, attaining a level far beyond show biz. He had seen only a sample of the Hamet/Horsecollar file. But imagine what the newspapers, the world tabloid press, could do with this material.

"So he was waiting to hear my proposition," said Sorella.

I said, "I'm trying to figure out just what you had in mind."

"Concluding a chapter in Harry's life. It should be concluded," said Sorella. "It was a part of the destruction of the Jews. On our side of the Atlantic, where we weren't threatened, we have a special duty to come to terms with it. . . ."

"Come to terms? Who, Billy Rose?"

"Well, he involved himself in it actively."

I recall that I shook my head and said, "You were asking too much. You couldn't have gotten very far with him."

"Well, he did say that Fonstein suffered much less than others. He wasn't in Auschwitz. He got a major break. He wasn't tattooed with a number. They didn't put him to work cremating the people that were gassed. I said to Billy that the Italian police must have been under orders to hand Jews over to the SS and that so many were shot in Rome, in the Ardeatine Caves."

"What did he say to this?"

"He said, 'Look, lady, why do *I* have to think about all of that? I'm not the kind of guy who's expected to. This is too much for me.' I said, 'I'm not asking you to make an enormous mental effort, only to sit down with my husband for fifteen minutes.' 'Suppose I do,' he said. 'What's your offer?' 'I'll hand over Deborah's whole file. I've got it right here.' 'And if I don't play ball?' 'Then I'll turn it over to some other party, or parties.' Then he burst out, 'You think you've got me by the knackers, don't you? You're taking an unfair terrible advantage of me. I don't want to talk dirty to a respectable person, but I call this kicking the shit out of a man. Right now I'm in an extrasensitive position, considering what's my purpose in Jerusalem. I want to contribute a memorial. Maybe it would be better not to leave any reminder of my life and I should be forgotten altogether. So at this moment you come along to take revenge from the grave for a jealous woman. I can imagine the record this crazy put together, about deals I made—I know she got the business part all wrong, and the bribery and arson would never stick. So that leaves things like the private clinical junk collected from show girls who bad-mouthed me. But let me say one thing, Missus: Even a geek has his human rights. Last of all, I haven't got all that many secrets left. It's all been told.' 'Almost all,' I said."

I observed, "You sure did bear down hard on him."

"Yes, I did," she admitted. "But he fought back. The libel suits he threatened were only bluff, and I told him so. I pointed out how little I was asking. Not even a note to Harry, just a telephone message would be enough, and then fifteen minutes of conversation. Mulling it over, with his eyes cast down and his little hands passive on the back of a sofa—he was on his feet, he wouldn't sit down, that would seem like a concession—he refused me again. Once and for all he said he wouldn't meet with Harry. 'I already did for him all I'm able to do.' 'Then you leave me no alternative,' I said."

On the striped chair in Billy's suite, Sorella opened her purse to look for a handkerchief. She touched herself on the temples and on the folds of her arms, at the elbow joint. The white handkerchief looked no bigger than a cabbage moth. She dried herself under the chin.

"He must have shouted at you," I said.

"He began to yell at me. It was what I anticipated, a screaming fit. He said no matter what you did, there was always somebody waiting with a switchblade to cut you, or acid to throw in your face, or claws to rip the clothes off you and leave you naked. That fucking old Hamet broad, whom he kept out of charity—as if her eyes weren't kooky enough, she put on those giant crooked round goggles. She hunted up those girls who swore he had the sexual development of a ten-year-old boy. It didn't matter for shit, because he was humiliated all his life long and you couldn't do more than was done already. There was relief in having no more to cover up. He didn't care what Hamet had written down, that bitch-eye mummy, spitting blood and saving the last glob for the man she hated most. As for me, I was a heap of fat filth!"

"You don't have to repeat it all, Sorella."

"Then I won't. But I did lose my temper. My dignity fell apart."

"Do you mean that you wanted to hit him?"

"I threw the document at him. I said, 'I don't *want* my husband to talk to the likes of you. You're not fit . . .' I aimed Deborah's packet at him. But I'm not much good at throwing, and it went through the open window."

"What a moment! What did Billy do then?"

"All the rage was wiped out instantly. He picked up the phone and got the desk. He said, 'A very important document was dropped from my window. I want it brought up right now. You understand? Immediately. This minute.' I went to the door. I don't suppose I wanted to make a gesture, but I am a Newark girl at bottom. I said, 'You're the filth. I want no part of you.' And I made the Italian gesture people used to make in a street fight, the edge of the palm on the middle of my arm."

Inconspicuously, and laughing as she did it, she made a small fist and drew the edge of her other hand across her biceps.

"A very American conclusion."

"Oh," she said, "from start to finish it was a one-hundred-percent American event, of our own generation. It'll be different for our children. A kid like our Gilbert, at his mathematics summer camp? Let him for the rest of his life do nothing but mathematics. Nothing could be more different from either East Side tenements or the back streets of Newark."

All this had happened toward the end of the Fonsteins' visit, and I'm sorry now that I didn't cancel a few Jerusalem appointments for their sake—give them dinner at Dagim Benny, a good fish restaurant. It would have been easy enough for me to clear the decks. What, to spend more time in Jerusalem with a couple from New Jersey named Fonstein? Yes is the answer. Today it's a matter of regret. The more I think of Sorella, the more charm she has for me.

I remember saying to her, "I'm sorry you didn't hit Billy with that packet."

My thought, then and later, was that she was too much hampered by fat under the arms to make an accurate throw.

She said, "As soon as the envelope left my hands I realized that I longed to get rid of it, and of everything connected with it. Poor Deborah—Mrs. Horsecollar, as you like to call her. I see that I was wrong to identify myself with her cause, her tragic life. It makes you think about the high and the low in people. Love is supposed to be high, but imagine falling for a creature like Billy. I didn't want a single thing that man could give Harry and me. Deborah recruited me, so I would continue her campaign against him, keep the heat on from the grave. He was right about that."

This was our very last conversation. Beside the King David driveway, she and I were waiting for Fonstein to come down. The luggage had been stowed in the

Mercedes—at that time, every other cab in Jerusalem was a Mercedes-Benz. Sorella said to me, "How do you see the whole Billy business?"

In those days I still had the Villager's weakness for theorizing—the profundity game so popular with middle-class boys and girls in their bohemian salad days. Ring anybody's bell, and he'd open the window and empty a basin full of thoughts on your head.

"Billy views everything as show biz," I said. "Nothing is real that isn't a show. And he wouldn't perform in your show because he's a producer, and producers don't perform."

To Sorella, this was not a significant statement, so I tried harder. "Maybe the most interesting thing about Billy is that he wouldn't meet with Harry," I said. "He wasn't able to be the counterexample in a case like Harry's. Couldn't begin to measure up."

Sorella said, "That may be a little more like it. But if you want my basic view, here it is: The Jews could survive everything that Europe threw at them. I mean the lucky remnant. But now comes the next test—America. Can they hold their ground, or will the U.S.A. be too much for them?"

This was our final meeting. I never saw Harry and Sorella again. In the sixties, Harry telephoned once to discuss Cal Tech with me. Sorella didn't want Gilbert to study so far from home. An only child, and all of that. Harry was full of the boy's perfect test scores. My heart doesn't warm to the parents of prodigies. I react badly. They're riding for a fall. I don't like parental boasting. So I was unable to be cordial toward Fonstein. My time just then was unusually valuable. Horribly valuable, as I now judge it. Not one of the attractive periods in the development (gestation) of a success.

I can't say that communication with the Fonsteins ceased. Except in Jerusalem, we hadn't had any. I *expected,* for thirty years, to see them again. They were excellent people. I admired Harry. A solid man, Harry, and very brave. As for Sorella, she was a woman with great powers of intelligence, and in these democratic times, whether you are conscious of it or not, you are continually in quest of higher types. I don't have to draw you maps and pictures. Everybody knows what standard products and interchangeable parts signify, understands the operation of the glaciers on the social landscape, planing off the hills, scrubbing away the irregularities. I'm not going to be tedious about this. Sorella was outstanding (or as one of my grandchildren says, "standing out"). So of course I meant to see more of her. But I saw nothing. She was in the warehouse of intentions. I was going to get around to the Fonsteins—write, telephone, have them for Thanksgiving, for Christmas. Perhaps for Passover. But that's what the Passover phenomenon is now—it never comes to pass.

Maybe the power of memory was to blame. Remembering them so well, did I need actually to *see* them? To keep them in a mental suspension was enough. They were a part of the permanent cast of characters, in absentia permanently. There wasn't a thing for them to do.

The next in this series of events occurred last March, when winter, with a grunt, gave up its grip on Philadelphia and began to go out in trickles of grimy slush. Then it was the turn of spring to thrive on the dirt of the city. The season at least produced crocuses, snowdrops, and new buds in my millionaire's private back garden. I pushed around my library ladder and brought down the poems of George Herbert, looking for the one that runs ". . . how clean, how pure are Thy returns," or words to that effect; and on my desk, fit for a Wasp of great wealth, the phone started to ring as I was climbing down. The following Jewish conversation began:

"This is Rabbi X [or Y]. My ministry"—what a Protestant term: he must be Reform, or Conservative at best; no Orthodox rabbi would say "ministry"—"is in Jerusalem. I have been approached by a party whose name is Fonstein. . . ."

"Not Harry," I said.

"No. I was calling to ask *you* about locating Harry. The Jerusalem Fonstein says that he is Harry's uncle. This man is Polish by birth, and he is in a mental institution. He is a very difficult eccentric and lives in a world of fantasy. Much of the time he hallucinates. His habits are dirty—filthy, even. He's totally without resources and well known as a beggar and local character who makes prophetic speeches on the sidewalk."

"I get the picture. Like one of our own homeless," I said.

"Precisely," said Rabbi X or Y, in that humane tone of voice one has to put up with.

"Can we come to the point?" I asked.

"Our Jerusalem Fonstein swears he is related to Harry, who is very rich. . . ."

"I've never seen Harry's financial statement."

"But in a position to help."

I went on, "That's just an opinion. At a hazard . . ." One does get pompous. A solitary, occupying a mansion, living up to his surroundings. I changed my tune; I dropped the "hazard" and said, "It's been years since Harry and I were in touch. You can't locate him?"

"I've tried. I'm on a two-week visit. Right now I'm in New York. But L.A. is my destination. Addressing . . ." (He gave an unfamiliar acronym.) Then he went on to say that the Jerusalem Fonstein needed help. Poor man, absolutely bananas, but under all the tatters, physical and mental

(I paraphrase), humanly so worthy. Abused out of his head by persecution, loss, death, and brutal history; beside himself, crying out for aid—human and supernatural, no matter in what mixture. There may have been something phony about the rabbi, but the case, the man he was describing, was a familiar type, was real enough.

"And you, too, are a relative?" he said.

"Indirectly. My father's second wife was Harry's aunt."

I never loved Aunt Mildred, nor even esteemed her. But, you understand, she had a place in my memory, and there must have been a good reason for that.

"May I ask you to find him for me and give him my number in L.A.? I'm carrying a list of family names and Harry Fonstein will recognize, will identify him. Or will not, if the man is *not* his uncle. It would be a mitzvah."

Christ, spare me these mitzvahs.

I said, "Okay, Rabbi, I'll trace Harry, for the sake of this pitiable lunatic."

The Jerusalem Fonstein gave me a pretext for getting in touch with the Fonsteins. (Or at least an incentive.) I entered the rabbi's number in my book, under the last address I had for Fonstein. At the moment, there were other needs and duties requiring my attention; besides, I wasn't yet ready to speak to Sorella and Harry. There were preparations to make. This, as it appears under my ballpoint, reminds me of the title of Stanislavski's famous book, *An Actor Prepares*—again, a datum relating to my memory, a resource, a vocation, to which a lifetime of cultivation has been devoted, and which in old age also oppresses me.

For just then (meaning now: "Now, now, very now") I was, I am, having difficulties with it. I had had a failure of memory the other morning, and it had driven me almost mad (not to hold back on an occurrence of such importance).

I had had a dental appointment downtown. I drove, because I was already late and couldn't rely on the radio cab to come on time. I parked in a lot blocks away, the best I could do on a busy morning, when closer lots were full. Then, walking back from the dentist's office, I found (under the influence of my walking rhythm, I presume) that I had a tune in my head. The words came to me:

> Way down upon the . . .
> Way down upon the . . .
> . . . upon the ——— River . . .

But what was the river called! A song I'd sung from childhood, upwards of seventy years, part of the foundations of one's mind. A classic song, known to all Americans. Of my generation anyway.

I stopped at the window of a sports shop, specializing, as it happened, in horsemen's boots, shining boots, both men's and women's, plaid saddle blankets, crimson coats, fox-hunting stuff—even brass horns. All objects on display were ultrasignificantly distinct. The colors of the plaid were especially bright and orderly—enviably orderly to a man whose mind was at that instant shattered.

What was that river's name!

I could easily recall the rest of the words:

> There's where my heart is yearning ever,
> That's where the old folks stay.
> All the world is [am?] sad and dreary
> Everywhere I roam.
> O darkies, how my heart grows weary . . .

And the rest.

All the world *was* dark and dreary. Fucking-A right! A

chip, a plug, had gone dead in the mental apparatus. A forerunning omen? Beginning of the end? There are psychic causes of forgetfulness, of course. I've lectured on those myself. Not everyone, needless to say, would take such a lapsus so to heart. A bridge was broken: I could not cross the ———— River. I had an impulse to hammer the window of the riding shop with the handle of my umbrella, and when people ran out, to cry to them, "Oh, God! You must tell me the words. I can't get past 'Way down upon the . . . upon the!' " They would—I saw it—throw that red saddle cloth, a brilliant red, threads of fire, over my shoulders and take me into the shop to wait for the ambulance.

At the parking lot, I wanted to ask the cashier—out of desperation. When she said, "Seven dollars," I would begin singing the tune through the round hole in the glass. But as the woman was black, she might be offended by "O darkies." And could I assume that she, like me, had been brought up on Stephen Foster? There were no grounds for this. For the same reason, I couldn't ask the car jockey either.

But at the wheel of the car, the faulty connection corrected itself, and I began to shout, "Swanee—Swanee—Swanee," punching the steering wheel. Behind the windows of your car, what you do doesn't matter. One of the privileges of liberty car ownership affords.

Of course! The Swanee. Or Suwannee (spelling preferred in the South). But this was a crisis in my mental life. I had had a double purpose in looking up George Herbert—not only the appropriateness of the season but as a test of my memory. So, too, my recollection of *Fonstein* v. *Rose* is in part a test of memory, and also a more general investigation of the same, for if you go back to the assertion that memory is life and forgetting death ("mercifully forgetting," the commonest adverb linked by writers with the participle, reflecting the preponderance of the opinion that so much of life *is* despair), I have established at the very least that I am still able to keep up my struggle for existence.

Hoping for victory? Well, what would a victory be?

I took Rabbi X/Y's word for it that the Fonsteins had moved away and were unlocatable. Probably they had, like me, retired. But whereas I am in Philadelphia, hanging in there, as the idiom puts it, they had very likely abandoned that ground of struggle the sullen North and gone to Sarasota or to Palm Springs. They had the money for it. America was good to Harry Fonstein, after all, and delivered on its splendid promises. He had been spared the worst we have here—routine industrial or clerical jobs and bureaucratic employment. As I wished the Fonsteins well, I was pleased for them. My much-appreciated in-absentia friends, so handsomely installed in my consciousness.

Not having heard from me, I assumed, they had given up on me, after three decades. Freud has laid down the principle that the *un*conscious does not recognize death. But as you see, consciousness is freaky too.

So I went to work digging up forgotten names of relatives from my potato-patch mind—Rosenberg, Rosenthal, Sorkin, Swerdlow, Bleistiff, Fradkin. Jewish surnames are another curious subject, so many of them imposed by German, Polish, or Russian officialdom (expecting bribes from applicants), others the invention of Jewish fantasy. How often the name of the rose was invoked, as in the case of Billy himself. There were few other words for flowers in the pale. *Margaritka,* for one. The daisy. Not a suitable family name for anybody.

Aunt Mildred, my stepmother, had been cared for during her last years by relatives in Elizabeth, the Rosensafts, and my investigations began with them. They weren't cordial or friendly on the phone, because I had seldom visited Mildred toward the last. I think she began to claim that she had brought me up and even put me through college. (The funds came from a Prudential policy paid for by my own mother.) This was a venial offense, which gave me the reasons for being standoffish that I was looking for. I wasn't fond of the Rosensafts either. They had taken my father's watch and chain after he died. But then one can live without these objects of sentimental value. Old Mrs. Rosensaft said she had lost track of the Fonsteins. She thought the Swerdlows in Morristown might know where Harry and Sorella had gone.

Information gave me Swerdlow's number. Dialing, I reached an answering machine. The voice of Mrs. Swerdlow, affecting an accent more suitable to upper-class Morristown than to her native Newark, asked me to leave my name, number, and the date of the call. I hate answering machines, so I hung up. Besides, I avoid giving my unlisted number.

As I went up to my second-floor office that night holding the classic Philadelphia banister, reflecting that I was pretty sick of the unshared grandeur of this mansion, I once more considered Sarasota or the sociable Florida Keys. Elephants and acrobats, circuses in winter quarters, would be more amusing. Moving to Palm Springs was out of the question. And while the Keys had a large homosexual population, I was more at home with gay people, thanks to my years in the Village, than with businessmen in California. In any case, I couldn't bear much more of these thirty-foot ceilings and all the mahogany solitude. This mansion demanded too much from me, and I was definitely conscious of a strain. My point had long ago been made—I could achieve such a dwelling place, possess it in style. Now take it away, I thought, in a paraphrase of the old tune "I'm so tired of roses, take them all away." I decided to discuss the subject again with my son, Henry. His wife didn't like the mansion; her tastes were modern, and she was satirical, too, about the transatlantic rivalry of parvenu American wealth with the titled wealth of Victorian London. She had turned me down dead flat when I tried to give the place to them.

What I was thinking was that if I could find Harry and Sorella, I'd join them in retirement, if they'd accept my company (forgiving the insult of neglect). For me it was natural to wonder whether I had not exaggerated (urged on by a desire for a woman of a deeper nature) Sorella's qualities in my reminiscences, and I gave further thought to this curious personality. I never had forgotten what she had said about the testing of Jewry by the American experience. Her interview with Billy Rose had itself been such an American thing. Again Billy: Weak? Weak! Vain? Oh, very! And trivial for sure. Creepy Billy. Still, in a childish way, big-minded—spacious; and spacious wasn't just a boast adjective from "America the Beautiful" (the spacious skies) but the dropping of fifteen to twenty actual millions on a rest-and-culture garden in Jerusalem, the core of Jewish history, the navel of the earth. This gesture of oddball magnificence was American. American and Oriental.

And even if I didn't in the end settle near the Fonsteins, I could pay them a visit. I couldn't help asking why I had turned away from such a terrific pair—Sorella, so mysteriously obese; Fonstein with his reddish skin (once stone white), his pomegranate face. I may as well include myself, as a third—a tall old man with a structural curl at the top like a fiddlehead fern or a bishop's crook.

Therefore I started looking for Harry and Sorella not merely because I had promised Rabbi X/Y, nor for the sake of the crazy old man in Jerusalem who was destitute. If it was only money that he needed, I could easily write a check or ask my banker to send him one. The bank charges eight bucks for this convenience, and a phone call would take care of it. But I preferred to attend to things in my own way, from my mansion office, dialing the numbers myself, by-passing the Mnemosyne Institute and its secretaries.

Using old address books, I called all over the place. (If only cemeteries had switchboards. "Hello, Operator, I'm calling area code 000.") I didn't want to involve the girls at the Institute in any of this, least of all in my investigations. When I reached a number, the conversation was bound to be odd, and a strain on the memory of the Founder. "Why, how are you?" somebody would ask whom I hadn't seen in three decades. "Do you remember my husband, Max? My daughter, Zoe?" Would I know what to say?

Yes, I would. But then again, why should I? How nice oblivion would be in such cases, and I could say, "Max? Zoe? No, I can't say that I do." On the fringes of the family, or in remote, time-dulled social circles, random memories can be an affliction. What you see first, retrospectively, are the psychopaths, the uglies, the cheapies, the stingies, the hypochondriacs, the family bores, humanoids, and tyrants. These have dramatic staying power. Harder to recover are the kind eyes, gentle faces, of the comedians who wanted to entertain you, gratis, divert you from troubles. An important part of my method is that memory chains are constructed thematically. Where themes are lacking there can be little or no recall. So, for instance, Billy, our friend Bellarosa, could not easily place Fonstein because of an unfortunate thinness of purely human themes—as contrasted with business, publicity, or sexual themes. To give a strongly negative example, there are murderers who can't recall their crimes because they have no interest in the existence or nonexistence of their victims. So, students, only pertinent themes assure full recollection.

Some of the old people I reached put me down spiritedly: "If you remember so much about me, how come I haven't seen you since the Korean War! . . ." "No, I can't tell you anything about Salkind's niece Sorella. Salkind came home to New Jersey after Castro took over. He died in an old people's nursing racket setup back in the late sixties."

One man commented, "The pages of calendars crumble away. They're like the dandruff of time. What d'you want from me?"

Calling from a Philadelphia mansion, I was at a disadvantage. A person in my position will discover, in contact with people from Passaic, Elizabeth, or Paterson, how many defenses he has organized against vulgarity or the lower grades of thought. I didn't want to talk about Medicare or social security checks or hearing aids or pacemakers or bypass surgery.

From a few sources I heard criticisms of Sorella. "Salkind was a bachelor, had no children, and that woman should have done something for the old fella."

"He never married?"

"Never," said the bitter lady I had on the line. "But he married *her* off, for his own brother's sake. Anyway, they've all checked out, so what's the diff."

"And you can't tell me where I might find Sorella?"

"I could care less."

"No," I said. "You couldn't care less."

So the matchmaker himself had been a lifelong bachelor. He had disinterestedly found a husband for his brother's daughter, bringing together two disadvantaged people.

Another lady said about Sorella, "She was remote. She looked down on my type of conversation. I think she was a snob. I tried to sign her up once for a group tour in Europe. My temple sisterhood put together a real good charter-flight package. Then Sorella told me that French was her second language, and she didn't need anybody to interpret for her in Paris. I should have told her, 'I knew you when no man would give you a second look and would even take back the first look if he could.' So that's how it was. Sorella was too good for everybody. . . ."

I saw what these ladies meant (this was a trend among my informants). They accused Mrs. Fonstein of being uppish, too grand. Almost all were offended. She preferred the company of Mrs. Hamet, the old actress with the paraffin-white tubercular face. Sorella was too grand for Billy too; hurling Mrs. Hamet's deadly dossier at him was the gesture of a superior person, a person of intelligence and taste. Queenly, imperial, and inevitably isolated. This was the consensus of all the gossips, the elderly people I telephoned from the triple isolation of my Philadelphia residence.

The Fonsteins and I were meant to be company for one another. They weren't going to force themselves on me, however. They assumed that I was above them socially, in upper-class Philadelphia, and that I didn't want their friendship. I don't suppose that my late wife, Deirdre, would have cared for Sorella, with her pince-nez and high manner, the working of her intellect and the problems of her cumulous body—trying to fit itself into a Hepplewhite chair in our dining room. Fonstein would have been comparatively easy for Deirdre to be with. Still, if I was not an assimilationist, I was at least an avoider of uncomfortable mixtures, and in the end I am stuck with these twenty empty rooms.

I can remember driving with my late father through western Pennsylvania. He was struck by the amount of land without a human figure in it. So much space! After long silence, in a traveler's trance resembling the chessboard trance, he said, "Ah, how many Jews might have been settled here! Room enough for everybody."

At times I feel like a socket that remembers its tooth.

As I made call after call, I was picturing my reunion with the Fonsteins. I had them placed mentally in Sarasota, Florida, and imagined the sunny strolls we might take in the winter quarters of Ringling or Hagenbeck, chatting about events long past at the King David Hotel—Billy Rose's lost suitcases, Noguchi's Oriental reserve. In old manila envelopes I found color snapshots from Jerusalem, among them a photograph of Fonstein and Sorella against the background of the Judean desert, the burning stones of Ezekiel, not yet (even today) entirely cooled, those stones of fire among which the cherubim had walked. In that fierce place, two modern persons, the man in a business suit, the woman in floating white, a married couple holding hands—her fat palm in his inventor's fingers. I couldn't help thinking that Sorella didn't have a real biography until Harry entered her life. And he, Harry, whom Hitler had intended to kill, had a biography insofar as Hitler had marked him for murder, insofar as he had fled, was saved by Billy, reached America, invented a better thermostat. And here they were in color, the Judean desert behind them, as husband and wife in a once-upon-a-time Coney Island might have posed against a painted backdrop or sitting on a slice of moon. As tourists in the Holy Land where were they, I wondered, biographically speaking? How memorable had this trip been for them? The question sent me back to myself and, Jewish style, answered itself with yet another question: What was there worth remembering?

When I got to the top of the stairs—this was the night before last—I couldn't bring myself to go to bed just yet. One does grow weary of taking care of this man-sized doll, the elderly retiree, giving him his pills, pulling on his socks, spooning up his cornflakes, shaving his face, seeing to it that he gets his sleep. Instead of opening the bedroom door, I went to my second-floor sitting room.

To save myself from distraction by concentrating every kind of business in a single office, I do bills, bank statements, legal correspondence on the ground floor, and my higher activities I carry upstairs. Deirdre had approved of this. It challenged her to furnish each setting appropriately. One of my diversions is to make the rounds of antiques shops and look at comparable pieces, examining and pricing them, noting what a shrewd buyer Deirdre had been. In doing this, I build a case against remaining in Philadelphia, a town in which a man finds little else to do with himself on a dull afternoon.

Even the telephone in my second-story room is a French instrument with a porcelain mouthpiece—blue and white Quimper. Deirdre had bought it on the Boulevard Haussmann, and Baron Charlus might have romanced his boyfriends with it, speaking low and scheming intricately into this very phone. It would have amused him, if he haunted objects of common use, to watch me dialing the Swerdlows' number again, pursuing my Fonstein inquiries.

On this *art nouveau* article—for those who escape from scientific ignorance (how *do* telephones operate?) with the aid of high-culture toys—I tried Morristown again, and this time Hyman Swerdlow himself answered. As soon as I heard his voice, he appeared before me, and presently his wife also was reborn in my memory and stood beside him. Swerdlow, who was directly related to Fonstein, had been an investment counselor. Trained on Wall Street, he settled in stylish New Jersey. He was a respectable, smooth person, very quiet in manner, "understated," to borrow a term from the interior decorators. His look was both saturnine and guilt-free. He probably didn't like what he had made of his life, but there was no way to revise that now. He settled for good manners—he was very polite, he wore Brooks Brothers grays and tans. His tone was casual. One could assimilate now *without* converting. You didn't have to choose between Jehovah and Jesus. I had known old Swerdlow. His son had inherited an ancient Jewish face from him, dark and craggy. Hyman had discovered a way to drain the Jewish charge from it. What replaced it was a look of perfect dependability. He was well-spoken. He could be trusted with your pension funds. He wouldn't dream of making a chancy investment. His children were a biochemist and a molecular biologist, respectively. His wife could now devote herself to her watercolor box.

I believe the Swerdlows were very intelligent. They may even have been deeply intelligent. What had happened to them couldn't have been helped.

"I can't tell you anything about Fonstein," Swerdlow said. "I've somehow lost track. . . ."

I realized that, like the Fonsteins, Swerdlow and his wife had isolated themselves. No deliberate choice was made. You went your own way, and you found yourself in Greater New York but beyond the bedroom communities, decently situated. Your history, too, became one of your options. Whether or not having a history was a "consideration" was entirely up to you.

Cool Swerdlow, who of course remembered me (I was rich, I might have become an important client; there was, however, no reproach detectable in his tone), now was asking what I wanted with Harry Fonstein. I said that a mad old man in Jerusalem needed Fonstein's help. Swerdlow dropped his inquiry then and there. "We never did develop a relationship," he said. "Harry was very decent. His wife, however, was somewhat overpowering."

Decoded, this meant that Edna Swerdlow had not taken to Sorella. One learns soon enough to fill in the simple statements to which men like Swerdlow limit themselves. They avoid putting themselves out and they shun (perhaps even hate) psychological elaboration.

"When did you last see the Fonsteins?"

"During the Lakewood period," said tactful Swerdlow—he avoided touching upon my father's death, possibly a painful subject. "I think it was when Sorella talked so much about Billy Rose."

"They were involved with him. *He* refused to be drawn in. . . . So you heard them talking about it?"

"Even sensible people lose their heads over celebrities. What claim did Harry have on Billy Rose, and why *should* Billy have done more than he did? A man like Rose has to ration the number of people he can take on."

"Like a sign in an elevator—'Maximum load twenty-eight hundred pounds'?"

"If you like."

"When I think of the Fonstein-Billy thing," I said, "I'm liable to see European Jewry also. What was all *that* about? To me, the operational term is Justice. Once and for all it was seen that this expectation, or reliance, had no foundation. You had to forget about justice . . . whether, taken seriously for so long, it could be taken seriously still."

Swerdlow could not allow me to go on. This was not his kind of conversation. "Put it any way you like—how does it apply to Billy? What was *he* supposed to do about it?"

Well, I didn't expect Billy to take this, or anything else, upon himself. From Hyman Swerdlow I felt that speaking of Justice was not only out of place but off the wall. And if the Baron Charlus had been listening, haunting his telephone with the Quimper mouthpiece, he would have turned from this conversation with contempt. I didn't greatly blame myself, and I certainly did not feel like a fool. At worst it had been inappropriate to call Swerdlow for information and then, without preparation, swerve wildly into such a subject, trying to carry him with me. These were matters I thought about privately, the subjective preoccupations of a person who lived alone in a great Philadelphia house in which he felt out of place, and who had lost sight of the difference between brooding and permissible conversation. I had no business out of the blue to talk to Swerdlow about Justice or Honor or the Platonic Ideas or the expectations of the Jews. Anyway, his tone now made it clear that he wanted to get rid of me, so I said, "This Rabbi X/Y from Jerusalem, who speaks better than fair English, got me to promise that I would locate Fonstein. He said he hadn't been able to find him."

"Are you sure that Fonstein isn't listed in the directory?"

No, I wasn't sure, was I? I hadn't looked. That was just like me, wasn't it? "I assumed the rabbi *had* looked," I said. "I feel chastened. I shouldn't have taken the man's word for it. *He* should have looked. I took it for granted. You're probably right."

"If I can be of further use . . . ?"

By pointing out how he would have gone about finding Fonstein, Swerdlow showed me how lopsided I was. Sure it was stupid of me not to look in the phone directory. Smart, smart, but a dope, as the old people used to say. For the Fonsteins *were* listed. Information gave me their number. There they were, as accessible as millions of others, in small print, row on row on row, the endless listings.

I dialed the Fonsteins, braced for a conversation—my opening words prepared, my excuses for neglecting them made with warmth, just such warmth as I actually felt. Should they be inclined to blame me—well, I was to blame.

But they were out, or had unplugged their line. Elderly people, they probably turned in early. After a dozen rings, I gave up and went to bed myself. And when I got into bed—without too much fear of being alone in this huge place, not that there aren't plenty of murdering housebreakers in the city—I picked up a book, preparing to settle in for a long read.

Deirdre's bedside books had now become mine. I was curious to know how she had read herself to sleep. What had been on her mind became important to me. In her last years she had turned to such books as *Koré Kosmu,* the *Hermetica* published by Oxford, and also selections from the Zohar. Like the heroine of Poe's story "Morella." Odd that

Deirdre had said so little about it. She was not a secretive lady, but like many others she kept her own counsel in matters of thought and religion. I loved to see her absorbed in a book, mummied up on her side of the antique bed, perfectly still under the covers. A pair of lamps on each side were like bronze thornbushes. I was always after Deirdre to get sensible reading lights. Nothing could persuade her— she was obstinate when her taste was challenged—and three years after she passed away I was still shopping: Those sculpture brambles never will be replaced.

Some men fall asleep on the sofa after dinner. This often results in insomnia, and as I hate to be up in the night, my routine is to read in bed until midnight, concentrating on passages marked by Deirdre and on her notes at the back of the book. It has become one of my sentimental rituals.

But on this night I passed out after a few sentences, and presently I began to dream.

There is great variety in my dreams. My nights are often busy. I have anxious dreams, amusing dreams, desire dreams, symbolic dreams. There are, however, dreams that are all business and go straight to the point. I suppose we have the dreams we deserve, and they may even be prepared in secret.

Without preliminaries, I found myself in a hole. Night, a dark plain, a pit, and from the start I was already trying to climb out. In fact, I had been working at it for some time. This was a dug hole, not a grave but a trap prepared for me by somebody who knew me well enough to anticipate that I would fall in. I could see over the edge, but I couldn't crawl out because my legs were tangled and caught in ropes or roots. I was clawing at the dirt for something I could grip. I had to rely on my arms. If I could hoist myself onto the edge, I might free the lower body. Only, I was already exhausted, winded, and if I did manage to pull myself out, I'd be too beat to fight. My struggles were watched by the person who had planned this for me. I could see his boots. Down the way, in a similar ditch, another man was also wearing himself out. He wasn't going to make it either. Despair was not principally what I felt, nor fear of death. What made the dream terrible was my complete conviction of error, my miscalculation of strength, and the recognition that my forces were drained to the bottom. The whole structure was knocked flat. There wasn't a muscle in me that I hadn't called on, and for the first time I was aware of them all, down to the tiniest, and the best they could do was not enough. I couldn't call on myself, couldn't meet the demand, couldn't put out. There's no reason why I should ask you to feel this with me, and I won't blame you for avoiding it; I've done that myself. I always avoid extremes, even during sleep. Besides, we all recognize the burden of my dream: Life so diverse, the Grand Masquerade of Mortality shriveling to a hole in the ground. Still, that did not exhaust the sense of the dream, and the remainder is essential to the interpretation of what I've set down about Fonstein, Sorella, or Billy even. I couldn't otherwise have described it. It isn't so much a dream as a communication. I was being shown—and I was aware of this in sleep—that I had made a mistake, a lifelong mistake: something wrong, false, now fully manifest.

Revelations in old age can shatter everything you've put in place from the beginning—all the wiliness of a lifetime of expertise and labor, interpreting and reinterpreting in patching your fortified delusions, the work of the swarm of your defensive shock troops, which will go on throwing up more perverse (or insane) barriers. All this is bypassed in a dream like this one. When you have one of these, all you can do is bow to the inevitable conclusions.

Your imagination of strength is connected to your apprehensions of brutality, where that brutality is fully manifested or absolute. Mine is a New World version of reality—granting me the presumption that there is anything real about it. In the New World, your strength *doesn't* give out. That was the reason why your European parents, your old people, fed you so well in this land of youth. They were trained in submission, but you were free and bred in liberty. You were equal, you were strong, and here you could not be put to death, as Jews *there* had been.

But your soul brought the truth to you so forcibly that you woke up in your fifty-fifty bed—half Jewish, half Wasp—since, thanks to the powers of memory, you were the owner of a Philadelphia mansion (too disproportionate a reward), and there the dream had just come to a stop. An old man resuming ordinary consciousness opened his still-frightened eyes and saw the bronze brier-bush lamp with bulbs glowing in it. His neck on two pillows, stacked for reading, was curved like a shepherd's crook.

It wasn't the dream alone that was so frightful, though that was bad enough; it was the accompanying revelation that was so hard to take. It wasn't death that had scared me, it was disclosure: I wasn't what I thought I was. I really didn't understand merciless brutality. And whom should I take this up with now? Deirdre was gone; I can't discuss things like this with my son—he's all administrator and executive. That left Fonstein and Sorella. Perhaps.

Sorella had said, I recall, that Fonstein, in his orthopedic boot, couldn't vault over walls and escape like Douglas Fairbanks. In the movies, Douglas Fairbanks was always too much for his enemies. They couldn't hold him. In *The Black Pirate* he disabled a sailing vessel all by himself. Holding a knife, he slid down the mainsail, slicing it in half. You couldn't have locked a man like that in a cattle car; he would have broken out. Sorella wasn't speaking of Douglas Fairbanks, nor did she refer to Fonstein only. Her remark was ultimately meant for me. Yes, she was talking of me and also of Billy Rose. For Fonstein was Fonstein—he was

Mitteleuropa. I, on the other hand, was from the Eastern Seaboard—born in New Jersey, educated at Washington Square College, a big mnemonic success in Philadelphia. I was a Jew of an entirely different breed. And therefore (yes, go on, you can't avoid it now) closer to Billy Rose and his rescue operation, the personal underground inspired by *The Scarlet Pimpernel*—the Hollywood of Leslie Howard, who acted the Pimpernel, substituted for the Hollywood of Douglas Fairbanks. There was no way, therefore, in which I could grasp the real facts in the case of Fonstein. I hadn't understood *Fonstein* v. *Rose,* and I badly wanted to say this to Harry and Sorella. You pay a price for being a child of the New World.

I decided to switch off the lamp, which, fleetingly, was associated with the thicket in which Abraham-*avinu* had found a ram caught by the horns—as you see, I was bombarded from too many sides. Now illuminated particles of Jewish history were coming at me.

An old man has had a lifetime to learn to control his jitters in the night. Whatever I was (and that, at this late stage, still remained to be seen), I would need strength in the morning to continue my investigation. So I had to take measures to avoid a fretful night. Great souls may welcome insomnia and are happy to think of God or Science in the dead of night, but I was too disturbed to think straight. An important teaching of the Mnemosyne System, however, is to learn to make your mind a blank. You will yourself to think nothing. You expel all the distractions. Tonight's distractions happened to be very serious. I had discovered for how long I had shielded myself from unbearable imaginations—no, not imaginations, but recognitions—of murder, of relish in torture, of the ground bass of brutality, without which no human music ever is performed.

So I applied my famous method. I willed myself to think

nothing. I shut out all thoughts. When you think nothing, consciousness is driven out. Consciousness being gone, you are asleep.

I conked out. It was a mercy.

In the morning, I found myself being supernormal. At the bathroom sink I rinsed my mouth, for it was parched (the elderly often suffer from such dryness). Shaved and brushed, I exercised on my ski machine (mustn't let the muscles go slack) and then I dressed and, when dressed, stuck my shoes under the revolving brush. Once more in rightful possession of a fine house, where Francis X. Biddle was once a neighbor and Emily Dickinson a guest at tea (there were other personages to list), I went down to breakfast. My housekeeper came from the kitchen with granola, strawberries, and black coffee. First the coffee, more than the usual morning fix.

"How did you sleep?" said Sarah, my old-fashioned caretaker. So much discretion, discernment, wisdom of life rolled up in this portly black lady. We didn't communicate in words, but we tacitly exchanged information at a fairly advanced level. From the amount of coffee I swallowed she could tell that I was shamming supernormalcy. From my side, I was aware that possibly I was crediting Sarah with very wide powers because I missed my wife, missed contact with womanly intelligence. I recognized also that I had begun to place my hopes and needs on Sorella Fonstein, whom I now was longing to see. My mind persisted in placing the Fonsteins in Sarasota, in winter quarters with the descendants of Hannibal's elephants, amid palm trees and hibiscus. An idealized Sarasota, where my heart apparently was yearning ever.

Sarah put more coffee before me in my study. Probably new lines had appeared in my face overnight—signs indicating the demolition of a long-standing structure. (How *could* I have been such a creep!)

At last my Fonstein call was answered—I was phoning on the half hour.

A young man spoke. "Hello, who is this?"

How clever of Swerdlow to suggest trying the old listed number.

"Is this the Fonstein residence?"

"That's what it is."

"Would you be Gilbert Fonstein, the son?"

"I would not," the young person said, breezy but amiable. He was, as they say, laid back. No suggestion that I was deranging him (Sorella entered into this—she liked to make bilingual puns). "I'm a friend of Gilbert's, house-sitting here. Walk the dog, water the plants, set the timed lights. And who are you?"

"An old relative—friend of the family. I see that I'll have to leave a message. Tell them that it has to do with another Fonstein who lives in Jerusalem and claims to be an uncle or cousin to Harry. I had a call from a rabbi—X/Y—who feels that something should be done, since the old guy is off the wall."

"In what way?"

"He's eccentric, deteriorated, prophetic, psychopathic. A decaying old man, but he's still ebullient and full of protest. . . ."

I paused briefly. You never can tell whom you're talking to, seen or unseen. What's more, I am one of those suggestible types, apt to take my cue from the other fellow and fall into his style of speech. I detected a certain freewheeling charm in the boy at the other end, and there was an exchange of charm for charm. Evidently I wanted to engage this young fellow's interest. In short, to imitate, to hit it off and get facts from him.

"This old Jerusalem character says he's a Fonstein and wants money?" he said. "You sound as if you yourself were in a position to help, so why not wire money."

"True. However, Harry could identify him, check his credentials, and naturally would want to hear that he's turned up alive. He may have been on the dead list. Are you only a house-sitter? You sound like a friend of the family."

"I see we're going to have a talk. Hold a minute while I find my bandanna. It's starting to be allergy time, and my whole head is raw. . . . Which relative are you?"

"I run an institute in Philadelphia."

"Oh, the memory man. I've heard of you. You go back to the time of Billy Rose—*that* flake. Harry disliked talking about it, but Sorella and Gilbert often did. . . . Can you hold on till I locate the handkerchief? Wiping my beard with Kleenex leaves crumbs of paper."

When he laid down the phone, I used the pause to place him plausibly. I formed an image of a heavy young man— a thick head of hair, a beer paunch, a T-shirt with a logo or slogan. *Act Up* was now a popular one. I pictured a representative member of the youth population seen on every street in every section of the country and even in the smallest of towns. Rough boots, stone-washed jeans, bristly cheeks—something like Leadville or Silverado miners of the last century, except that these young people were not laboring, never would labor with picks. It must have diverted him to chat me up. An old gent in Philadelphia, moderately famous and worth lots of money. He couldn't have imagined the mansion, the splendid room where I sat holding the French phone, expensively rewired, an instrument once the property of a descendant of the Merovingian nobility. (I wouldn't give up on the Baron Charlus.)

The young man was not a hang-loose, hippie handyman untroubled by intelligence, whatever else. I was certain of that. He had much to tell me. Whether he was malicious I had no way of saying. He was manipulative, however, and he had already succeeded in setting the tone of our exchange.

Finally, he had information about the Fonsteins, and it was information I wanted.

"I do go back a long way," I said. "I've been out of touch with the Fonsteins for too many years. How have they arranged their retirement? Do they divide their year between New Jersey and a warm climate? Somehow I fancy them in Sarasota."

"You need a new astrologer."

He wasn't being satirical—protective rather. He now treated me like a senior citizen. He gentled me.

"I was surprised lately when I reckoned up the dates and realized the Fonsteins and I last met about thirty years ago, in Jerusalem. But emotionally I was in contact—that does happen." I tried to persuade him, and I felt in reality that it was true.

Curiously, he agreed. "It would make a dissertation subject," he said. "Out of sight isn't necessarily out of mind. People withdraw into themselves, and then they work up imaginary affections. It's a common American condition."

"Because of the continental U.S.A.—the terrific distances?"

"Pennsylvania and New Jersey are neighboring states."

"I do seem to have closed out New Jersey mentally," I admitted. "You sound as though you have studied . . . ?"

"Gilbert and I were at school together."

"Didn't he do physics at Cal Tech?"

"He switched to mathematics—probability theory."

"There I'm totally ignorant."

"That makes two of us," he said, adding, "I find you kind of interesting to talk to."

"One is always looking for someone to have a real exchange with."

He seemed to agree. He said, "I'm inclined to make the time for it, whenever possible."

He had described himself as a house-sitter, without mentioning another occupation. In a sense I was a house-sitter myself, notwithstanding that I owned the property. My son and his wife may also have seen me in such a light. A nice corollary was that my soul played the role of sitter in my body.

It did in fact cross my mind that the young man wasn't altogether disinterested. That I was undergoing an examination or evaluation. So far, he had told me nothing about the Fonsteins except that they didn't winter in Sarasota and that Gilbert had studied mathematics. He didn't say that he himself had attended Cal Tech. And when he said that out of sight wasn't invariably out of mind, I thought his dissertation, if he had written one, might have been in the field of psychology or sociology.

I recognized that I was half afraid of asking direct questions about the Fonsteins. By neglecting them, I had compromised my right to ask freely. There were things I did and did not want to hear. The house-sitter sensed this, it amused him, and he led me on. He was light and made sporty talk, but I began to feel there was a grim side to him.

I decided that it was time to speak up, and I said, "Where can I reach Harry and Sorella, or is there a reason you can't give out their number?"

"I haven't got one."

"Please don't talk riddles."

"They can't be reached."

"What are you telling me! Did I put it off too long?"

"I'm afraid so."

"They're dead, then."

I was shocked. Something essential in me caved in, broke down. At my age, a man is well prepared to hear news of death. What I felt most sharply and immediately was that I had abandoned two extraordinary people whom I had always said I valued and held dear. I found myself making a list of names: Billy is dead; Mrs. Hamet, dead; Sorella, dead; Harry, dead. All the principals, dead.

"Were they sick? Did Sorella have cancer?"

"They died about six months ago, on the Jersey Turnpike. The way it's told, a truck and trailer went out of control. But I wish I didn't have to tell you this, sir. As a relative, you'll take it hard. They were killed instantly. And thank God, because their car folded on them and it took welders to cut the bodies free— This must be hard for somebody who knew them well."

He was, incidentally, giving me the business. To some extent, I had it coming. But at any moment during these thirty years, any of us might have died in an instant. I too might have. And he was wrong to assume that I was a Jew of the old type, bound to react sentimentally to such news as this.

"You *are* a senior citizen, you said. You'd have to be, given the numbers."

My voice was low. I said I was one. "Where were the Fonsteins going?"

"They were driving from New York, bound for Atlantic City."

I saw the bloodstained bodies delivered from the car and stretched out on the grass slope—the police flares, the crush of diverted traffic and the wavering of the dark, gassed atmosphere, the sucking shrieks of the ambulance, the paramedics and their body bags. Last summer's heat was tormenting. You might say the dead sweated blood.

If you're deciding which is the gloomiest expressway in the country, the Jersey Pike is certainly a front runner. This was no place for Sorella, who loved Europe, to be killed. Harry's forty American years of compensation for the destruction of his family in Poland suddenly were up.

"Why were they going to Atlantic City?"

"Their son was there, having trouble."

"Was he gambling?"

"It was pretty widely known, so I'm able to say. After all, he wrote a mathematical study on winning at blackjack. Math mavens say it's quite a piece of work. On the real-life side, he's gotten into trouble over this."

They were rushing to the aid of their American son when they were killed.

"It must be very dreary to hear this," the young man said.

"I looked forward to seeing them again. I'd been promising myself to resume contact."

"I don't suppose death is the worst . . . ," he said.

I wasn't about to go into eschatology with this kid on the telephone and start delineating the various grades of evil. Although, God knows, the phone may encourage many forms of disclosure, and you may hear as much if not more from the soul by long distance as face to face.

"Which one was driving?"

"Mrs. Fonstein was, and maybe being reckless."

"I see—an emergency, and a mother in a terrible hurry. Was she still huge?"

"The same for years, and right up against the wheel. But there weren't many people like Sorella Fonstein. You don't want to criticize."

"I'm not criticizing," I said. "I would have gone to the funeral to pay my respects."

"Too bad you didn't come and speak. It wasn't much of a memorial service."

"I might have told the Billy Rose story to a gathering of friends in the chapel."

"There was no gathering," the young man said. "And did you know that when Billy died, they say that he couldn't be buried for a long time. He had to wait until the court decided what to do about the million-dollar tomb provision in his will. There was a legal battle over it."

"I never heard."

"Because you don't read the *News,* or *Newsday.* Not even the *Post.*"

"Was *that* what happened!"

"He was kept on ice. This used to be discussed by the Fonsteins. They wondered about the Jewish burial rules."

"Does Gilbert take any interest in his Jewish background—for instance, in his father's history?"

Gilbert's friend hesitated ever so slightly—just enough to make me think that he was Jewish himself. I don't say that he disowned being a Jew. Evidently he didn't want to reckon with it. The only life he cared to lead was that of an American. So hugely absorbing, that. So absorbing that one existence was too little for it. It could drink up a hundred existences, if you had them to offer, and reach out for more.

"What you just asked is—I translate—whether Gilbert is one of those science freaks with minimal human motivation," he said. "You have to remember what a big thing gambling is to him. It never could be *my* thing. You couldn't pay me to go to Atlantic City, especially since the double-deck disaster. They put a double-deck bus on the road, filled with passengers bound for the casino. It was too high to clear one of the viaducts, and the top was torn away."

"Did many die? Were heads sheared off?"

"You'd have to check the *Times* to find out."

"I wouldn't care to. But where is Gilbert now? He inherited, I suppose."

"Well, sure he did, and right now he's in Las Vegas. He took a young lady with him. She's trained in his method, which involves memorizing the deck in every deal. You keep mental lists of cards that have been played, and you apply various probability factors. They tell me that the math of it is just genius."

"The system depends on memorizing?"

"Yes. That's up your alley. Is Gilbert the girl's lover? is the next consideration. Well, this wouldn't work without sex interest. The gambling alone wouldn't hold a young woman for long. Does she enjoy Las Vegas? How could she not? It's the biggest showplace in the world—the heart of the American entertainment industry. Which city today is closest to a holy city—like Lhasa or Calcutta or Chartres or Jerusalem? Here it could be New York for money, Washington for power, or Las Vegas attracting people by the millions. Nothing to compare with it in the history of the whole world."

"Ah," I said. "It's more in the Billy Rose vein than in the Harry Fonstein vein. But how is Gilbert making out?"

"I haven't finished talking about the sex yet," said the bitter-witty young man. "Is the gambling a turn-on for sex, or does sex fuel the gambling? Figuring it as a sublimation. Let's assume that for Gilbert, abstraction is dominant. But past a certain abstraction point, people are said to be definitely mad."

"Poor Sorella—poor Harry! Maybe it was their death that threw him."

"I can't make myself responsible for a diagnosis. My own narcissistic problem is plenty severe. I confess I expected a token legacy, because I was damn near a family member and looked after Gilbert."

"I see."

"You don't see. This brings my faith in feelings face to face with the real conditions of existence."

"Your feelings for Fonstein and Sorella?"

"The feelings Sorella led me to believe she had for me."

"Counting on you to take care of Gilbert."

"Well . . . this has been a neat conversation. Good to talk to a person from the past who was so fond of the Fonsteins. We'll all miss them. Harry had the dignity, but Sorella had the dynamism. I can see why you'd be upset—your timing was off. But don't pine too much."

On this commiseration, I cradled the phone, and there it was, on its high mount, a conversation piece from another epoch sitting before a man with an acute need for conversation. Stung by the words of the house-sitter. I also considered that owing to Gilbert, the Fonsteins from their side had avoided me—he was so promising, the prodigy they had had the marvelous luck to produce and who for mysterious reasons (Fonstein would have felt them to be mysterious American reasons) had gone awry. They wouldn't have wanted me to know about this.

As for pining—well, that young man had been putting me on. He was one of those lesser devils that come out of every pore of society. All you have to do is press the social soil. He was taunting me—for my Jewish sentiments. Dear, dear! Two more old friends gone, just when I was ready after thirty years of silence to open my arms to them: Let's sit down together and recall the past and speak again of Billy Rose—"sad stories of the death of kings." And the "sitter" had been putting it to me, existentialist style. Like: Whose disappearance will fill you with despair, sir? Whom can you not live without? Whom do you painfully long for? Which of your dead hangs over you daily? Show me where and how death has mutilated you. Where are your wounds? Whom would you pursue beyond the gates of death?

What a young moron! Doesn't he think I know all that?

I had a good mind to phone the boy back and call him on his low-grade cheap-shot nihilism. But it would be an absurd thing to do if improvement of the understanding (*his* understanding) was my aim. You can never dismantle all these modern mental structures. There are so many of them that they face you like an interminable vast city.

Suppose I were to talk to him about the roots of memory in feeling—about the themes that collect and hold the memory; if I were to tell him what retention of the past really means. Things like: "If sleep is forgetting, forgetting is also sleep, and sleep is to consciousness what death is to life. So that the Jews ask even God to remember, *'Yiskor Elohim.'*"

God doesn't forget, but your prayer requests him particularly to remember your dead. But how was I to make an impression on a kid like that? I chose instead to record everything I could remember of the Bellarosa Connection, and set it all down with a Mnemosyne flourish.

A

THEFT

———

TO MY SON,

DANIEL O. BELLOW

Clara Velde, to begin with what was conspicuous about her, had short blond hair, fashionably cut, growing upon a head unusually big. In a person of an inert character a head of such size might have seemed a deformity; in Clara, because she had so much personal force, it came across as ruggedly handsome. She needed that head; a mind like hers demanded space. She was big-boned; her shoulders were not broad but high. Her blue eyes, exceptionally large, grew prominent when she brooded. The nose was small—ancestrally a North Sea nose. The mouth was very good but stretched extremely wide when she grinned, when she wept. Her forehead was powerful. When she came to the threshold of middle age, the lines of her naive charm deepened; they would be permanent now. Really, everything about her was conspicuous, not only the size and shape of her head. She must have decided long ago that for the likes of her there could be no cover-up; she couldn't divert energy into disguises. So there she was, a rawboned American woman. She had very good legs—who knows what you would have seen if pioneer women had worn shorter skirts. She bought her clothes in the best shops and was knowledgeable about cosmetics. Nevertheless the backcountry look never left her. She came from the sticks; there could be no mistake about that. Her people? Indiana and Illinois farmers and small-town businessmen who were very religious. Clara was brought up on the Bible: prayers at breakfast, grace at every meal, psalms learned by heart, the Gospels, chapter and verse—old-time religion. Her father owned small department stores in southern Indiana. The children were sent to good schools. Clara had studied Greek at Bloomington and Elizabethan-Jacobean literature at Wellesley. A disappointing love affair in Cambridge led to a suicide attempt. The family decided not to bring her back to Indiana. When she threatened to swallow more sleeping pills they allowed her to attend Columbia University, and she lived in New York under close supervision—the regimen organized by her parents. She, however, found ways to do exactly as she pleased. She feared hellfire but she did it just the same.

After a year at Columbia she went to work at Reuters, then she taught in a private school and later wrote American feature articles for British and Australian papers. By the age of forty she had formed a company of her own—a journalistic agency specializing in high fashion for women—and eventually she sold this company to an international publishing group and became one of its executives. In the boardroom she was referred to by some as "a good corporate person," by others as "the czarina of fashion writing." By now she was also the attentive mother of three small girls. The first of these was conceived with some difficulty (the professional assistance of gynecologists made it possible). The father of these children was Clara's fourth husband.

Three of the four had been no more than that—men who fell into the husband class. Only one, the third, had been something like the real thing. That was Spontini the oil tycoon, a close friend of the billionaire leftist and terrorist Giangiacomo F., who blew himself up in the seventies. (Some Italians said, predictably, that the government had set him up to explode.) Mike Spontini was not political, but then he wasn't born rich, like Giangiacomo, whose role model had been Fidel Castro. Spontini made his own fortune. His looks, his town houses and châteaus and yachts, would have qualified him for a role in *La Dolce Vita*. Scores of women were in pursuit. Clara had won the fight to marry him but lost the fight to keep him. Recognizing at last that he was getting rid of her, she didn't oppose this difficult, arbitrary man and surrendered all property rights in the settlement—a nonsettlement really. He took away the terrific gifts he had made her, down to the last bracelet. No sooner had the divorce come through than Mike was bombed out by two strokes. He was half paralyzed now and couldn't form his words. An Italian Sairey Gamp type took care of him in Venice, where Clara occasionally went to see him. Her ex-husband would give her an animal growl, one glare of rage, and then resume his look of imbecility. He would rather be an imbecile on the Grand Canal than a husband on Fifth Avenue.

The other husbands—one married in a full-dress church wedding, the others routine city hall jobs—were . . . well, to be plain about it, gesture-husbands. Velde was big and handsome, indolent, defiantly incompetent. He worked on the average no longer than six months at any job. By then everybody in the organization wanted to kill him.

His excuse for being in and out of work was that his true talent was for campaign strategies. Elections brought out the best in him: getting media attention for his candidate, who never, ever, won in the primaries. But then, he disliked being away from home, and an election is a traveling show. "Very sweet," went one of Clara's summaries to Laura Wong, the Chinese-American dress designer who was her confidante. "An affectionate father as long as the kids don't bother him, what Wilder mostly does is sit reading paperbacks—thrillers, science fiction, and pop biographies. I think he feels that all will be well as long as he keeps sitting there on his cushions. To him inertia is the same as stability. Meantime I run the house single-handed: mortgage, maintenance, housemaids, au pair girls from France or Scandinavia—Austrian the latest. I dream up projects for the children, I do the school bit, do the dentist and the pediatrician, plus playmates, outings, psychological tests, doll dressing, cutting and pasting valentines. What else . . . ? Work with their secret worries, sort out their quarrels, encourage their minds, wipe tears. Love them. Wilder just goes on reading P. D. James, or whoever, till I'm ready to snatch the book and throw it in the street."

One Sunday afternoon she did exactly that—opened the window first and skimmed his paperback into Park Avenue.

"Was he astonished?" asked Ms. Wong.

"Not absolutely. He sees how provoking he is. What he doesn't allow is that I have reason to be provoked. He's *there,* isn't he? What else do I want? In all the turbulence, he's the point of calm. And for all the wild times and miseries I had in the love game—about which he has full information—he's the answer. A sexy woman who couldn't find the place to put her emotionality, and appealing to brilliant men who couldn't do what she really wanted done."

"And he *does* do?"

"He's the overweening overlord, and for no other reason than sexual performance. It's stud power that makes him so confident. He's not the type to think it out. *I* have to do that. A sexy woman may delude herself about the gratification of a mental life. But what really settles everything, according to him, is masculine bulk. As close as he comes to spelling it out, his view is that I wasted time on Jaguar nonstarters. Lucky for me I came across a genuine Rolls-Royce. But he's got the wrong car," she said, crossing the kitchen with efficient haste to take the kettle off the boil. Her stride was powerful, her awkward, shapely legs going too quickly for the heels to keep pace. "Maybe a Lincoln

Continental would be more like it. Anyway, no woman wants her bedroom to be a garage, and least of all for a boring car."

What was a civilized lady like Laura Wong making of such confidences? The raised Chinese cheek with the Chinese eye let into it, the tiny degree of heaviness of the epicanthic fold all the whiter over the black of the eye, and the light of that eye, so foreign to see and at the same time superfamiliar in its sense . . . What could be more human than the recognition of this familiar sense? And yet Laura Wong was very much a New York lady in her general understanding of things. She did not confide in Clara as fully as Clara confided in her. But then who did, who *could* make a clean breast so totally? What Ms. Wong's rich eyes suggested, Clara in her awkwardness tried in fact to say. To do.

"Yes, the books," said Laura. "You can't miss that." She had also seen Wilder Velde pedaling his Exercycle while the TV ran at full volume.

"He can't understand what's wrong, since what I make looks like enough for us. But I don't earn *all* that much, with three kids in private schools. So family money has to be spent. That involves my old parents—sweet old Bible Hoosiers. I can't make him see that I can't afford an unemployed husband, and there isn't a headhunter in New York who'll talk to Wilder after one look at his curriculum vitae and his job record. Three months here, five months there. Because it's upsetting me, and for *my* sake, my bosses are trying to place him somewhere. I'm important enough to the corporation for that. If he loves elections so much, maybe he should run for office. He *looks* congressional, and what do I care if he screws up in the House of Representatives. I've been with congressmen, I even married one, and he's no dumber than they are. But he won't admit that anything is wrong; he's got that kind of confidence in himself—so much that he can even take a friendly interest in the men I've been involved with. They're like failed competitors to the guy who won the silver trophy. He's proud to claim a connection with the famous ones, and when I went to visit poor Mike in Venice, he flew with me."

"So he isn't jealous," said Laura Wong.

"The opposite. The people I've been intimate with, to him are like the folks in a history book. And suppose Richard III or Metternich had gotten into *your* wife's pants when she was a girl? Wilder is a name dropper, and the names he most enjoys dropping are the ones he came into by becoming my husband. Especially the headliners . . ."

Laura Wong was of course aware that it was not for her to mention the most significant name of all, the name that haunted all of Clara's confidences. That was for Clara herself to bring up. Whether it was appropriate, whether she could summon the strength to deal with the most persistent of her preoccupations, whether she would call on Laura to bear with her one more time . . . these were choices you had to trust her to make tactfully.

". . . whom he sometimes tapes when they're being interviewed on CBS or the MacNeil/Lehrer programs. Teddy Regler always the foremost."

Yes, there was the name. Mike Spontini mattered greatly, but you had to see him still in the husband category. Ithiel Regler stood much higher with Clara than any of the husbands. "On a scale of ten," she liked to say to Laura, "he *was* ten."

"Is ten?" Laura had suggested.

"I'd not only be irrational but psycho to keep Teddy in the active present tense," Clara had said. This was a clouded denial. Wilder Velde continued to be judged by a standard from which Ithiel Regler could never be removed. It did not make, it never could make, good sense to speak of irrationality and recklessness. Clara never would be safe or prudent, and she wouldn't have dreamed of expelling Ithiel's influence—not even if God's angel had offered her the option. She might have answered: You might as well try to replace my own sense of touch with somebody else's. And the matter would have had to stop there.

So Velde, by taping Ithiel's programs for her, proved how unassailable he was in his position as the final husband, the one who couldn't in the scheme of things be bettered. "And I'm glad the man thinks that," said Clara. "It's best for all of us. He wouldn't believe that I might be unfaithful. You've got to admire *that*. So here's a double-mystery couple. Which is the more mysterious one? Wilder actually enjoys watching Ithiel being so expert and smart from Washington. And meantime, Laura, I have no sinful ideas of being unfaithful. I don't even think about such things, they don't figure in my conscious mind. Wilder and I have a sex life no marriage counselor in the world could fault. We have three children, and I'm a loving mother, I bring them up conscientiously. But when Ithiel comes to town and I see him at lunch, I start to flow for him. He used to make me come by stroking my cheek. It can happen when he talks to me. Or even when I see him on TV or just hear his voice. *He* doesn't know it—I think not—and anyway Ithiel wouldn't want to do harm, interfere, dominate or exploit— that's not the way he is. We have this total, delicious connection, which is also a disaster. But even to a woman raised on the Bible, which in the city of New York in this day and age is a pretty remote influence, you couldn't call my attachment an evil that rates punishment after death. It's not the sex offenses that will trip you up, because by now nobody can draw the line between natural and unnatural in sex. Anyway, it couldn't be a woman's hysteria that would send her to hell. It would be something else. . . ."

"What else?" Laura asked. But Clara was silent, and Laura wondered whether it wasn't Teddy Regler who should be asked what Clara considered a mortal sin. He had known Clara so well, over so many years, that perhaps he could explain what she meant.

This Austrian au pair girl, Miss Wegman—Clara gave herself the pleasure of sizing her up. She checked off the points: dressed appropriately for an interview, hair freshly washed, no long nails, no conspicuous polish. Clara herself was gotten up as a tailored matron, in a tortoiseshell-motif suit and a white blouse with a ruff under the chin. From her teaching days she commanded a taskmistress's way of putting questions ("Now, Willie, pick up the *Catiline* and give me the tense of *abutere* in Cicero's opening sentence"): it was the disciplinarian's armor worn by a softy. This Austrian chick made a pleasing impression. The father was a Viennese bank official and the kid was correct, civil and sweet. You had to put it out of your head that Vienna was a hatchery of psychopaths and Hitlerites. Think instead of that dear beauty in the double suicide with the crown prince. This child, who had an Italian mother, was called Gina. She spoke English fluently and probably wasn't faking when she said she could assume responsibility for three little girls. Not laying secret plans to con everybody, not actually full of dislike for defiant, obstinate, mutely resistant kids like Clara's eldest, Lucy, a stout little girl needing help. A secretly vicious young woman could do terrible damage to a kid like Lucy, give her wounds that would never heal. The two little skinny girls laughed at their sister. They scooped up their snickers in their hands while Lucy held herself like a Roman soldier. Her face was heated with boredom and grievances.

The foreign young lady made all the right moves, came up with the correct answers—why not? since the questions made them obvious. Clara realized how remote from present-day "facts of life" and current history her "responsible" assumptions were—those were based on her small-town Republican churchgoing upbringing, the nickel-and-dime discipline of her mother, who clicked out your allowance from the bus conductor's changemaker hanging from her neck. Life in that Indiana town was already as out of date as ancient Egypt. The "decent people" there were the natives from whom television evangelists raised big money to pay for their stretch limos and Miami-style vices. Those were Clara's preposterous dear folks, by whom she had felt stifled in childhood and for whom she now felt a boundless love. In Lucy she saw her own people, rawboned, stubborn, silent—she saw herself. Much could be made of such beginnings. But how did you coach a kid like this, what could you do for her in New York City?

"Now—is it all right to call you Gina?—what was your purpose, Gina, in coming to New York?"

"To perfect my English. I'm registered in a music course at Columbia. And to learn about the U.S.A."

A well-brought-up and vulnerable European girl would have done better to go to Bemidji, Minnesota. Any idea of the explosive dangers girls faced here? They could be blown up from within. When she was young (and not only then), Clara had made reckless experiments—all those chancy relationships; anything might have happened; much did; and all for the honor of running risks. This led her to resurvey Miss Wegman, to estimate what might be done to a face like hers, its hair, her figure, the bust—to the Arabian Nights treasure that nubile girls (innocent up to a point) were sitting on. So many dangerous attractions—and such ignorance! Naturally Clara felt that she herself would do everything (up to a point) to protect a young woman in her household, and everything possible meant using all the resources of an experienced person. At the same time it was a fixed belief with Clara that no *in*experienced woman of mature years could be taken seriously. So could it be a serious Mrs. Wegman back in Vienna, the mother, who had given this Gina permission to spend a year in Gogmagogsville? In the alternative, a rebellious Gina was chancing it on her own. Again, for the honor of running risks.

Clara, playing matron, lady of the house, nodded to agree with her own thoughts, and this nod may have been interpreted by the girl to mean that it was okay, she was as good as hired. She'd have her own decent room in this vast Park Avenue co-op apartment, a fair wage, house privileges, two free evenings, two afternoons for the music-history classes, parts of the morning while the children were at school. Austrian acquaintances, eligible young people, were encouraged to visit, and American friends vetted by Clara. By special arrangement, Gina could even give a small party. You can be democratic and still have discipline.

The first months, Clara watched her new au pair girl closely, and then she was able to tell friends at lunch, people in the office, and even her psychiatrist, Dr. Gladstone, how lucky she had been to find this Viennese Miss Wegman with darling manners. What a desirable role model she was, and also such a calming influence on the hyperexcitable tots. "As you have said, Doctor, they set off hysterical tendencies in one another."

You didn't expect replies from these doctors. You paid them to lend you their ears. Clara said as much to Ithiel Regler, with whom she remained very much in touch— frequent phone calls, occasional letters, and when Ithiel came up from Washington they had drinks, even dinner from time to time.

"If you think this Gladstone is really helping . . . I suppose some of those guys *can* be okay," said Ithiel, neutral in tone. With him there was no trivial meddling. He never tried to tell you what to do, never advised on family matters.

"It's mostly to relieve my heart," said Clara. "If you and I had become husband and wife that wouldn't have been necessary. I might not be so overcharged. But even so, we have open lines of communication to this day. In fact, you went through a shrink period yourself."

"I sure did. But my doctor had even more frailties than me."

"Does that matter?"

"I guess not. But it occurred to me one day that he couldn't tell me how to be Teddy Regler. And nothing would go well unless I *was* Teddy Regler. Not that I make cosmic claims for precious Teddy, but there never was anybody else for me to be."

Because he thought things out he spoke confidently, and because of his confidence he sounded full of himself. But there was less conceit about Ithiel than people imputed to him. In company, Clara, speaking as one who knew, really *knew* him—and she made no secret of that—would say, when his name was mentioned, when he was put down by some restless spirit or other, that Ithiel Regler was more plainspoken about his own faults than anybody who felt it necessary to show him up.

At this turn in their psychiatry conversation, Clara made a move utterly familiar to Ithiel. Seated, she inclined her upper body toward him. "*Tell* me!" she said. When she did that, he once more saw the country girl in all the dryness of her ignorance, appealing for instruction. Her mouth would be slightly open as he made his answer. She would watch and listen with critical concentration. "Tell!" was one of her code words.

Ithiel said, "The other night I watched a child-abuse program on TV, and after a while I began to think how much they were putting under that heading short of sexual molestation or *deadly* abuse—mutilation and murder. Most of what they showed was normal punishment in my time. So today I could be a child-abuse case and my father might have been arrested as a child-beater. When he was in a rage he was transformed—he was like moonshine from the hills compared to store-bought booze. The kids, all of us, were slammed two-handed, from both sides simultaneously, and without mercy. So? Forty years later I have to watch a TV show to see that I, too, was abused. Only, I loved my late father. Beating was only an incident, a single item between us. I still love him. Now, to tell you what this signifies: I can't apply the going terms to my case without damage to reality. My father beat me passionately. When he did it, I hated him like poison and murder. I also loved him with a passion, and I'll *never* think myself an abused child. I suspect that your psychiatrist would egg me on to hate, not turn hate into passivity. So he'd be telling me from the height of his theoretical assumptions how Teddy Regler should be Teddy Regler. The real Teddy, however, rejects this grudge against a dead man, whom he more than half expects to see in the land of the dead. If that were to happen, it would be because we loved each other and wished for it. Besides, after the age of forty a moratorium has to be declared—earlier, if possible. You can't afford to be a damaged child forever. That's my argument with psychiatry: it encourages you to build on abuses and keeps you infantile. Now the heart of this whole country aches for itself. There may be occult political causes for this as well. Foreshadowings of the fate of this huge superpower . . ."

Clara said, *"Tell!"* and then she listened like a country girl. That side of her would never go away, thank God, Ithiel thought; while Clara's secret observation was, How well we've come to understand each other. If only we'd been like this twenty years back.

It wasn't as if she hadn't been able to follow him in the early years. She always had understood what Ithiel was saying. If she hadn't he wouldn't have taken the trouble to speak—why waste words? But she also recognized the comic appeal of being the openmouthed rube. Gee! Yeah!

Of course! And I could kick myself in the head for not having thought of this myself! But all the while the big-city Clara had been in the making, stockpiling ideas for survival in Gogmagogsville.

"But let me tell you," she said, "what I was too astonished to mention when we were first acquainted . . . when we lay in bed naked in Chelsea, and you sent thoughts going around the world, but then they always came back to *us*, in bed. In *bed*, which in my mind was for rest, or sex, or reading a novel. And back to *me*, whom you never overlooked, wherever your ideas may have gone."

This Ithiel, completely black-haired then, and now grizzled, had put some weight on. His face had filled, rounded out at the bottom. It had more of an urn shape. Otherwise his looks were remarkably unchanged. He said, "I really didn't have such a lot of good news about the world. I think you were hunting among the obscure things I talked about for openings to lead back to your one and only subject: love and happiness. I often feel as much curiosity about love and happiness now as you did then listening to my brainstorms."

Between jobs, Ithiel had been able to find time to spend long months with Clara—in Washington, his main base, in New York, on Nantucket, and in Montauk. After three years together, she had actually pressured him into buying an engagement ring. She was at that time, as she herself would tell you, terribly driven and demanding (as if she wasn't now). "I needed a symbolic declaration at least," she would say, "and I put such heat on him, saying that he had dragged me around so long as his girl, his lay, that at last I got this capitulation from him." He took Clara to Madison Hamilton's shop in the diamond district and bought her an emerald ring—the real thing, conspicuously clear, color perfect, top of its class, as appraisers later told Clara. Twelve hundred dollars he paid for it, a big price in the sixties, when he was especially strapped. He was like that, though: hard to convince, but once decided, he dismissed the cheaper items. "Take away all this other shit," he muttered. Proper Mr. Hamilton probably had heard this. Madison Hamilton was a gentleman, and reputable and dignified in a decade when some of those qualities were still around: "Before our fellow Americans had lied themselves into a state of hallucination—bullshitted themselves into inanity," said Ithiel. He said also, still speaking of Hamilton, who sold antique jewelry, "I think the weird moniker my parents gave me predisposed me favorably toward vanishing types like Hamilton—Wasps with good manners. . . . For all I know, he might have been an Armenian, passing."

Clara held out her engagement finger, and Ithiel put on the ring. When the check was written and Mr. Hamilton asked for identification, Ithiel was able to show not only a driver's license but a Pentagon pass. It made a great impression. At that time Ithiel was flying high as a wunderkind in nuclear strategy, and he might have gone all the way to the top, to the negotiating table in Geneva, facing the Russians, if he had been less quirky. People of great power set a high value on his smarts. Well, you only had to look at the size and the evenness of his dark eyes—"The eyes of Hera in my Homeric grammar," said Clara. "Except that he was anything but effeminate. No way!" All she meant was that he had a classic level look.

"At Hamilton's that afternoon, I wore a miniskirt suit that showed my knees touching. I haven't got knock-knees, just this minor peculiarity about the inside of my legs. . . . If this is a deformity, it did me good. Ithiel was crazy about it."

At a later time, she mentioned this as "the unforeseen usefulness of anomalies." She wrote that on a piece of paper and let it drift about the house with other pieces of paper, so that if asked what it meant, she could say she had forgotten.

Although Ithiel now and again might mention "game theory" or "MAD," he wouldn't give out information that might be classified, and she didn't even try to understand what he did in Washington. Now and then his name turned up in the *Times* as a consultant on international security, and for a couple of years he was an adviser to the chairman of a Senate committee. She let politics alone, asking no questions. The more hidden his activities, the better she felt about him. Power, danger, secrecy made him even sexier. No loose talk. A woman could feel safe with a man like Ithiel.

It was marvelous luck that the little apartment in Chelsea should be so near Penn Station. When he blew into town he telephoned, and in fifteen minutes he was there, holding his briefcase. It was his habit when he arrived to remove his necktie and stuff it in among his documents. It was her habit when she hung up the phone to take the ring from its locked drawer, admire it on her finger, and kiss it when the doorbell rang.

No, Ithiel didn't make a big public career, he wasn't a team player, he had no talent for administration; he was too special in his thinking, and there was no chance that he would reach cabinet level. Anyway, it was too easy for him to do well as a free agent; he wouldn't latch on to politicians with presidential ambitions: the smart ones never would make it. "And besides," he said, "I like to stay mobile." A change of continent when he wanted fresh air. He took on such assignments as pleased the operator in him, the behind-the-scenes Teddy Regler: in the Persian Gulf, with a Japanese whiskey firm looking for a South American market, with the Italian police tracking terrorists. None of these activities compromised his Washington reputation for dependability. He testified before congressional investigative committees as an expert witness.

In their days of intimacy, Clara more than once helped

him to make a deadline. Then they were Teddy and Clara, a superteam working around the clock. He knew how dependable she was, a dervish for work, how quickly she grasped unfamiliar ideas, how tactful she could be. From her side, she was aware how analytically deep he could go, what a range of information he had, how good his reports were. He outclassed everybody, it seemed to her. Once, at the Hotel Cristallo in Cortina d'Ampezzo, they did a document together, to the puncturing rhythm of the tennis court below. He had to read the pages she was typing for him over the transatlantic telephone. While he spoke, he let her run ahead on the machine. He could trust her to organize his notes and write them up in a style resembling his own (not that style mattered in Washington). All but the restricted material. She'd do any amount of labor—long dizzy days at the tinny lightweight Olivetti—to link herself with him.

As she told Ms. Wong, she had seen a book many years ago in the stacks of the Columbia library. A single title had detached itself from the rest, from thousands: *The Human Pair*. Well, the big-boned blond student doing *research* and feeling (unaware) so volcanic that one of her controls was to hold her breath—at the sight of those gilded words on the spine of a book she was able to breathe again. She breathed. She didn't take the book down; she didn't want to read it. "I wanted *not* to read it."

She described this to Laura Wong, who was too polite to limit her, too discreet to direct her confidences into suitable channels. You had to listen to everything that came out of Clara's wild head when she was turned on. Ms. Wong applied these personal revelations to her own experience of life, as anybody else would have done. She had been married too. Five years an American wife. Maybe she had even been in love. She never said. You'd never know.

"The full title was *The Human Pair in the Novels of Thomas*

Hardy. At school I loved Hardy, but now all I wanted of that book was the title. It came back to me at Cortina. Ithiel and I were the Human Pair. We took a picnic lunch up to the forest behind the Cristallo—cheese, bread, cold cuts, pickles and wine. I rolled on top of Ithiel and fed him. Later I found out when I tried it myself how hard it is to swallow in that position.

"I now feel, looking back, that I was carrying too much of an electrical charge. It's conceivable that the world-spirit gets into mere girls and makes them its demon interpreters. I mentioned this to Ithiel a while back—he and I are old enough now to discuss such subjects—and he said that one of his Russian dissident pals had been talking to him about something called 'superliterature'—literature being the tragedy or comedy of private lives, while superliterature was about the possible end of the world. Beyond personal history. In Cortina I thought I was acting from personal emotions, but those emotions were so devouring, fervid, that they may have been suprapersonal—a wholesome young woman in love expressing the tragedy or comedy of the world concluding. A fever using love as its carrier.

"After the holiday we drove down to Milan. Actually, that's where I met Spontini. We were at a fancy after-dinner party, and he said, 'Let me give you a ride back to your hotel.' So Ithiel and I got into his Jaguar with him, and we were escorted by carloads of cops, fore and aft. He was proud of his security; this was when the Red Brigades were kidnapping the rich. It wasn't so *easy* to be rich—rich enough for ransom. Mike said, 'For all I know, my own friend Giangiacomo may have a plan to abduct me. Not Giangiacomo personally but the outfit he belongs to.'

"On that same trip Ithiel and I also spent some time with Giangiacomo the billionaire revolutionist himself. He was a kind, pleasant man, good-looking except for his preposterous Fidel Castro getup, like a little kid from Queens in a cowboy suit. He wore a forage cap, and in a corner of his fancy office there was a machine gun on the floor. He invited Ithiel and me to his château, about eighty kilometers away, eighteenth-century rococo: it might have been a set for *The Marriage of Figaro,* except for the swimming pool with algae in it and a sauna alongside, in the dank part of the garden far down the hill. At lunch, the butler was leaning over with truffles from Giangiacomo's own estate to grate over the *crème veloutée,* and he couldn't because Giangiacomo was waving his arms, going on about revolutionary insurgency, the subject of the book he was writing. Then, when Ithiel told him that there were no views like his in Karl Marx, Giangiacomo said, 'I never read Marx, and it's too late now to do it; it's urgent to act.' He drove us back to Milan in the afternoon at about five hundred miles an hour. Lots of action, let me tell you. I covered my emerald and gripped it with my right hand, to protect it, maybe, in a crash.

"Next day, when we flew out, Giangiacomo was at the airport in battle dress with a group of boutique girls, all in minis. A year or two later he blew himself up while trying to dynamite power lines. I was sad about it."

When they returned to New York in stuffy August, back to the apartment in Chelsea, Clara cooked Ithiel a fine Italian dinner of veal with lemon and capers, as good as, or better than, the Milan restaurants served, or Giangiacomo's chef at the lovely toy château. At work in the narrow New York galley-style kitchen, Clara was naked and wore clogs. To make it tender, she banged the meat with a red cast-iron skillet. In those days she wore her hair long. Whether she was dressed or nude, her movements always were energetic; she didn't know the meaning of slow-time.

Stretched on the bed, Ithiel studied his dangerous documents (all those forbidden facts) while she cooked and the music played; the shades were down, the lights were on, and they enjoyed a wonderful privacy. "When I was a kid

and we went on holidays to the Jersey coast during the war,"
Clara recalled, "we had black window blinds because of the
German submarines hiding out there under the Atlantic, but
we could play our radios as loud as we wanted." She liked
to fancy that she was concealing Ithiel and his secret documents—not that the deadly information affected Ithiel
enough to change the expression of his straight profile:
"concentrating like Jascha Heifetz." Could anybody have
been tailing him? Guys with zoom lenses or telescopic sights
on the Chelsea rooftops? Ithiel smiled, and pooh-poohed
this. He wasn't that important. "I'm not rich like Spontini."
They might rather be trained on Clara, zeroing in on a
Daughter of Albion without a stitch on, he said.

In those days he came frequently from Washington to
visit his young son, who lived with his mother on East
Tenth Street. Ithiel's ex-wife, who now used her maiden
name, Etta Wolfenstein, went out of her way to be friendly
to Clara, chatted her up on the telephone. Etta had informants in Washington, who kept an eye on Ithiel. Ithiel was
indifferent to gossip. "I'm not the president," he would say,
"that bulletins should go out about my moods and movements."

"I shouldn't have blamed Ithiel for taking a woman out
to dinner now and then in Washington. He needed plain,
ordinary quiet times. I turned on so much power in those
days. Especially after midnight, my favorite time to examine
my psyche—what love was; and death; and hell and eternal
punishment; and what Ithiel was going to cost me in the
judgment of God when I closed my eyes on this world
forever. All my revivalist emotions came out after one A.M.,
whole nights of tears, anguish and hysteria. I drove him out
of his head. To put a stop to this, he'd have to marry me.
Then he'd never again have to worry. All my demon power
would be at his service. But meanwhile if he got an hour's
sleep toward morning and time enough to shave before his

first appointment, he'd swallow his coffee, saying that he looked like Lazarus in his shroud. He was vain of his good looks too," said Clara to Ms. Wong. "Maybe that's why I chose that kind of punishment, to put rings under his eyes. Once he said that he had to outline a piece of legislation for the Fiat people—they were trying to get a bill passed in Congress—and they'd think he'd spent the night at an orgy and now couldn't get his act together."

Clara wasn't about to tell Teddy that in Milan when Mike Spontini had invited her to sit in front with him, she had found the palm of his hand waiting for her on the seat, and she had lifted herself up immediately and given him her evening bag to hold. In the dark his fingers soon closed on her thigh. Then she pushed in the cigarette lighter and he guessed what she would do with it when the coil was hot, so he stopped, he let her be. You didn't mention such incidents to the man you were with. It was anyway commonplace stuff to a man who thought world politics continually.

In the accounts heard by Ms. Wong (who had so much American sensitivity, despite her air of Oriental distance and the Chinese cut of her clothes), Clara's frankness may have made *her* seem foreign. Clara went beyond the conventions of American openness. The emerald ring appeased her for a time, but Ithiel was not inclined to move forward, and Clara became more difficult. She told him she had decided that they would be buried in the same grave. She said, "I'd rather go into the ground with the man I loved than share a bed with somebody indifferent. Yes, I think we should be in the same coffin. Or two coffins, but the one who dies last will be on the top. Side by side is also possible. Holding hands, if that could be arranged." Another frequent topic was the sex and the name of their first child. An Old Testament name was what she preferred—Zebulon or Gad or Asher or Naftali. For a girl, Michal, perhaps, or Naomi.

He vetoed Michal because she had mocked David for his naked victory dance, and then he refused to take part in such talk at all. He didn't want to make any happy plans. He was glum with her when she said that there was a lovely country cemetery back in Indiana with big horse chestnuts all around.

When he went off to South America on business, she learned from Etta Wolfenstein that he had taken a Washington secretary with him for assistance and (knowing Teddy) everything else. To show him what was what, Clara had an affair with a young Jean-Claude just over from Paris, and within a week he was sharing her apartment. He was very good-looking, but he seldom washed. His dirt was so ingrained that she couldn't get him clean in the shower stall. She had to take a room at the Plaza to force him into the tub. Then for a while she could bear the smell of him. He appealed to her to help get a work permit, and she took him to Steinsalz, Ithiel's lawyer. Later Jean-Claude refused to return her house key, and she had to go to Steinsalz again. "Have your lock changed, dear girl," said Steinsalz, and he asked whether she wanted Ithiel billed for these consultations. He was a friend and admired Ithiel.

"But Ithiel told me you never charged him for your services."

Clara had discovered how amused New Yorkers were by her ignorance.

"Since you took up with this Frenchie, have you missed anything around the house?"

She seemed slow to understand, but that was simply a put-on. She had locked the emerald ring in her deposit box (this, too, an act suggestive of burial).

She said firmly, "Jean-Claude is no bum."

Steinsalz liked Clara too, for her passionate character. Somehow he knew, also, that her family had money—a real-estate fortune, and this gained her a certain consideration with him. Jean-Claude was not the Steinsalz type. He advised Clara to patch up her differences with Ithiel. "Not to use sex for spite," he said. Clara could not help but look at the lawyer's lap, where because he was obese his sex organ was outlined by the pressure of his fat. It made her think of one of those objects that appeared when art-lovers on their knees made rubbings on a church floor. The figure of a knight dead for centuries.

"Then why can't Ithiel stay faithful?"

Steinsalz's first name was Bobby. He was a great economist. He ran a million-dollar practice, and it cost him not a cent. He sublet a corner office space from a flashy accountant and paid him in legal advice.

Steinsalz said, "Teddy is a genius. If he didn't prefer to hang loose, he could name his position in Washington. He values his freedom, so that when he wanted to visit Mr. Leakey in the Olduvai Gorge, he just picked up and went. He thinks no more about going to Iran than I do about Coney Island. The Shah likes to talk to him. He sent for him once just to be briefed on Kissinger. I tell you this, Clara, so that you won't hold Ithiel on too short a leash. He truly appreciates you, but he irks easy. A little consideration of his needs would fill him with gratitude. A good idea is not to get too clamorous around him. Let me tell you, there are curators in the zoo who give more thought to the needs of a fruit bat than any of us give our fellowman."

Clara answered him, "There are animals who come in pairs. So suppose the female pines?"

That was a good talk, and Clara remembered Steinsalz gratefully.

"Everybody knows how to advise lovers," said Steinsalz. "But only the lovers can say what's what."

A bookish bachelor, he lived with his eighty-year-old mother, who had to be taken to the toilet in her wheelchair.

He liked to list the famous men he had gone to high school with—Holz the philosopher, Buchman the Nobel physicist, Lashover the crystallographer. "And yours truly, whose appellate briefs have made legal history."

Clara said, "I sort of loved old Steinsalz too. He was like a Santa Claus with an empty sack who comes down your chimney to steal everything in the house—that's one of Ithiel's wisecracks, about Steinsalz and property. In his own off-the-wall way, Steinsalz was generous."

Clara took advice from the lawyer and made peace with Ithiel on his return. Then the same mistakes overtook them. "I was a damn recidivist. When Jean-Claude left I was glad of it. Getting into the tub with him at the Plaza was a kind of frolic—a private camp event. They say the Sun King stank. If so, Jean-Claude could have gone straight to the top of Versailles. But my family are cleanliness freaks. Before she would sit in your car, my Granny would force you to whisk-broom the seat, under the floor mat too, to make sure her serge wouldn't pick up any dust." By the way, Clara locked up the ring not for fear that Jean-Claude would steal it but to protect it from contamination by her wrongful behavior in bed.

But when Ithiel came back, his relations with Clara were not what they had been. Two outside parties had come between them, even though Ithiel seemed indifferent to Jean-Claude. Jealous and hurt, Clara could not forgive the little twit from Washington, of whom Etta Wolfenstein had given her a full picture. That girl was stupid but had very big boobs. When Ithiel talked about his mission to Betancourt in Venezuela, Clara was unimpressed. An American woman in love was far more important than any South American hotshot. "And did you take your little helper along to the president's palace to show off her chest development?"

Ithiel sensibly said, "Let's not beat on each other too

much," and Clara repented and agreed. But soon she set up another obstacle course of tests and rules, and asserted herself unreasonably. When Ithiel had his hair cut, Clara said, "That's not the way I like it, but then I'm not the one you're pleasing." She'd say, "You're grooming yourself more than you used to. I'm sure Jascha Heifetz doesn't take such care of his hands." She made mistakes. You didn't send a man with eyes from Greek mythology to the bathroom to cut his fingernails, even if you did have a horror of clippings on the carpet—she'd forget that she and Ithiel were the Human Pair.

But at the time she couldn't be sure that Ithiel was thinking as she did about "Human." To sound him out, she assumed a greater interest in politics and got him to talk about Africa, China and Russia. What emerged was the insignificance of the personal factor. Clara repeated and tried out words like Kremlin or Lubyanka in her mind (they sounded like the living end) while she heard Ithiel tell of people who couldn't explain why they were in prison, never rid of lice and bedbugs, never free from dysentery and TB, and finally hallucinating. They make an example of them, she thought, to show that nobody is anybody, everybody is expendable. And even here, when Ithiel was pushed to say it, he admitted that here in the U.S., the status of the individual was weakening and probably in irreversible decline. Felons getting special consideration was a sign of it. He could be remote about such judgments, as if his soul were one of a dozen similar souls in a jury box, hearing evidence: to find us innocent would be nice, but guilty couldn't shock him much. She concluded that he was in a dangerous moral state and that it was up to her to rescue him from it. The Human Pair was also a rescue operation.

"A terrible crisis threatened to pinch us both to death."

At the time, she was not advanced enough to think this to a conclusion. Later she would have known how to put it: You couldn't separate love from being. You could Be, even though you were alone. But in that case, you loved only yourself. If so, everybody else was a phantom, and then world politics was a shadow play. Therefore she, Clara, was the only key to politics that Ithiel was likely to find. Otherwise he might as well stop bothering his head about his grotesque game theories, ideology, treaties, and the rest of it. Why bother to line up so many phantoms?

But this was not a time for things to go well. He missed the point, although it was as big as a boulder to her. They had bad arguments—"It was a mistake not to let him sleep"—and after a few oppressive months, he made plans to leave the country with yet another of his outlandish lady friends.

Clara heard, again from Etta Wolfenstein, that Ithiel was staying in a fleabag hotel in the Forties west of Broadway, where he'd be hard to find. " 'Safety in sleaze,' Etta said— *She* was a piece of work." He was to meet the new girlfriend at Kennedy next afternoon.

At once Clara went uptown in a cab and walked into the cramped lobby, dirty tile like a public lavatory. She pressed with both hands on the desk and lied that she was Ithiel's wife, saying that he had sent her to check him out and take his luggage. "They believed me. You're never so cool as when you're burned up completely. They didn't even ask for identification, since I paid cash and tipped everybody five bucks apiece. When I went upstairs I was astonished that he could bring himself to sit down on such a bed, much less sleep in those grungy sheets. The morgue would have been nicer."

Then she returned to her apartment with his suitcase— the one they took to Cortina, where she had been so happy. She waited until after dark, and he turned up at about seven o'clock. Cool with her, which meant that he was boiling.

"Where do you get off, pulling this on me?"

"You didn't say you were coming to New York. You were sneaking out of the country."

"Since when do I have to punch the clock in and out like an employee!"

She stood up to him without fear. In fact she was desperate. She shouted at him the Old Testament names of their unborn children. "You're betraying Michal and Naomi."

As a rule, Ithiel was self-possessed to an unusual degree, "unless we were making love. It was cold anger at first," as Clara was to tell it. "He spoke like a man in a three-piece suit. I reminded him that the destiny of both our races depended on those children. I said they were supposed to be a merger of two high types. I'm not against other types, but they'd be there anyway, and more numerous—I'm no racist."

"I can't have you check me out of my hotel and take my suitcase. Nobody is going to supervise me. And I suppose you went through my things."

"I wouldn't do that. I was protecting you. You're making the mistake of your life."

At that moment Clara's look was hollow. You saw the bones of her face, especially the orbital ones. The inflammation of her eyes would have shocked Ithiel if he hadn't been bent on teaching her a lesson. Time to draw the line, was what he was saying to himself.

"You're not going back to that horrible hotel!" she said when he picked up his bag.

"I have a reservation in another place."

"Teddy, take off your coat. Don't go now, I'm in a bad way. I love you with my soul." She said it again, when the door swung shut after him.

He told himself it would set a bad precedent to let her control him with her fits.

The luxury of the Park Avenue room didn't sit well with

him—the gilded wall fixtures, the striped upholstery, the horror of the fresco painting, the bed turned back like the color photograph in the brochure, with two tablets of chocolate mint on the night table. The bathroom was walled with mirrors, the brightwork shone, and he felt the life going out of him. He went to the bed and sat on the edge but did not lie down. It was not in the cards for him to sleep that night. The phone rang—it was a mean sound, a thin rattle—and Etta said, "Clara has swallowed a bottle of sleeping pills. She called me and I sent the ambulance. You'd better go to Bellevue; you may be needed. Are you alone there?"

He went immediately to the hospital, hurrying through gray corridors, stopping to ask directions until he found himself in the waiting space for relatives and friends, by a narrow horizontal window. He saw bodies on stretchers, no one resembling Clara. A young man in a dog collar presently joined him. He said he was Clara's minister.

"I didn't realize that she had one."

"She often comes to talk to me. Yes, she's in my parish."

"Has her stomach been pumped?"

"That—oh, yes. But she took a big dose, and they're not certain yet. You're Ithiel Regler, I suppose?"

"I am."

The young minister asked no other questions. No discussions occurred. You couldn't help but be thankful for his tact. Also for the information he brought from the nurses. Word came in the morning that she would live. They were moving her upstairs to a women's ward.

When she was able, she sent word through her clergyman friend that she didn't want to see Ithiel, had no wish to hear from him, ever. After a day of self-torment in the luxury of the hotel on Park Avenue, he canceled his trip to Europe. He fended off the sympathy of Etta Wolfenstein, avid to hear about his torments, and went back to Washington. The clergyman made a point of seeing him off at Penn Station. There he was, extra tall, in his dickey and clerical collar. Baldness had just come over him, he had decided not to wear a hat, and he kept reaching for vanished or vanishing tufts of hair. Ithiel was made uncomfortable by his sympathy. Because the young man had nothing at all to tell him except that he shouldn't blame himself. He may have been saying: "You with your sins, your not very good heart. I with my hair loss." This took no verbal form. Only a mute urgency in his decent face. He said, "She's ambulatory already. She goes around the ward and tapes back their IV needles when they work loose. She's a help to old derelicts."

You can always get a remedy, you can tap into solace when you need it, you can locate a mental fix. America is generous in this regard. The air is full of helpful hints. Ithiel was too proud to accept any handy fix. Like: "Suicide is a power move." "Suicide is punitive." "The poor kids never mean it." "It's all the drama of rescue." You could tell yourself such things; they didn't mean a damn. In all the world, now, there wasn't a civilized place left where a woman would say, "I love you with my soul." Only this backcountry girl was that way still. If no more mystical sacredness remained in the world, she hadn't been informed yet. Straight-nosed Ithiel, heading for Washington and the Capitol dome, symbolic of a nation swollen with world significance, set a greater value on Clara than on anything in *this* place, or any place. He thought, This is what I opted for, and this is what I deserve. Walking into that room at the Regency, I got what I had coming.

It was after this that Clara's marriages began—first the church wedding in her granny's gown, the arrangements elaborate, Tiffany engravings, Limoges china, Lalique glassware. Mom and Dad figured that after two suicide attempts, the fullest effort must be made to provide a stable life for their Clara. They were dear about it. There were no economies. Husband One was an educational psychologist who tested schoolchildren. His name was a good one—Monserrat. On the stationery she had printed, Clara was Mme de Monserrat. But as she was to say to Ithiel: "This marriage was like a Thanksgiving turkey. After a month the bird is drying out and you're still eating breast of turkey. It needs more and more Russian dressing, and pretty soon the sharpest knife in the city won't slice it." If there was anything she could do to perfection, it was to invent such descriptions. "Pretty soon you're trying to eat threads of bird meat," she said.

Her second husband was a Southern boy who went to Congress and even ran in a few presidential primaries. They lived out in Virginia for about a year, and she saw something of Ithiel in Washington. She was not very kind to him then. "Frankly," she told him at lunch one day, "I can't imagine why I ever wanted to embrace you. I look at you, and I say, Yuch!"

"There probably is a *yuch* aspect to me," said Ithiel, perfectly level. "It does no harm to learn about your repulsive side."

She couldn't flap him. In the glance she then gave him, there was a glimmer of respect.

"I was a little crazy," she would say later.

At that time she and her Southern husband were trying to have a child. She telephoned Ithiel and described the difficulties they were having. "I thought maybe you would oblige me," she said.

"Out of the question. It would be grotesque."

"A child with classic Greek eyes. Listen, Teddy, as I sit here, what do you think I'm doing to myself? Where do you suppose my hand is, and what am I touching?"

"I've already done my bit for the species," he said. "Why breed more sinners?"

"What do you suggest?"

"These utility husbands are not the answer."

"But for you and me, it wasn't in the cards, Ithiel. Why did you have so many women?"

"For you there were quite a few men—maybe it has something to do with democracy. There are so many eligibles, such handsome choices. Mix with your equals. And why limit yourself?"

"Okay, but it comes out so unhappy. . . . And why shouldn't I be pregnant by you? Alistair and I aren't compatible that way. Haven't you forgiven me for what I said that day about your being *yuch*? I was just being perverse. Ithiel, if you were here now . . ."

"But I'm not going to be."

"Just for procreation. There are even surrogate mothers these days."

"I can see a black dude motorcycle messenger in boots, belt and helmet, waiting with a warm box for the condom full of sperm. 'Here you are, Billy. Rush this to the lady.' "

"You shouldn't make fun. You should think of the old Stoic who told his buddies when they caught him in the act, 'Mock not, I plant a Man.' Oh, I talk this way to make an impression on you. It's not real. I ask you—and now I'm serious—what should I do?"

"It should be Alistair's child."

But she divorced Alistair and married Mike Spontini, whom she had threatened in Milan to burn with the dashboard lighter coil. For Spontini she had real feeling, she said. "Even though I caught him humping another woman just before we were married."

"He wasn't meant to be a husband."

"I thought once he got to know my quality I'd mean more to him. He'd finally *see* it. I don't say that I'm better than other women. I'm not superior. I'm nutty, also. But I am in touch with the *me* in myself. There's so much I could do for a man that I loved. How *could* Mike, in my bed, with the door unlocked and me in the house, ball such an awful tramp as that? *Tell* me."

"Well, people have to be done with disorder, finally, and by the time they're done they're also finished. When they back off to take a new leap, they realize they've torn too many ligaments. It's all over."

Mike Spontini intended to do right by Clara. He bought a handsome place in Connecticut with a view of the sea. He never invested badly, never lost a penny. He doubled his money in Connecticut. The Fifth Avenue apartment was a good deal too. In the country, Clara became a gardener. She must have hoped that there was sympathetic magic in flowers and vegetables, or that the odor of soil would calm Mike's jetting soul, bring down his fever. The marriage lasted three years. He paid the wretchedness fee, he did bad time, as convicts say, then he filed for divorce and liquidated the real estate. It took a stroke to stop Mad Mike. The left side of his face was disfigured in such a manner (this was Clara speaking) that it became a fixed commentary on the life strategy he had followed: "his failed concept." But Clara was strong on loyalty, and she was loyal even to a stricken ex-husband. You don't cut all bonds after years of intimacy. After his stroke, she arranged a birthday party for him at the hospital; she sent a cake to the room. However, the doctor asked her not to come.

When you were down, busted, blasted, burnt out, dying, you saw the best of Clara.

So it was odd that she should also have become an executive, highly paid and influential. She could make fashionable talk, she dressed with originality, she knew a lot and at first hand about decadence, but at any moment she could set aside the "czarina" and become the hayseed, the dupe of traveling salesmen or grifters who wanted to lure her up to the hayloft. In her you might see suddenly a girl from a remote town, from the vestigial America of one-room schoolhouses, constables, covered-dish suppers, one of those communities bypassed by technology and urban development. Her father, remember, was still a vestryman, and her mother sent checks to TV fundamentalists. In a sophisticated boardroom Clara could be as plain as cornmeal mush, and in such a mood, when she opened her mouth, you couldn't guess whether she would speak or blow bubble gum. Yet anybody who had it in mind to get around her was letting himself in for lots of bad news.

She was prepared always to acknowledge total ignorance, saying, as she had so often said to Ithiel Regler, "*Tell* me!" The girl from the backwoods was also sentimental; she kept souvenirs, family photographs, lace valentines, and she cherished the ring Ithiel had bought her. She held on to it through four marriages. When she had it appraised for insurance, she found that it had become very valuable. It was covered for fifteen thousand dollars. Ithiel had never been smart about money. He was a bad investor—unlucky, careless. On Forty-seventh Street twenty years ago, Madison Hamilton had goofed, uncharacteristically, in pricing his emerald. But Clara was careless as well, for the ring disappeared while she was carrying Patsy. Forgotten on a washstand, maybe, or stolen from a bench at the tennis club. The loss depressed her; her depression deepened as she searched for it in handbags, drawers, upholstery crevices, shag rugs, pill bottles.

Laura Wong remembered how upset Clara had been. "*That* put you back on the couch," she said, with Oriental gentleness.

Clara had been hoping to free herself from Dr. Gladstone. She had said as much. "Now that I'm expecting for the third time I should be able to go it alone at last. A drink with Ithiel when I'm low does more for me. I've already got more doctors than any woman should need. Gladstone will ask me why this Ithiel symbol should still be so powerful. And what will there be to say? When the bag of your Hoover fills with dust, you replace it with another. Why not get rid of feeling-dust too. Yet . . . even a technician like Gladstone knows better. What he wants is to desensitize me. I was ready to die for love. Okay, I'm still living, have a husband, expect another baby. I'm as those theology people say, all those divinity fudges: *situated*. If, finally, you get situated, why go into mourning over a ring?"

In the end Clara did telephone Ithiel to tell him about the emerald. "Such a link between us," she said. "And it makes me guilty to bother you with it now, when things aren't going well for you with Francine."

"Never so bad that I can't spare some words of support," said Ithiel, so dependable. He disliked grieving over his own troubles. And he was so highly organized—as if living up to the classic balance of his face; such a pair of eyes seemed to call for a particular, maybe even an administered, sort of restraint. Ithiel could be hard on himself. He blamed himself about Clara and for his failed marriages, including the present one. And yet the choices he made showed him to be reckless too. He was committed to high civility, structure, order; nevertheless he took chances with women, he was a gambler, something of an anarchist. There was anarchy on both sides. Nevertheless, his attachment, his feeling for her was—to his own surprise—permanent. His continually increasing respect for her came over the horizon like a moon taking decades to rise.

"Seven marriages between us, and we still love each other," she said. Ten years before, it would have been a risky thing to say, it would have stirred a gust of fear in him. Now she was sure that he would agree, as indeed he did.

"That is true."

"How do you interpret the ring, then?"

"I don't," said Ithiel. "It's a pretty bad idea to wring what happens to get every drop of meaning out of it. The way people twist their emotional laundry is not to be believed. *I* don't feel that you wronged me by losing that ring. You say it was insured?"

"Damn right."

"Then file a claim. The companies charge enough. Your premiums must be out of sight."

"I'm really torn up about it," said Clara.

"That's your tenth-century soul. Much your doctor can do about that!"

"He helps, in some respects."

"Those guys!" said Ithiel. "If a millipede came into the office, he'd leave with an infinitesimal crutch for each leg."

Reporting this conversation to Ms. Wong, Clara said, "That did it. That's the anarchist in Ithiel busting out. It gives me such a boost to chat with him even for five minutes."

The insurance company paid her fifteen thousand dollars, and then, a year later, the missing ring turned up.

In one of her fanatical fits of spring cleaning, she found it beneath the bed, above the caster, held in the frame to which the small braking lever was attached. It was on her side of the bed. She must have been groping for a paper tissue and knocked it off the bedside table. For what purpose she had been groping, now that it was discovered, she didn't care to guess. She held the ring to her face, felt actually as if she were inhaling the green essence of this ice—no, ice was diamond; still, this emerald also was an ice. In it Ithiel's pledge was frozen. Or else it represented the permanent form of the passion she had had for this man. The hot form would have been red, like a node inside the body, in the sexual parts. That you'd see as a ruby. The cool form was this concentrate of clear green. This was not one of her fancies; it was as real as the green of the ocean, as the mountains in whose innards such gems are mined. She thought these locations (the Atlantic, the Andes) as she thought the inside of her own body. In her summary fashion, she said, "Maybe what it comes to is that I am an infant mine." She had three small girls to prove it.

The insurance company was not notified. Clara was not prepared to return the money. By now it simply wasn't there. It had been spent on a piano, a carpet, yet another set of Limoges china—God knows what else. So the ring couldn't be reinsured, but that didn't matter much. Exultingly glad, she told Ithiel on the telephone, "*Incredible, where that ring fell! Right under me, as I lay there suffering over it. I could have touched it by dropping my arm. I could have poked it with my finger."

"How many of us can say anything like that?" said Ithiel. "That you can lie in bed and have the cure for what ails you within reach."

"Only you don't know it . . ." said Clara. "I thought you'd be pleased."

"Oh, I am. I think it's great. It's like adding ten years to your life to have it back."

"I'll have to take double good care of it. It's not insurable. . . . I'm never sure how important an item like this ring can be to a man who has to think about the Atlantic Alliance and all that other stuff. Deterrence, theater nuclear forces . . . completely incomprehensible to me."

"If only the answers were under my bed," said Ithiel. "But you shouldn't think I can't take a ring seriously, or that I'm so snooty about world significance or Lenin's 'decisive correlation of forces'—that you're just a kid and I indulge you like a big daddy. I like you better than I do the president, or the national security adviser."

"Yes, I can see that, and why, humanly, you'd rather have me to deal with."

"Just think, if you didn't do your own spring cleaning, your help might have found the ring."

"My help wouldn't dream of going under the bed at any season of the year; that's why I took time off from the office. I had to work around Wilder, who's been reading John le Carré. Sitting in the middle of his female household like a Sioux Indian in his wickiup. Like Sitting Bull. All the same, he's often very sweet. Even when he acts like the reigning male. And he'd be totally at sea if I weren't . . . oops!"

"If you weren't manning the ship," said Ithiel.

Well, it was a feminine household, and for that reason perhaps Gina felt less foreign in New York. She said that she loved the city, it had so many accommodations for women specifically. Everybody who arrived, moreover, already knew the place because of movies and magazines, and when John Kennedy said he was a Berliner, all of Berlin could have answered, "So? We are New Yorkers." There was no such thing as being strange here, in Gina's opinion.

"That's what *you* think, baby," was Clara's response, although it was not made to Gina Wegman, it was made to Ms. Wong. "And let's hope she never finds out what this town can do to a young person. But when you think about such a pretty child and the Italian charm of her looks, so innocent—although innocence is a tricky thing to prove. You can't expect her to forget about being a girl just because the surroundings are so dangerous."

"Do you let her ride the subway?"

"*Let* her!" said Clara. "When the young things go into the street, where's your control over them? All I can do is pray she'll be safe. I told her if she was going to wear a short skirt she should also put on a coat. But what good is advice without a slum background? What a woman needs today is some slum experience. However, it's up to me to keep an eye on the child, and I must assume she's innocent and doesn't *want* to be rubbed up against in the rush hours by dirty-sex delinquents."

"It's hard to be in the responsible-adult position," said Laura.

"It's the old-time religion in me. Stewardship." Clara said this partly in fun. Yet when she invoked her background, her formative years, she became for a moment the girl with the wide forehead, the large eyes, the smallish nose, who had been forced by her parents to memorize long passages from Galatians and Corinthians.

"She suits the children," said Ms. Wong.

"They're very comfortable with her, and there's no strain with Lucy." For Clara, Lucy was the main thing. At this stage she was so sullen—overweight, shy of making friends, jealous, resistant, troubled. Hard to move. Clara had often suggested that Lucy's hair be cut, the heavy curls that bounded her face. "The child has hair like Jupiter," said Clara in one of her sessions with Laura. "Sometimes I think she must be as strong—potentially—as a hod carrier."

"Wouldn't she like it short and trim, like yours?"

"I don't want a storm over it," said Clara.

The child was clumsy certainly (although her legs were going to be good—you could already see that). But there was a lot of power under this clumsiness. Lucy complained that her little sisters united against her. It looked that way, Clara agreed. Patsy and Selma were graceful children, and they made Lucy seem burly, awkward before the awkward age. She would be awkward after it too, just as her mother had been, and eruptive, defiant and prickly. When Clara got through to her (the superlarge eyes of her slender face had to bear down on the kid till she opened up—"You can always talk to Mother about what goes on, what's cooking inside"), then Lucy sobbed that all the girls in her class snubbed and made fun of her.

"Little bitches," said Clara to Ms. Wong. "Amazing how

early it all starts. Even Selma and Patsy, affectionate kids, are developing at Lucy's expense. Her 'grossness'—you know what a word 'gross' is with children—makes ladies of them. And the little sisters are far from dumb, but I believe Lucy is the one with the brains. There's something *major* in Lucy. Gina Wegman agrees with me. Lucy acts like a small she-brute. It's not just that Roman hairdo. She's greedy and bears grudges. God, she does! That's where Gina comes in, because Gina has so much class, and Gina *likes* her. As much as I can, with executive responsibilities and bearing the brunt of the household, I mother those girls. Also, I have sessions with the school psychologists—I was once married to one of those characters—and discussions with other mothers. Maybe putting them in the 'best' schools is a big mistake. The influence of the top stock-brokers and lawyers in town has to be overcome there. I'm saying it as I see it. . . ."

What Clara couldn't say, because Laura Wong's upbringing was so different from her own (and it was her own that seemed the more alien), had to do with Matthew 16:18: "the gates of hell shall not prevail against it"—*it* being love, against which no door can be closed. This was more of the primitive stuff that Clara had brought from the backcountry and was part of her confused inner life. Explaining it to her confidante would be more trouble than it was worth, if you considered that in the end Ms. Wong would still be in the dark—the second dark being darker than the first. Here Clara couldn't say it as she saw it.

"There's a lot of woman in that child. A handsome, powerful woman. Gina Wegman intuits the same about her," said Clara.

She was much drawn to Gina, only it wouldn't be wise to make a younger friend of her; that would lie too close to adoption and perhaps cause rivalry with the children. You had to keep your distance—avoid intimacies, avoid confidences especially. Yet there was nothing wrong with an occasional treat, as long as the treat was educational. For instance, you asked the au pair girl to bring some papers to your office, and then you could show her around the suite, give her a nice tea. She let Gina attend a trade briefing on shoulder pads and hear arguments for this or that type of padding, the degree of the lift, the desirability of a straighter line in the hang of one's clothes; the new trends in size in the designs of Armani, Christian Lacroix, Sonia Rykiel. She took the girl to a show of the latest spring fashions from Italy, where she heard lots of discussion about the desirability of over-the-knee boots, and of the layering of the skirts of Gianni Versace over puffy knickers. Agitprop spokesmen putting across short garments of puckered silk, or jackets of cunningly imitated ocelot, or simulated beaver capes—all this the ingenious work of millionaire artisans, billionaire designer commissars. Gina came suitably dressed, a pretty girl, very young. Clara couldn't say how this fashion display impressed her. It was best, Clara thought, to underplay the whole show: the luxurious setting, the star cast of Italians, and the pomp of the experts—somewhat subdued by the presence of the impassive czarina.

"Well, what should I say about these things?" said Clara, again confiding to Laura Wong. "This glitter is our living, and nice women grow old and glum, cynical too, in all this glitz of fur, silk, leather, cosmetics, et cetera, of the glamour trades. Meanwhile my family responsibilities are what count. How to protect my children."

"And you wanted to give your Gina a treat," said Ms. Wong.

"And I'm glad about the playfulness," said Clara. "We have to have that. But the sums it costs! And who gets what! Besides, Laura, if it has to be slathered onto women . . . If a woman is beautiful and you add beautiful dress, that's one thing: you're adding beauty to beauty. But if the operation comes from the outside only, it has curious effects. And that's the way it generally happens. Of course there will be barefaced schemers or people in despair looking glorious. But in most cases of decoration, the effect is hell. It's a variation on that Auden line I love so much about 'the will of the insane to suffer.' " When she had said this she looked blankly violent. She had gone farther than she had intended, farther than Ms. Wong was prepared to follow. Here Clara might well have added the words from Matthew 16.

Her Chinese-American confidante was used to such sudden zooming. Clara was not being stagy when she expressed such ideas about clothing; she was brooding audibly, and very often she had Ithiel Regler in mind, the women he had gone off with, the women he had married. Among them were several "fancy women"—she meant that they were overdressed sexpots, gaudy and dizzy, "ground-dragging titzers," on whom a man like Ithiel should never have squandered his substance. And he had been married three times and had two children. What a waste! Why should there have been seven marriages, five children! Even Mike Spontini, for all his powers and attractions, had been a waste—a Mediterranean, an Italian husband who came back to his wife when he saw fit, that is, when he was tired of business and of playing around. *All* the others had been dummy husbands, humanly unserious—you could get no real masculine resonance out of any of them.

What a pity! thought Laura Wong. Teddy Regler should have married Clara. Apply any measure—need, sympathy, feeling, you name it—and the two profiles (that was the Wong woman's way of putting it) were just about identical. And Ithiel was doing very badly now. Just after Gina became her au pair girl, Clara learned from the Wolfenstein woman, Teddy's first wife, who had her scouts in Washington, that the third Mrs. Regler had hired a moving van and emptied the house one morning as soon as Teddy left for the office.

Coming home in the evening, he found nothing but the bed they had shared the night before (stripped of bedding) and a few insignificant kitchen items. Francine, the third wife, had had no child to take care of. She had spent her days wandering around department stores. That much was true. He didn't let her feel that she was sharing his life. Yet the man was stunned, wiped out—depressed, then ill. He had been mourning his mother. Francine had made her move a week after his mother's funeral. One week to the day.

Clara and Laura together had decided that Francine couldn't bear his grieving. She had no such emotions herself, and she disliked them. "Some people just can't grasp grief," was what Clara said. Possibly, too, there was another man in the picture, and it would have been awkward, after an afternoon with this man, to come home to a husband absorbed in dark thoughts or needing consolation. "I can easily picture this from the wife's side," said Laura. Her own divorce had been a disagreeable one. Her husband, a man named Odo Fenger, a dermatologist, had been one of those ruddy, blond, fleshy baby-men who have to engross you in their emotions (eyes changing from baby blue to whiskey blue) and so centuple the agonies of breaking away. So why *not* send a van to the house and move straight into the future—future being interpreted as never (never in this life) meeting the other party again. "That Francine didn't have it in her to see him through, after the feeling had been killed out of *her*. Each age has its own way of dealing with these things. As you said before, in the Renaissance you used poison. When the feeling is killed, the other party becomes physically unbearable."

Clara didn't entirely attend to what Laura was saying. Her only comment was, "I suppose there *has* been progress. Better moving than murdering. At least both parties go on living."

By now Ms. Wong wanted no husbands, no children.

She had withdrawn from all that. But she respected Clara Velde. Perhaps her curiosity was even deeper than her respect, and she was most curious about Clara and Ithiel Regler. She collected newspaper clippings about Regler and like Wilder Velde didn't miss his TV interviews, if she could help it.

When Clara heard about Francine and her moving van, she flew down to Washington as soon as she could get to the shuttle. Gina was there to take charge of the children. Clara never felt so secure as when dependable Gina was looking after them. As a backup Clara had Mrs. Peralta, the cleaning woman, who had also become a family friend.

Clara found Ithiel in a state of sick dignity. He was affectionate with her but reserved about his troubles, thanked her somewhat formally for her visit, and told her that he would rather not go into the history of his relations with Francine.

"Just as you like," said Clara. "But you haven't got anybody here; there's just me in New York. I'll look after you if you should need it."

"I'm glad you've come. I've been despondent. What I've learned, though, is that when people get to talking about their private troubles, they go into a winding spiral about relationships, and they absolutely stupefy everybody with boredom. I'm sure that I can turn myself around."

"Of course. You're resilient," said Clara, proud of him. "So we won't say too much about it. Only, that woman didn't have to wait until your mother was dead. She might have done it earlier. You don't wait until a man is down, then dump on him."

"Shall we have a good dinner? Middle Eastern, Chinese, Italian or French? I see you're wearing the emerald."

"I hoped you'd notice. Now tell me, Ithiel, are you giving up your place? Did she leave it very bare?"

"I can camp there until some money comes in and then refit the living room."

"There ought to be somebody taking care of you."

"If there's one thing I can do without, it's this picture of poor me, deep in the dumps, and some faithful female who makes my heart swell with gratitude." Being rigorous with his heart gave him satisfaction.

"He likes to look at the human family as it is," Clara was to explain.

"You wouldn't marry a woman who did value you," said Clara at dinner. "Like Groucho Marx saying he wouldn't join a club that accepted him for membership."

"Let me tell you," said Ithiel, and she understood that he had drawn back to the periphery in order to return to the center from one of his strange angles. "When the president has to go to Walter Reed Hospital for surgery and the papers are full of sketches of his bladder and his prostate—I can remember the horrible drawings of Eisenhower's ileitis— then I'm glad there are no diagrams of my vitals in the press and the great public isn't staring at my anus. For the same reason, I've always discouraged small talk about my psyche. It's only fair that Francine shouldn't have valued me. I would have lived out the rest of my life with her. I was patient. . . ."

"You mean you gave up, you resigned yourself."

"I was affectionate," Ithiel insisted.

"You had to fake it. You saw your mistake and were ready to pay for it. She didn't give a squat for your affection."

"I was faithful."

"No, you were licked," said Clara. "You went to your office hideaway and did your thing about Russia or Iran. Those crazy characters from Libya or Lebanon are *some* fun to follow. What did she do for fun?"

"I suppose that every morning she had to decide where to go with her credit cards. She liked auctions and furniture shows. She bought an ostrich-skin outfit, complete with boots and purse."

"What else did she do for fun?"

Ithiel was silent and reserved, moving crumbs back and forth with the blade of his knife. Clara thought, She cheated on him. Precious Francine had no idea what a husband she had. And what did it matter what a woman like that did with her gross organs. Clara didn't get a rise out of Ithiel with her suggestive question. She might just as well have been talking to one of those Minoans dug up by Evans or Schliemann or whoever, characters like those in the silent films, painted with eye-lengthening makeup. If Clara was from the Middle Ages, Ithiel was from antiquity. Imagine a low-down woman who felt that *he* didn't appreciate *her*! Why, Ithiel could be the Gibbon or the Tacitus of the American Empire. *He* wouldn't have thought it, but she remembered to this day how he would speak about Keynes's sketches of Clemenceau, Lloyd George and Woodrow Wilson. If he wanted, he could do with Nixon, Johnson, Kennedy or Kissinger, with the Shah or de Gaulle, what Keynes had done with the Allies at Versailles. World figures had found Ithiel worth their while. Sometimes he let slip a comment or a judgment: "Neither the Russians nor the Americans can manage the world. Not capable of organizing the future." When she came into her own, Clara thought, she'd set up a fund for him so he could write his views.

She said, "If you'd like me to stay over, Wilder has gone to Minnesota to see some peewee politician who needs a set of speeches. Gina is entertaining a few friends at the house."

"Do I look as if I needed friendly first aid?"

"You are *down*. What's the disgrace in that?"

Ithiel drove her to the airport. For the moment the parkways were empty. Ahead were airport lights, and in the slanting planes seated travelers by the thousands came in, went up.

Clara asked what job he was doing. "Not who you're doing it for, but the subject."

He said he was making a survey of the opinions of émigrés on the new Soviet regime—he seemed glad to change the subject, although he had always been a bit reluctant to talk politics to her. Politics were not her thing, he didn't like to waste words on uncomprehending idle questioners, but he seemed to have his emotional reasons tonight for saying just what it was that he was up to. "Some of the smartest émigrés are saying that the Russians didn't announce liberalization until they had crushed the dissidents. Then they co-opted the dissidents' ideas. After you've gotten rid of your enemies, you're ready to abolish capital punishment—that's how Alexander Zinoviev puts it. And it wasn't only the KGB that destroyed the dissident movement but the whole party organization, and the party was supported by the Soviet people. They strangled the opposition, and now they're pretending to be *it*. You have the Soviet leaders themselves criticizing Soviet society. When it has to be done, they take over. And the West is thrilled by all the reforms."

"So we're going to be bamboozled again," said Clara.

But there were other matters, more pressing, to discuss on the way to the airport. Plenty of time. Ithiel drove very slowly. The next shuttle flight wouldn't be taking off until nine o'clock. Clara was glad they didn't have to rush.

"You don't mind my wearing this ring tonight?" said Clara.

"Because this is a bad time to remind me of the way it might have gone with us? No. You came down to see how I was and what you could do for me."

"Next time, Ithiel, if there is a next time, you'll let me

check the woman out. You may be big in political analysis . . . No need to finish *that* sentence. Besides, my own judgment hasn't been one hundred percent."

"If anybody were to ask me, Clara, I'd say that you were a strange case—a woman who hasn't been corrupted, who developed her own moral logic, worked it out independently by her own solar power and from her own feminine premises. You hear I've had a calamity and you come down on the next shuttle. And how few people take this Washington flight for a human purpose. Most everybody comes on business. Some to see the sights, a few because of the pictures at the National Gallery, a good percentage to get laid. How many come because they're deep?"

He parked his car so that he could walk with her to the gate.

"You're a dear man," she said. "We have to look out for each other."

On the plane, she pulled her seat belt tight in order to control her feelings, and she opened a copy of *Vogue,* but only to keep her face in it. No magazine now had anything to tell her.

When she got back to Park Avenue, the superintendent's wife, a Latino lady, was waiting. Mrs. Peralta was there too. Clara had asked the cleaning lady to help Gina entertain (to keep an eye on) her friends. The elevator operator-doorman was with the ladies, a small group under the marquee. The sidewalks of Park Avenue are twice as broad as any others, and the median strip was nicely planted with flowers of the season. When the doorman helped Clara from the yellow cab, the women immediately began to tell her about the huge bash Gina had given. "A real mix of people," said Mrs. Peralta.

"And the girls?"

"Oh, we were careful with them, kept them away from

those East Harlem types. We're here because Mr. Regler called to say what flight you'd be on."

"I asked him to do that," said Clara.

"I don't think Gina thought so many were coming. Friends, and friends of friends, of her boyfriend, I guess."

"Boyfriend? Now, who would he be? This is news to me."

"I asked Marta Elvia to come and see for herself," said Antonia Peralta. Marta Elvia, the super's wife, was related somehow to Antonia.

They were taken up in the elevator. Marta Elvia, eight months pregnant and filling up much of the space, was saying what a grungy mob had turned up. It was an open house.

"But tell me, quickly, who is the boyfriend?" said Clara.

The man was described as coming from the West Indies; he was French-speaking, dark-skinned, very good-looking, "arrogant like," said Mrs. Peralta.

"And how long has he been coming to the house?"

"Couple of weeks, just."

When she entered the living room, Clara's first impression was: So this is what can be done here. It doesn't have to be the use I put it to. She had limited the drawing room to polite behavior.

The party was mostly over; there were only four or five couples left. As Clara described it, the young women looked gaudy. "The room was more like a car of the West Side subway. Lots of muscle on the boys, as if they did aerobics. And I used to be able to identify the smell of pot, but I'm in the dark, totally, on the new drugs. Crack is completely beyond me; I can't even say what it is, much less describe how it works and does it have a smell. The whole scene was like a mirage to me, how they were haberdashed. Gina's special friend, Frederic, was a good-looking boy, black, and he did have an attractive French accent. Gina tried to behave as if nothing at all was wrong, and she couldn't quite swing that. I wasn't going to fuss at her, though. At the back of the apartment, I had three children sleeping. At a time like this your history books come back to you—how a pioneer woman dealt with an Indian war party when her husband was away. So I put myself out to make time pass pleasantly, toned down the music, ventilated the smoke, and soon the party petered out."

While Mrs. Peralta was cleaning up, Clara had a talk with Gina Wegman. She said she had imagined a smaller gathering—a few acquaintances, not a random sample of the street population.

"Frederic asked if he could bring some friends."

Well, Clara was willing to believe that this was simply a European misconception of partying in New York—carefree musical young people, racially mixed, dancing to reggae music. In Vienna, as elsewhere, such pictures of American life were on TV—America as the place where you let yourself go.

"Anyway, I must tell you, Gina, that I can't allow this kind of thing—like scenes from some lewd dance movie."

"I'm sorry, Mrs. Velde."

"Where did you meet Frederic?"

"Through friends from Austria. They work at the UN."

"Is that where he works too?"

"I never asked."

"And do you see a lot of him? You don't have to answer—I can tell you're taken with him. You never asked what he does? He's not a student?"

"It never came up."

Clara thought, judging by Gina's looks, that what came up was Gina's skirt. Clara herself knew all too well how that was. We've been through it. What can be more natural in a foreign place than to accept exotic experiences? Otherwise why leave home at all?

Clifford, a convict in Attica, still sent Clara a Christmas card without fail. She hadn't seen him in twenty-five years. They had no other connection. Frederic, to go by appearances, wouldn't even have sent a card. Generational differences. Clifford had been a country boy.

We must see to it that it doesn't end badly, was what Clara told herself.

But then we must learn what sort of person Gina is, really, she thought. What makes her tick, and if this is the whole sum of what she wants. I didn't take her for a little hotpants type.

"I suppose things are done differently in Vienna," Clara said. "As to bringing strangers into the house . . ."

"No. But then you're personally friendly with the colored lady who works here."

"Mrs. Peralta is no stranger."

"She brings her children here at Thanksgiving, and they eat with the girls at the same table."

"And why not? But yes," said Clara, "I can see that this is a mixture that might puzzle somebody just over from Europe for the first time. My husband and I are not rashists. . . ." (This was a pronunciation Clara could not alter.) "However, Mrs. Peralta is a trusted member of this household."

"But Frederic's friends might steal . . . ?"

"I haven't accused anyone. You couldn't vouch for anybody, though. You've just met these guests yourself. And haven't you noticed the security arrangements—the doors, the buzzer system, everybody inspected?"

Gina said, speaking quietly and low, "I noticed. I didn't apply it to myself."

Not *herself*. Gina hadn't considered Frederic in this light.

And she couldn't allow him to be viewed with suspicion. Clara gave her a good mark for loyalty. Ten on a scale of ten, she thought, and warmed toward Gina. "It's not a color question. The corporation I'm in has even divested itself in South Africa." This was not a strong statement. To Clara, South Africa was about as close as Xanadu. But she said to herself that they were being diverted into absurdities, and what she and Gina were telling each other was only so much fluff. The girl had come to New York to learn about such guys as Frederic, and there wasn't all that much to learn. This was simply an incident, and not even a good incident. Just a lot of exciting trouble. Then she made a mental note to take all this up with Ithiel and also get his opinion on divestiture.

"Well," she said, "I'm afraid I'm going to set a limit on the size of the group you can entertain."

The girl nodded. That made sense. She couldn't deny it.

No more scolding. And a blend of firmness and concern for the girl. If she were to send her away, the kids would cry. And I'd miss her myself, Clara admitted. So she stood up (mistress terminating a painful interview was how Clara perceived it; she saw that she really had come to depend on certain lady-of-the-house postures). When Gina had gone to her room, Clara ran a check: the Jensen ashtray, the silver letter opener, mantelpiece knickknacks; and for the nth time she wished that there were someone to share her burdens. Wilder was no good to her that way. If he got fifty speech commissions he couldn't make up the money he had sunk in mining stocks—Homestake and Sunshine. Supposedly, precious metals were a hedge, but there was less and less principal for the shrinking hedge to hedge.

The inspection over, Clara talked to Antonia Peralta before Antonia turned on the noisy vacuum cleaner. How often had Gina's young man been in the apartment? Antonia jabbed at her cheek with a rigid finger, meaning that a sharp lookout was necessary. Her message was: "Count on me, Mrs. Velde." Well, she was part of a pretty smart subculture. Between them, she and Marta Elvia would police the joint. On Gina Wegman herself Antonia Peralta did not comment. But then she wasn't always around, she had her days off. And remember, Antonia hadn't cleaned under the bed. And if she *had* been thorough she would have found the missing ring. In that case, would she have handed it over? She was an honest lady, according to her lights, but there probably were certain corners into which those lights never were turned. The insurance company had paid up, and Clara would have been none the wiser if Antonia had silently pocketed a lost object. No, the Spanish ladies were honest enough. Marta Elvia was bonded, triple certified, and Antonia Peralta had never taken so much as a handkerchief.

"In my own house," Clara was to explain later, "I object to locking up valuables. A house where there is no basic trust is not what I call a house. I just can't live with a bunch of keys, like a French or Italian person. Women have told me that they couldn't sleep nights if their jewelry weren't locked up. *I* couldn't sleep if it were."

She said to Gina, "I'm taking your word for it that nothing bad will happen." She was bound to make this clear, while recognizing that there was no way to avoid giving offense.

Gina had no high looks, no sharp manner. She simply said, "Are you telling me not to have Frederic here?"

Clara's reaction was, Better here than *there*. She tried to imagine what Frederic's pad must be like. That was not too difficult. She had, after all, herself been a young woman in New York. Gina was giving her a foretaste of what she would have to face when her own girls grew up. Unless heaven itself were to decree that Gogmagogsville had gone far enough, and checked the decline—time to lower the boom, send in the Atlantic to wash it away. Not a possibility you could count on.

"By no means," said Clara. "I will ask you, though, to take full charge when Antonia is off."

"You don't want Frederic here when the children are with me?"

"Right."

"He wouldn't harm them."

Clara did not see fit to say more.

She spoke to Ms. Wong about it, stopping at her place after work for a brief drink, a breather on the way home. Ms. Wong had an unsuitably furnished Madison Avenue apartment, Scandinavian design, not an Oriental touch about it except some Chinese prints framed in blond wood. Holding her iced Scotch in a dampening paper napkin, Clara said, "I hate to be the one enforcing the rules on that girl. I feel for her a lot more than I care to."

"You identify all that much with her?"

"She's got to learn, of course," said Clara. "Just as I did. And I don't think much of mature women who have evaded it. But sometimes the schooling we have to undergo is too rough."

"Seems to you *now* . . ."

"No, it takes far too much out of a young girl."

"You're thinking of three daughters," said Ms. Wong, accurate enough.

"I'm thinking how it is that you have to go on for twenty years before you understand—maybe understand—what there was to preserve."

Somewhat dissatisfied with her visit to Laura (it was so *New York!*), she walked home, there to be told by Mrs. Peralta that she had found Gina and Frederic stretched out on the living room sofa. Doing what? Oh, only petting, but the young man with the silk pillows under his combat boots. Clara could see why Antonia should be offended.

The young man was putting down the Veldes and their fine upholstery, spreading himself about and being arrogant. And perhaps it wasn't even that. He may not have reached *that* level of intentional offensiveness.

"You talk to the girl?"

"I don't believe I will. No," said Clara, and risked being a contemptible American in Mrs. Peralta's eyes, one of those people who let themselves be run over in their own homes. Largely to herself, Clara explained, "I'd rather put up with him here than have the girl do it in his pad." No sooner had she said this than she was dead certain that there was nothing to keep Gina from doing whatever they did in both places. She would have said to Gina, "Making the most of New York—this not-for-Vienna behavior. No boys lying on top of you in your mother's drawing room." "Land of opportunity," she might have said, but she said this only to herself after thinking matters through, considering deeply in a trancelike private stillness and moistening the center of her upper lip with the tip of her tongue. Why did it go so dry right at the center? Imagining sexual things sometimes did that to her. She didn't envy Gina; the woman who had made such personal sexual disclosures to Ms. Wong didn't have to envy anyone. No, she was curious about this pretty, plump girl. She sensed that she was a deep one. *How* deep was what Clara was trying to guess when she went so still.

And so she closed her eyes briefly, nodding, when Marta Elvia, who sometimes waited for her in the lobby, pressed close with her pregnant belly to say that Frederic had come in at one o'clock and left just before Mrs. Velde was expected.

(There were anomalies in Clara's face when you saw it frontally. Viewing it in profile, you would find yourself trying to decide which of the Flemish masters would have painted her best.)

"Thanks, Marta Elvia," she said. "I've got the situation under control."

She shouldn't have been so sure about it, for that very evening when she was dressing for dinner—a formal corporate once-a-year affair—she was standing before the long mirror in her room, when suddenly she knew that her ring had been stolen. She kept it in the top drawer of her dresser—unlocked, of course. Its place was a dish Jean-Claude had given her years ago. The young Frenchman, Ithiel's temporary replacement recklessly chosen in anger, had called this gift a *vide-poches*. At bedtime you emptied your pockets into it. It was meant for men; women didn't use that kind of object; but it was one of those mementos Clara couldn't part with—she kept schoolday valentines in a box, too. She looked, of course, into the dish. The ring wasn't there. She hadn't expected it to be. She expected nothing. She said that the sudden knowledge that it was gone came over her like death and she felt as if the life had been vacuumed out of her.

Wilder, already in evening clothes, was reading one of his thrillers in a corner where the back end of the grand piano hid him. With her rapid, dry decisionmaker's look, Clara went to the kitchen, where the kids were at dinner. Under Gina's influence they behaved so well at table. "May I see you for a moment?" said Clara, and Gina immediately got up and followed her to the master bedroom. There Clara shut both doors, and lowering her head so that she seemed to be examining Gina's eyes, "Well, Gina, something has happened," she said. "My ring is gone."

"You mean the emerald that was lost and found again? Oh, Mrs. Velde, I am sorry. Is it gone? I'm sure you have looked. Did Mr. Velde help you?"

"I haven't told him yet."

"Then let's look together."

"Yes, let's. But it's always in the same place, in this room.

In that top drawer under my stockings. Since I found it again, I've been extra careful. And of course I want to examine the shag rug. I want to crawl and hunt for it. But I'd have to take off this tight dress to get on my knees. And my hair is fixed for going out."

Gina, stooping, combed through the carpet near the dresser. Clara, silent, let her look, staring down, her eyes superdilated, her mouth stern. She said, at last, "It's no use." She had let Gina go through the motions.

"Should you call the police to report it?"

"I'm not going to do that," said Clara. She was not so foolish as to tell the young woman about the insurance. "Perhaps that makes you feel better, not having the police."

"I think, Mrs. Velde, you should have locked up your valuable objects."

"In my own home, I shouldn't have to."

"Yes, but there are other people also to consider."

"I consider, Gina, that a woman has a right in her own bedroom . . . it's for a woman *herself* to decide who comes in. I made it explicit what the household rules were. I would have vouched for you, and you must vouch for your friend."

Gina was shaken. Both women trembled. After all, thought Clara, a human being can be sketched in three or four lines, but then when the sockets are empty, no amount of ingenuity can refill them. Not her brown, not my blue.

"I understand you," said Gina with an air of being humiliated by a woman whose kindness she counted on. "Are you sure the ring isn't misplaced again?"

"Are *you* sure . . . ?" Clara answered. "And try to think of my side of it. That was an engagement ring from a man who loved me. It's not just an object worth X dollars. It's also a life support, my dear." She was about to say that it was involved with her very grip on existence, but she didn't want any kind of cry to come out or to betray a fear of total slippage. She said instead, "The ring was here yesterday.

And a person I don't know wandering around the house and—why not?—coming into my room . . ."

"Why don't you say it?" said Gina.

"I'd have to be a fool not to. To be too nice for such things, I'd have to be a moron. Frederic was here all afternoon. Has he got a job somewhere?"

The girl had no answer to this.

"You can't say. But you don't believe he's a thief. You don't think he'd put you in this position. And don't try to tell me he's being accused because of his color."

"I didn't try. People *are* nasty about the Haitians."

"You'd better go and talk to him. If he's got the ring, tell him he has to return it. I want you to produce it tomorrow. Marta Elvia can sit with the girls if you have to go out tonight. Where does he live?"

"One hundred twenty-eighth Street."

"And a telephone? You can't go up there alone after dark. Not even by day. Not alone. And where does he hang out? I can ask Antonia's husband to take you by cab. . . . Now Wilder's coming down the corridor, and I've got to go."

"I'll wait here for the concierge."

"For Marta Elvia. I'll talk to her on the way out. *You* wouldn't steal, Gina. And Mrs. Peralta has been here eight years without a coffee spoon missing."

Later Clara took it out on herself: What did I do to that girl, like ordering her to go to Harlem, where she could be raped or killed, because of my goddam ring, the rottenest part of town in the rotten middle of the night, frantic mad and (what it comes down to) over Ithiel, who balked at marrying me twenty years ago! A real person understands how to cut losses, not let her whole life be wound around to the end by a single desire, because under it all is the uglitude of this one hang-up. Four husbands and three kids haven't cured me of Ithiel. And finally this love-toy emerald, personal sentimentality, makes me turn like a maniac on this Austrian kid. She may think I grudge her the excitement of her romance with that disgusting girl-fucker who used her as his cover to get into the house and now sticks her with this theft.

Nevertheless Clara had fixed convictions about domestic and maternal responsibilities. She had already gone too far in letting Gina bring Frederic into the apartment and infect the whole place, spraying it with sexual excitement. And, as it now turned out, even become involved in crime. A fling in the U.S.A. was all very well for a young lady from bourgeois Vienna—like the poor Russian hippie, that diplomat's son who fell in love with Mick Jagger. "Tell Mick Jagger goodbye," he said, boarding the plane. This city had become the center, the symbol of worldwide adolescent revolt.

In the middle of the corporate evening Clara was attacked by one of her fierce migraines, and a head as conspicuous as hers, dominating a dinner table, affected everybody when it began to ache, so that the whole party stood up when she rose and hurried out. The Veldes went straight home. Swallowing a handful of white pills from the medicine chest, Clara went immediately to Gina's room. To her relief, the girl was there, in bed. The reading lamp was on, but she wasn't reading, only sitting up, her hands thoughtfully folded.

"I'm glad you didn't go to Harlem!"

"I reached Frederic on the phone. He was with some of our UN friends."

"And you'll see him tomorrow . . . ?"

"I didn't mention the ring. But I am prepared to move out. You told me I had to bring it back or leave."

"Going where . . . !" Clara was taken by surprise. Next she was aware of the girl's brown gaze, the exceptional fixity of it. Unshed tears were killing her. "But if Frederic gives back the ring, you'll stay." While she was speaking, Clara with some shame recognized how dumb she sounded. It was the hereditary peasant in her saying this. The guy would deny the theft, and if eventually he admitted it, he still would not return the ring. This very moment he might be taking a thousand bucks for it. These people came up from the tropical slums to outsmart New York, and with all the rules crumbling here as elsewhere, so that nobody could any longer be clear in his mind about anything, they could do it.

Left standing were only property rights. With murder in second place. A stolen ring. A corpse to account for. Such were the only universals recognized, and very few others could be acknowledged. So where did love fit in? Love was down in the catacombs, those catacombs being the personal neuroses of women like herself.

She said to Gina, as one crypto lover to another, "What will you do?"

Gina said, but without resentment, not a hint of accusation in her voice, "That I can't say. I've only had a couple of hours to think. There are places."

She'd move in with her Haitian, Clara guessed, plausibly enough. But this was not sayable. Clara was learning to refrain. You didn't *say* everything. "Discover silence," she instructed herself.

Next day she rushed home from work in a cab and found Marta Elvia baby-sitting. Clara had already been in touch with an agency, and there was a new girl coming tomorrow. Best she could do on short notice. Lucy was upset, predictably, and Clara had to take her aside for special explanations. She said, "Gina suddenly had to go. It was an emergency. She didn't *want* to. When she can, she'll come back. It's not *your* fault." There was no guessing just how rattled Lucy was. She was silent, stoical.

Clara had rehearsed this on the telephone with the psychiatrist, Dr. Gladstone.

"With working parents," she said to Lucy, "such problems do come up."

"But Daddy isn't working now."

You're telling *me*! thought Clara. He was doping out the upcoming primaries in New Hampshire.

As soon as possible, she went to see Dr. Gladstone. He was about to take one of his holidays and would be away three weeks. They had discussed this absence in the last session. In the waiting room, she studied the notes she had prepared: Where is Gina? How can I find out, keep track? Protect?

She acknowledged to Dr. Gladstone that she was in a near-hysterical state over the second disappearance, the theft. She was discovering that she had come to base her stability entirely on the ring. Such dependency was fearful. He asked how she saw this, and how Ithiel figured in it. She said, "The men I meet don't seem to be real persons. Nobody really is anybody. There may be more somebodies than I've been able to see. I don't want to write off about one half of our species. And concentrated desire for so many years may have affected my judgment. Anyway, for me, what a man is seems to be defined by Ithiel. Also, I am *his* truest friend, and he understands that and responds emotionally."

Involuntarily Clara fell into Dr. Gladstone's way of talking. To herself, she would never say "responds emotionally." As the sessions were short, she adopted his lingo to save time, notwithstanding the danger of false statements. Hope brought her here, every effort must be made, but when she looked, looked with all her might at Dr. Gladstone, she could not justify the trust she was asked to place in that samurai beard, the bared teeth it framed, the big fashionable specs, his often baseless confidence in his science. However, it would take the better part of a year to acquaint a new doctor with the fundamentals of her case. She was stuck with this one.

"And I'm very worried about Gina. How do I find out what's happening to her? Should I hire a private investigator? A girl like that survive in Spanish Harlem? No way."

"An expensive proposition," said Dr. Gladstone. "Any alternatives in mind?"

"Wilder does nothing. He could get on the case. Like shadow her, make practical use of the thrillers he's read. But he's negotiating with some hopeless wimp who wants to go for the White House."

"Let's get back to the theft, if it *is* a theft."

"It *has* to be. I didn't misplace it again."

"However, it gave you daily anxiety. Why did it occupy so big a place in you?"

"What did I come up with last time we discussed it? I cheated the insurance company and had the ring *and* the money. You could call that white-collar crime. It all added to the importance of my emerald, but I would never have guessed that it would be so shattering to lose it."

"I can suggest a coincidence," said the doctor. "At this bad moment for you I am going on a holiday. My support is removed. And my name is Glad*stone*. Is that why you take the loss so hard?"

Astonished, she gave him a real stare, not a fitting or becoming one. She said, "You may be a stone, but you're not a gem."

When she returned to her office she telephoned Ithiel, her only dependable adviser, to discuss matters.

"I wish you were coming up to New York," she said. "I used to call on Steinsalz when things were urgent."

"He was a great loss to me too."

"He took such interest in people. Short of lending them

money. He'd treat you to dinner but never lend a cent. He did listen, though."

"It so happens," said Ithiel (when he was being method-ical, a sort of broken flatness entered his voice), "that I have a lunch date next Tuesday with a man in New York."

"Let's say half-past three, then?"

Their customary meeting place was St. Patrick's cathe-dral, near Clara's office, a central location and a shelter in bad weather. "Like a drop for secret agents," Ithiel said. They left the cathedral and went directly to the Helmsley Palace. A quiet corner of the bar was still available at that early hour. "This is on my Gold Card," said Clara. "Now let's see how you look—somewhere between a Spanish grandee and a Mennonite."

Then with executive rapidity she set forth the main facts.

"What's your opinion of Frederic—an occasional stealer or a pro?"

"I think he improvises," said Clara. "Dope? Probably."

"You could find out about his police record, if any. Then ask the Austrian consulate about her. Not telephone her folks in Vienna."

"I knew it would be a relief to talk to you. Now tell me . . . about the ring."

"A loss, I'd guess. Write it off."

"I suppose I'll have to. I indulged myself about it, and look at the trouble it made. There's nothing appropriate. For instance, this luxury bar that fits neither you nor me. In my true feelings you and I are as naked as Adam and Eve. I'm not being suggestive, either. It's not an erotic suggestion, just a simile."

Talk like this, the hint of wildness in it, had the effect of forcing him into earnestness. She could see him applying his good mind to her difficulties, like a person outside pressing his forehead on the windowpane to see what's going on.

As she figured it, he counted on the executive Clara to gain on the subjective Clara. She *did* have the ability to put her house in order. Yet his sympathy for the subjective, personal Clara was very strong. Considering the greater tumult in her, she had done better than he. Even now her life was more coherent than his.

"For a few hundred bucks, I think you can find out where the girl is. Investigators are easy to hire."

"Tell me! I can see why General Haig and such people call on you to analyze the Iranians or the Russians. By the way, Wilder thought you were great on TV with Dobrynin, week before last."

When Ithiel smiled, his teeth were so good you suspected Hollywood dentistry, but they were all his own.

"Dobrynin has some genius, of a low kind. He convinces Americans that Russians are exactly like them. Sometimes he behaves as if he were the senior senator from a fifty-first, all-Russian state. Just a slight accent, but the guys from the Deep South have one also. He sold Gorbachev on this completely, and Gorbachev is selling the whole U.S.A. Which craves to be sold. Deceived, if you prefer."

"Like me, in a way, about the Human Pair."

"You're close to that girl, I see."

"Very close. It would be easy for you to put her down as a well-brought-up kid with a taste for low sex. Resembling me. You'd be wrong. Too bad you can't see her yourself. Your opinion would interest me."

"So she isn't like you?"

"I sure hope not." Clara made a gesture, as if saying, Wipe out these Helmsley Palace surroundings and listen to me. "Don't forget my two suicide attempts. I have a spoonful of something wild in my mixture, my whole sense of . . ."

"Of life . . ."

"Listen to me. You have no idea really how wild and

how mixed, or how much territory it takes in. The territory stretches over into death. When I'm drunk with agitation—and it is like being drunk—there's one pulse in me that's a death-beat pulse, and it tempts me to make out with death. It says, Why wait! When I get as intense as that, existence won't hold me. That's the internal horror side of the thing. I'm open to seduction by death. Now you're going to remind me that I'm the mother of three kids."

"Exactly what I was about to do."

"There's no one in the world but you that I'd say this to. You're the one human being I fully confide in. Neither do you have secrets from me. Whatever you didn't admit I saw for myself."

"You certainly did, Clara."

"But we'll never be man and wife. Oh, you don't have to say anything. You love me, but the rest is counterindicated. It's one of those damn paradoxes that have to be waited out. There may even be a parallel to it in your field, in politics. We have the power to destroy ourselves, and maybe the desire, and we keep ourselves in permanent suspense—waiting. Isn't that wild, too? You could tell *me*. You're the expert. You're going to write the book of books about it."

"Now you're making fun of me."

"Not really, Ithiel. If it is the book of books on the subject, it should be written. You may be the man to write it, and I'm not making fun. For *me* it would be funny. Think of a great odalisque, nude and beautiful. And now think of her in eyeglasses and writing books on a lap board."

Over the table they smiled briefly at each other.

"But I want to get back to Gina," said Clara. "You're going to find me a dependable investigator to check out Frederic, and the rest of it. I doubt that she is like me, except in taking chances. But when I told her that the ring was given by a man who loved me, the fact registered completely. What I didn't add was that I bullied you into giving it to me. Don't deny it. I twisted your arm. Then I sentimentalized it. Then I figured out that you continued to love me *because* we didn't marry. And now the ring . . . The girl understands about the ring. The love part of it."

Teddy was stirred, and looked aside. He wasn't ready, and perhaps never would be ready, to go farther. No, they never would be man and wife. When they stood up to go, they kissed like friends.

"You'll get me an investigator with a little class . . . the minimum sleaze?"

"I'll tell the man to go to your office, so you can look him over."

"A few things have to be done for you too," said Clara. "That Francine left you in bad shape. You have that somber look that you get when you're up against it."

"Is that what you mean by the Mennonite?"

"There were plenty of Mennonites in Indiana—I can tell that you didn't have any business in New York today except me."

Within ten days she had Gina's address—a fourth-floor walk-up on East 128th Street, care of F. Vigneron. She had a phone number as well. Call? No, she wouldn't speak to her yet. She brought her executive judgment to bear on this, and the advice from this source was to send a note. In her note, she wrote that the children asked for Gina often. Lucy missed her. Even so, she had done Lucy good. You could see the improvements. There was a lot of woman in that small girl, already visible. Then, speaking for herself, she said that she was sorry to have come down so hard on a matter that needn't be spelled out now. She had left Gina few options. She had had no choice but to go. The mystery was why she had gone "uptown" when other choices were possible. However, Gina owed her no explanations. And

Clara hoped that she would not feel that she had to turn away from her forever or decide that she, Clara, was an enemy. Anything but a hostile judge, Clara respected her sense of honor.

Asked for a reference on her unlisted mental line, Clara, when reached, would have said about Gina: soft face, soft bust, brown bourgeois-maiden gaze, but firm at decision time. Absolutely ten on a scale of ten.

But in the note she sent to Gina she went on, ladylike, matronly and fair-minded, to wish her well, and concluded, "You should have had some notice, and I believe it only fair that the month should have been rounded out, so since I am not absolutely certain of the correct address, I will leave an envelope with Marta Elvia. Two hundred dollars in cash."

Frederic Vigneron would send her for the money, if he got wind of it.

Gottschalk, the private eye, did his job responsibly; that was about the best that could be said of him. Perhaps half an eye. And not much more ear. Still, he did obtain the facts she asked for. He said of the building in East Harlem, "Of course the city can't run around and condemn every joint it should, or there'd be lots more street people sleeping in the West Side terminal. But I wouldn't want any nieces of mine living there."

Having done what you could, you went ahead with your life: showered and powdered with talcum in the morning, put on underthings and stockings, chose a skirt and blouse for the day, made up your face for the office, took in the paper, and, if Wilder was sleeping in (he did often), ground your coffee and as the water dripped turned the pages of the *Times* professionally. For a group of magazines owned by a publishing corporation, she was the lady overseeing women's matters. Almost too influential to have a personal life, as she sometimes observed to Ms. Wong. High enough in the power structure, you can be excused from having one, "an option lots of people are glad to exercise."

Nobody called for the money envelope. Marta Elvia's instructions were to give it to Gina only. After a period of keen interest, Clara stopped asking about it. Gottschalk, doing little, sent an occasional memo: "Status quo unchanged." To go with his Latin, Clara figured that Gina had found a modus vivendi with her young Haitian. The weeks, week after week, subdued Clara. You can say that you're waiting only if there is something definite to wait for. During this time it often seemed there wasn't anything. And, "I never feel so bad as when the life I lead stops being characteristic—when it could be anybody else's life," she told Laura Wong.

But coming home one afternoon after a session with Dr. Gladstone (things were so bad that she was seeing him regularly again), she entered her bedroom for an hour's rest before the kids returned from ballet class. She had dropped her shoes and was crawling toward the pillows, her mouth open in the blindness of fatigue, surrendering to the worst of feelings, when she saw that her ring had been placed on the night table. It had been set on a handkerchief, a new object from a good shop. She slipped on her ring and lunged for the phone across the bed, rapidly punching out Marta Elvia's number.

"Marta Elvia," she said, "has anybody been here today? Did anybody come to leave an article for me?" Fifteen years in the U.S. and the woman still spoke incomplete English. "Listen," said Clara. "Did Gina come here today? Did you or anybody let Gina into the apartment? . . . No? Somebody did come in, and Gina gave up her house keys when she left. . . . Sure she could have made a duplicate—she or her boyfriend. . . . Of course I should have changed the lock. . . . No, nothing was taken. On the contrary, the person gave back something. I'm glad I didn't change the lock."

Now Marta Elvia was upset that an outside somebody had got in. Security in this building was one hundred percent. She was sending her husband up to make sure the door hadn't been jimmied open.

"No, no!" said Clara. "There hasn't been illegal entry. What a wild idea!"

Her own ideas at this moment were not less wild. She rang Gina's number in East Harlem. What she got was an answering machine, from which came Frederic's voice, whose Frenchy slickness was offensive. (Clara disliked those telephone devices anyway, and her prejudice extended to the sound of the signal—in this instance a pig squeal.) "This is Mrs. Wilder Velde calling Miss Wegman." Inasmuch as Gina might have prevailed by reasonable means over him, Clara was ready to revise her opinion of Frederic too. (On her scale of ten, she could upgrade him from less than zero to one.)

Next Clara phoned Gottschalk and entered on his tape her request that he call back. She then tried Laura Wong, and finally Wilder in New Hampshire. It was primary time up there; his candidate lagged far behind the field, and you couldn't expect Wilder to be in his hotel room. Ithiel was in Central America. There was no one to share the recovery of the ring with. The strongest lights in the house were in the bathroom, and she turned them on, pressing against the sink to examine the stone and the setting, making sure that the small diamonds were all there. Since Mrs. Peralta had been in that day, she tried her number— she had a crying need to talk with somebody—and this time actually succeeded. "Did anybody come into the house today?"

"Only deliveries, by the service elevator."

During this unsatisfactory conversation Clara had a view of herself in the hall mirror—a bony woman, not young, blond but not fair, gaunt, a long face, a hollow cheek, not rejoicing, and pressing the ringed hand under the arm that held the phone. The big eyes ached, and looked it. Feeling so high, why did she appear so low? But did she think that recovering the ring would make her young?

What she believed—and it was more than a belief; there was triumph in it—was that Gina Wegman had come into the bedroom and placed the ring on the nightstand.

And how had Gina obtained the ring, what had she had to promise, or sacrifice, or pay? Maybe her parents had wired money from Vienna. Suppose that her only purpose during four months had been nothing but restitution, and that the girl had done her time in East Harlem for no other reason? It struck Clara that if Gina had stolen the emerald back from Frederic and run away, then leaving a message on his machine had been a bad mistake. He might put it all together and come after Gina with a gun. There was even a private eye in this quickly fermenting plot. Except that Gottschalk was no Philip Marlowe in a Raymond Chandler story. Nevertheless he was a detective of some kind. He must be licensed to carry a gun. And everybody's mind ran in these psychopathic-melodrama channels streaming with blood, or children's fingerpaints, or blood that naive people took for fingerpaint. The fancy (or hope) that Gottschalk would kill Frederic in a shoot-out was so preposterous that it helped Clara to calm herself.

When she received Gottschalk in her office next day, she was wearing the ring and showed it to him. He said, "That's a high-value object. I hope you don't take public transportation to work." She looked disdainful. There was a livery service. He didn't seem to realize how high her executive bracket was. But he said, "There are people in top positions who insist on using the subway. I could name you a Wall Street woman who goes to work disguised as a bag lady so it isn't worthwhile to hassle her."

"I believe Gina Wegman entered my apartment yesterday and left the emerald by my bed."

"Must've been her."

Gottschalk's personal observation was that Mrs. Velde hadn't slept last night.

"It couldn't have been the *man*," she said. "What's your professional conclusion about him?"

"Casual criminal. Not enough muscle for street crime."

"She didn't marry him, did she?"

"I could run a check on that. My guess is no."

"What you can find out for me is whether she's still on One hundred twenty-eighth Street. If she grabbed the ring and brought it back, he may do her some harm."

"Well, ma'am, he's been in the slammer a few times for petty stuff. He wouldn't do anything major." Frederic had been one of those boat people lucky enough to reach Florida a few years back. So much Clara knew.

"After stealing your ring, he didn't even know how to fence it."

Clara said, "I have to find out where she's living. I have to see the girl. Get hold of her. I'll pay a bonus—within reason."

"Send her to your house?"

"That might embarrass her—the girls, Mrs. Peralta, my husband. Say I want to have lunch with her. Ask her whether she received my note."

"Let me look into it."

"Quickly. I don't want this dragging on."

"Top priority," said Gottschalk.

She counted on the suite of offices to impress him, and she was glad now that she had paid his bills promptly. Keeping on his good side, taking care from every standpoint to be a desirable client. As for Gottschalk, he was exactly what she had ordered from Ithiel—minimum sleaze. Not much more.

"I'd like a progress report by Friday," she said.

That afternoon she met with Ms. Wong. Moved to talk. And with the gesture of a woman newly engaged, she held out her hand, saying, "Here's the ring. I thought it had gone into the muck for good. It's getting to be a fairy-tale object. With me it's had the funny effect of those trick films they used to show kids—first a building demolished by dynamite. They show it coming down. Then they reverse it in slow motion, and it's put together again."

"Done by means of a magic ring?" said Ms. Wong.

It occurred to Clara that Laura was a mysterious lady too. She was exotic in externals, but in what she said she was perfectly conventional. While your heart was moved, she would still murmur along. If you came and told her you were going to kill yourself, what would she do? Probably nothing. Yet one must talk.

"I can't say what state I'm in," said Clara, "whether I'm pre-dynamite or post-dynamite. I don't suppose I look demolished. . . ."

"Certainly not."

"Yet I feel as if something had come down. There are changes. Gina, for instance, was a girl I took into the house to help with the kids. Little was ever said. I didn't think well of her Caribbean romance, or sex experiment. Just another case of being at sea amongst collapsing cultures—I sound like Ithiel now, and I don't actually take much stock in the collapsing-culture bit: I'm beginning to see it instead as the conduct of life without input from your soul. Essential parts of people getting mislaid or crowded out—don't ask me for specifics; I can't give them. They're always flitting by me. But what I started to say was how I've come to love that girl. Just as she immediately understood Lucy, how needy Lucy was, in one minute she also got the whole meaning of this ring. And on the decision to get it back for me she left the house. Moving to East Harlem, yet."

"If her Vienna family had a notion . . ."

"I intend to do something for her. That's a special young woman. I certainly will do something. I have to think what it should be. Now, I don't expect her to describe what she went through, and I don't intend to ask her. There are things I wouldn't want anybody to ask me," said Clara. Clifford from Attica was on her mind. On the whole, she kept this deliberately remote, yet if pressed she could recover quite a lot from her memory.

"Have you any idea . . . ?" said Laura Wong.

"About her, not yet, not until I've spoken to her. About myself, however, I do have different views as a result of this. Twice losing and recovering this ring is a sign, a message. It forces me to interpret. For instance, when Francine came in a van and emptied Ithiel's house—that woman is about as human as a toilet plunger!—Ithiel didn't turn to me. He didn't come and say, 'You're unhappy with Wilder. And between us we've had seven marriages. Now, shouldn't you and I . . . ?' "

"Clara, you wouldn't have done that?" said Laura. For once her voice was more real. Clara was struck by the difference.

"I *might* have done it. So far it's been change and change and change. There's pleasure change, and acquisitive change, and there's the dynamic of . . . oh, I don't know. Perhaps of power. Is there no point of rest? Won't the dynamic ever let you go? I felt that Ithiel might be a point of rest. Or I for him. But that was simply goofy. I have an anti-rest character. I think there's too much basic discord in me."

"So the ring stood for hope of Teddy Regler," said Laura Wong.

"The one exception. Teddy. A repeatedly proven exception. There must be others, but I never came across them."

"And do you think . . . ?"

"He'll ever accomplish his aim? I can't say. He can't, either. What he says is that no trained historian will ever do it, only a singular person with a singular eye. Looking at the century with his singular inborn eye, with a genius for observing politics: That's about the way he says it, and perhaps he'll take hold one day and do a wrap-up of the century, the wrap-up of wrap-ups. As for me," said Clara, "I have the kids, with perhaps Wilder thrown in as a fourth child. The last has been unacceptable. What I'd most like now is a quiet life."

"The point of rest?"

"No, I don't expect that. A quiet life in lieu of the point of rest. The point of rest might have been with Ithiel. I have to settle for what I can get—peaceful evenings. Let there be a convent atmosphere, when the kids have gone to bed and I can disconnect the phones and concentrate on Yeats or somebody like that. Not to be too ambitious; it would be enough to get rid of your demons—they're like patients who drift in and out of the mental hospital. In short, come to terms with my anti-rest character."

"So all these years you've never given up hope that Teddy Regler and you . . ."

"Might make a life together, in the end . . . ?" said Clara. Something caused her to hesitate. As they had always done in problematic situations, her eyes turned sideways, looking for an exit, and her country-girl mouth was open but silent.

On Madison Avenue, walking uptown, Clara was thinking, saying to herself in her contralto grumble, This is *totally* off the wall. There's no limit, is there? She wanted me to say that Ithiel and I were finished, so that she could put her own moves on him. Everybody feels free to picture what they like, and I talked Ithiel up until he became too desirable for her to resist, and how long has the little bitch been dreaming of having him for herself! No way! Clara was angry, but she was also laughing about this. So I choose friends, so I choose lovers, so I choose husbands and bankers and accountants and psychiatrists and ministers, all the way down the line. And just now lost my principal confidante. But I have to spin her off very slowly, for if I cut the relationship, she's in a position to hurt me with Wilder. There's also the insurance company, remember, the real owner of this ring. Also, she's so gifted professionally. We still need her layouts.

Meanwhile she had in mind an exceptional, a generous action.

From her office next day, on her private line, she had a preliminary talk about it with Ithiel, just back from Central America. Naturally she couldn't tell him what her goal was. She began by describing the return of her ring, all the strange circumstances. "This very minute, I'm looking at it. Wearing it, I don't feel especially girlish. I'm more like contemplating it."

She could see Ithiel trying on this new development, matching the contemplative Clara against the Clara who had once sunk her long nails into his forearm and left scars that he might have shown General Haig or Henry Kissinger if he had wanted to emphasize a point about violence. He had quite a sense of humor, Ithiel did. He enjoyed telling how, in a men's room at the White House, Mr. Armand Hammer was at the next urinal, and about the discussion on Soviet intentions they had had between the opening and the closing zips.

Or thinking back to the passionate Clara, or to the Clara who had wanted them buried side by side or even in the same grave. This had lately begun to amuse him.

From her New York office, she had continued to talk. So far he had had little to say other than to congratulate her on the recovery of this major symbol, Madison Hamilton's emerald. "This Gina is a special young woman, Ithiel," she told him. "You would have expected such behavior from a Sicilian or a Spanish woman, and not a contemporary, either, but a romantic Stendhal character—a Happy Few type, or a young woman of the Italian Renaissance in one of those Venetian chronicles the Elizabethans took from."

"Not what you would expect from the Vienna of Kurt Waldheim," he said.

"You've got it. And a young person of that quality shouldn't go on tending kids in New York—Gogmagogsville. Now, what I want to suggest is that she go to Washington."

"And you'd like me to find her a job?"

"That wouldn't be easy. She has a student visa, not a green card. I need to get her away from here."

"Save her from the Haitian. I see. However, she may not want to be saved."

"I'll have to find out how she sees it. My hunch is that the Haitian episode is over and she's ready for some higher education. . . ."

"And that's where I come in, isn't it?"

"Don't be light with me about this. I'm asking you to take me seriously. Remember what you said to me not long ago about my moral logic, worked out on my own feminine premises under my own power. . . . Now, I've never known you to talk through your hat on any real subject."

She had been centered, unified, concentrated, heartened, oriented by his description of her, and she couldn't let him withdraw any part of it.

"What I saw was what I said. Years of observation to back it. Does she want to come to Washington?"

"Well, Ithiel, I haven't had an opportunity to ask her. But . . . so that you'll understand me, I've come to love that girl. I've examined minutely every aspect of what probably happened, and I believe that the man stole the ring because their relationship was coming to an end. Their affair was about over. So he made her an accessory to the theft and she went with him only to get my emerald back."

Ithiel said, "And why do you believe this . . . this scenario of yours—that she was through with him, and he was so cunning, and she had such a great sense of honor, or responsibility? All of it sounds more like *you* than like any sample of the general population."

"But what I'm telling you," she said with special emphasis, "is that Gina isn't a sample from the population, and that I love her."

"And you want us to meet. And she'll come under my influence. She'll fall in love with me. So you and I will increase our number. She'll enlist with us. And she and I will cherish each other, and you will have the comfort of seeing me in safe hands, and this will be your blessing poured over the two of us."

"Teddy, you're making fun of me," she said, but she knew perfectly well that he wasn't making fun, that wasn't where the accent fell, and his interpretation was more or less correct, as far as it went.

"We'll never get each other out of trouble," said Ithiel. "Not the amount of trouble we're in. And even that is not so exceptional. And we all know what to expect. Only a few mavericks fight on. That's you I'm speaking of. I like to think that I'm at home with what is real. Your idea of the real is different. Maybe it's deeper than mine. Now, if your young lady has her own reasons for moving down here to Washington, I'll be happy to meet her for your sake and talk to her. But the sort of arrangements that are ideal for your little children—play school, parties, and concerned teachers—can't be extended to the rest of us."

"Oh, Teddy, I'm not such a fool as you take me for," Clara said.

After this conversation, she drew up a memo pad to try to summarize Ithiel's underlying view: The assumptions we make as to one another's motives are so circumscribed, our understanding of the universe and its forces is so false, that the more we analyze, the more injury we do. She knew perfectly well that this memo, like all the others, would disappear. She'd ask herself, "What was I thinking after my talk with Teddy?" and she'd never see this paper anymore.

Now she had to arrange a meeting with Gina Wegman, and that turned out to be a difficult thing to do. She would never have anticipated that it would be so hard. She repeatedly called Gottschalk, who said he was in touch with Gina. He hadn't actually seen her yet. He now had a midtown number for her and occasionally was able to reach her. "Have you said that I'd like a meeting?" said Clara. She thought, It's shame. The poor kid is ashamed.

"She said she was extremely busy, and I believe there's a plan for her to go home."

"To Austria?"

"She speaks English okay, only I'm not getting a clear signal."

Unkindly, Clara muttered that if he'd keep his glasses clean he'd see more. Also, to increase his importance and his fees, he was keeping information from her—or pretending that he had more information than he actually did have. "If you'd give me the number, I could try a direct call," she said. "Now, is the young man with her, there in midtown?"

"That wouldn't be my guess. I think she's with friends, relatives, and I think she's going back to Vienna real soon. I'll give you her number, but before you call her, let me have a few hours more to get supplementary information for you."

"Fine," said Clara, and as soon as Gottschalk was off the line she dialed Gina. She reached her at once. As simple as that.

"Oh, Mrs. Velde. I meant to call you," said Gina. "I was a little put off by that Mr. Gottschalk. He's a detective, and I worried about your attitude, that you thought it was a police matter."

"He's not police at all, he's strictly private. I needed to find out. I would never have threatened. I wanted to know where you were. The man's a moron. Never mind about him. Is it true, Gina, that you're going to Vienna?"

The young woman said, "Tonight, Lufthansa. Via Munich."

"Without seeing me? Why, that's not possible. I must have made you angry. But it's not anger that I feel toward you; just the opposite. And we have to meet before you leave. You must be rushed with last-minute things." Horrified to be losing her, and dilated with heat and breath, her heart swelling suddenly, she was hardly able to speak because of the emotional stoppage of her throat. "Won't you make some time for me, Gina? There's so much to work out, so much between us. Why the rush home?"

"And I would very much like to see you, Mrs. Velde. The hurry is my engagement and marriage."

Clara wildly guessed, She's pregnant. "Are you marrying Frederic?" she said. It was a charged question, nearly a prayer: Don't let her be as crazy as that. Gina was not prepared to answer. She seemed to be considering. But presently she said, "I wouldn't have to go to Vienna, in that case. My fiancé is a man from my father's bank."

Whether or not to explain herself must have been the issue. Explanations, in Clara's opinion, should be made. Gina had been wavering, but now she agreed, she decided to see Clara after all. Yes, she was going to do it. "Some friends are giving me a cocktail send-off. That's on Madison in the low Seventies. Maybe half an hour beforehand? . . . In your way, you *were* very kind," Clara heard the girl saying.

"Let's make it at the Westbury, then. When? At four o'clock."

Kind, in my way . . . Signifying what? She feels I was crude. But these side issues could be dealt with later. Right now Clara's appointment with Dr. Gladstone must be canceled. Since the fee would have to be paid notwithstanding, he'd have an hour to think deep analytic thoughts, ponder identity problems, Clara told herself with more than a drop of hatred. Was there anybody who was somebody? How was a man like Gladstone to know! Plumbers was what Ithiel called these Gladstone types. He had quit analysis because nobody was able to tell him what it took to be Ithiel Regler. This sounded haughty, but actually it was the only reasonable thing. It was no more than true. It applied to her as well.

That she should be so firm and assertive was strange, seeing that she was in a fever, trying to regulate an outflow of mingled soiled emotions. In the cab—one of ten thousand cars creeping uptown—she leaned her long neck backward to relieve it of the weight of her head and to control the wildness of her mind, threatened with panic. These gridlocks on Madison Avenue, these absolutely unnecessary mobs, the vehicles that didn't have to be here, carrying idle shoppers or old people with no urgent purpose except to break out of confinement or go and scold someone. Clara was suffocated by this stalling and delay. She exploded engines in her mind, got out at corners and pulled down stoplights with terrible strength. Five of the thirty minutes Gina could give her were already down the drain. Two blocks from the Westbury, she could no longer bear the traffic, and she got out and trotted the rest of the way, the insides of her knees rubbing together as they always did when she was in a rush.

She passed through the four-quartered door into the lobby and there was Gina Wegman just getting up from the tall chair, and how beautiful the girl looked in her round black glossy straw hat with a half veil dropped onto the bridge of her nose. She certainly wasn't gotten up to look contrite, in a dress that showed off her bust and the full lines of her bottom. On the other hand, she wasn't defiant, either. Lively, yes, and brilliant too. She approached Clara with an affectionate gesture so that when they kissed on the cheek Clara captured part of what a passionate man might feel toward a girl like this.

Clara, as she blamed her lateness on the rush hour, was at the same instant dissatisfied with the dress she had put on that day—those big flowers were a mistake, a bad call, and belonged in her poor-judgment closet.

They sat down in the cocktail lounge. At once one of those smothering New York waiters was upon them. Clara wasted no time on him. She ordered a Campari, and as he wrote down the drinks, she said, "Bring them and then don't bother us; we have to cover lots of ground." Then she leaned toward Gina—two heads of fine hair, each with its distinct design. The girl put up her veil. "Now, Gina . . . *tell* me," said Clara.

"The ring looks wonderful on your hand. I'm glad to see it there."

No longer the au pair girl waiting to be spoken to, she held herself like a different person—equal-equal, and more. It was a great thing she had done in America.

"How did you get it into the house?"

"Where did you find it?" asked Gina.

"What does *that* mean?" Clara wanted to know. In her surprise, she fell back on the country girl's simpleminded flat tone of challenge and suspicion. "It was on my night table."

"Yes. Okay then," said Gina.

"One thing I feel terrible about is the hard assignment I gave you. Just about impossible," said Clara. "The alternative was to turn the case over to the police. I suppose you know by now that Frederic has a criminal record—no serious crimes, but they had him on Rikers Island and in the Bronx jail. That would have made trouble, an investigation would have been hard on you, and I wouldn't do that." She lowered her hand to her legs and felt the startling prominence of the muscles at the knee.

Gina did not look embarrassed by this mention of Rikers Island. She must have taken a decision not to be.

Clara never would find out what the affair with Frederic was about. Gina went no further than to acknowledge that her boyfriend had taken the ring. "He said he was walking around the apartment . . ." Imagine, a man like that, lewd and klepto, at large in her home! "He saw the ring, so he put it in his pocket, not even thinking. I said it was given to you by someone you loved, who loved you"—so she definitely *did* understand about the love!—"and I felt responsible because it was me that brought Frederic into the house."

"That made him look blank, I suppose."

"He said that people on Park Avenue didn't understand anything. They didn't like trouble and relied on security to protect them. Once you got past the security arrangements in the lobby, why, they were just as helpless as chickens. Lucky if they weren't killed. No idea of defense."

Clara's gaze was clear and sober. Her upturned nose added dryness to her look. She said, "I have to agree. In my own place I didn't feel that I should lock away the valuables. But he may be right about Park Avenue. This is a class of people that won't think and can't admit. So it is lucky that somebody more vicious than Frederic didn't get in. Maybe Haitians are more lighthearted than some others in Harlem or the Bronx."

"Your class of Park Avenue people?"

"Yes," said Clara. She looked great-eyed again, grimly

thinking, My God, what will my kids be up against! "I should thank the man for only stealing, I suppose."

"We have no time to talk about this side of it," said Gina.

These minutes in the bar seemed to be going according to Gina's deliberate plan. Frederic was not to be discussed. Suddenly Clara's impulse was to come down hard on Gina. Why, she was like the carnal woman in the Book of Proverbs who eats and drinks and wipes away all signs of lust with her napkin. But she couldn't sustain this critical impulse. Who could say how the girl got sucked in and how she managed, or what she had to do to recover the ring from such a fellow. I *owe* her. Also, with the kids she was trustworthy. Now then, what are we looking at here? There is some pride in this Gina. She stood up to the New York scene, a young upper-class Vienna girl. There *is* a certain vainglory playing through. It's false to do the carnal woman number on her. Let's not get so Old Testament. My regular Christmas card from Attica is still arriving. Before marrying this man from Daddy's bank the girl owed herself some excitement, and Gogmagogsville is the ideal place for it. Dr. Gladstone might have pointed out that Clara's thoughts were taking on a hostile color—envious of youth, perhaps. She didn't think so. Nobody, but nobody, can withstand modern temptations. (Try and print your personal currency, and see what you can get for it.) She still felt that her affection for the girl was not misplaced. "Are you sure you want to go flying back—would you think of staying?"

"What should I stay for?"

"I only wondered. If you wanted a different experience of America, you might find it in Washington, D.C."

"What would I be doing there?"

"Serious work. And don't be put off by 'serious'; it wouldn't be dull. I did some of it myself in Cortina d'Ampezzo years ago and had one of the greatest summers of my life. This friend of mine in Washington, the one I did it for, may possibly be a dark horse in the history of the American mind. I think perhaps he's the one with the gifts to put it all in perspective. Everything. If you met him, you'd agree that he was a fascinating man. . . ." Here Clara stopped herself. Without warning, she had sped into a complex intersection, a cloverleaf without a single sign. A pause was imposed on her, and she considered in a silence of many levels where her enthusiasm for this Austrian girl—a pretty girl and a sound one, basically (maybe)—was leading. Did she want to give Ithiel to her? She wanted to reward Gina. All right. And she wanted to find a suitable woman for Ithiel. It was a scandal, the wives he chose. (Or my husbands; not much better.) Again, all right. But what about Frederic? What had she done that she had to veto all discussion of the Haitian connection? And why was this conversation with Clara cramped into twenty minutes? Why was she not invited to the farewell cocktail party? Who would be there?

Now came any number of skeptical scenarios: Gina's parents had come to America to take her home. They had paid Frederic off, and an incidental part of the deal was that he should surrender the ring. Clara could readily imagine such a package. The girl had plenty of reasons to keep Clara away from her friends—possibly her parents. Brash Clara with her hick candor might have put the case point-blank to the rich parents with all their Mitteleuropa culture (bullshit culture, Ithiel might have said). Oh, let them have their party undisturbed. But she wasn't about to send Gina to Washington all done up in gift wrapping—only the present with ribbons would have been Ithiel, handed over to this young woman. No way! Clara decided. Let me be as crude as she accused me of being. I am sure not going to make a marriage to rankle me for life. She stopped the matchmaking pitch she had begun, in her softheaded goodness. Yes, Gina was an unusual girl—that conviction was

unchanged—but if Teddy Regler was the man in pros-
pect, no.

"I haven't met him, have I?" Gina said.

"No."

Nor will you ever.

"You'd like to do something for me, wouldn't you?" Gina
spoke in earnest.

"Yes, if there were something feasible," said Clara.

"You're a generous woman—exceptionally so. I'm not
in a position to go to Washington. Otherwise I might be
glad to. And I have to leave you soon, I'm sorry to say. I
really am sorry. There's no time to talk about it, but you
have meant a lot to me."

That's one thing, Clara was thinking. The people you
mean a lot to just haven't got the time to speak to you about
it. "Let me tell you quickly," said Clara, "since it has to be
quick, what I've been thinking of the stages a woman like
me has gone through in her life. Stage one: Everybody is
kindly, basically good; you treat 'em right, they'll treat you
right—that's baby time. Stage two: Everybody is a brute,
butcher, barbarian, rapist, crook, liar, killer and monster.
Stage three: Cynicism *also* is unacceptable, and you begin
to put together an improved judgment based on minimal
leads or certain selected instances. I don't know what, if
anything, you can make of that. . . . Now, before you leave
you're going to satisfy my curiosity at least on one point:
how you got the ring back. If it cost you money, I want to
pay every cent of it. I insist. Tell me how much, and to
whom. And how did you get into the apartment? Nobody
saw you. Not with a key?"

"Don't talk about costs; there's no money owing," said
Gina. "The one thing I have to tell you is how the ring got
to your bedside. I went to Lucy's school and gave it to her."

"You gave an emerald to Lucy! To a young child?"

"I made sure to arrive before her new sitter came for her,

and I explained to Lucy what had to be done: Here's your mother's ring, it has to be put on her night table, and here's a nice Madeira handkerchief to put it on."

"What else did you say?"

"There wasn't much else that needed saying. She knew the ring was lost. Well, it was found now. I folded the handkerchief around the ring and put it in her schoolbag."

"And she understood?"

"She's a lot like you."

"How's that? *Tell* me!"

"The same type as you. You mentioned that to me several times. Did I think so? And presently I did begin to think so."

"You could trust her to carry it out, and not to say, not to tell. Why, I was beside myself when the ring turned up on the handkerchief. Where did it drop from! Who could have done it! I even wondered if a burglar had been hired to come in and put it there. Not a word from the kid. She looked straight ahead like a Roman sentry. You asked her not to say?"

"Well, yes. It was better that way. It never occurred to you to ask her about it?"

"How would that ever come up?" said Clara. Not once. My own kid, capable of that.

"I told her to come down to the street again and report to me afterward," said Gina. "I walked behind them from school—Lucy and the new girl, who doesn't know me. And in about fifteen minutes Lucy came to me at the corner and said she had put it where I told her. . . . You're pleased, aren't you?"

"I'm mystified. I'm moved. Frankly, Gina, I don't believe you and I will ever meet again. . . ." The girl didn't disagree, and Clara said, "So I'm going to speak my mind. You weren't going to describe or discuss your experiences in New York—in Harlem: I suppose you were being firm according to your private lights. Your intimacies are your business, but the word I used to describe your attitude was 'vainglory'—the pride of a European girl in New York who gets into a mess and takes credit for getting herself out. But it's far beyond that." Tears fell from Clara's eyes as she took Gina's hand. "I see how you brought it all together through my own child. You gave her something significant to do, and she was equal to it. Most amazing to me is the fact that she didn't talk, she only watched. That level of observation and control in a girl of ten . . . how do you suppose it feels to discover that?"

Gina had been getting ready to stand up, but she briefly sat down again. She said, "I think you found the right word—right for both of us. When I came to be interviewed, the vainglory was all around—you were waving it over me. I wondered whether the lady of the house was like that in America. But you're not an American lady of the house. You have a manner, Mrs. Velde. As if you were directing traffic. 'Turn left, go right—do this, do that.' You have definite ideas."

"Pernickety, maybe?" said Clara. "Did I hurt your feelings?"

"If that means bossy, no. My feelings weren't hurt when I knew you better. You were firm, according to *your* lights. I decided that you were a complete person, and the orders you gave you gave for that reason."

"Oh, wait a minute, I don't see any complete persons. In luckier times I'm sure complete persons did exist. But now? Now that's just the problem. You look around for something to take hold of, and where is it?"

"I see it in you," said Gina. She stood up and took her purse. "You may be reluctant to believe it, because of the disappointment and confusion. Which people are the lost people? This is the hardest thing of all to decide, even about oneself. The day of the fashion show we had lunch, and you made a remark like 'Nobody is anybody.' You were just muttering, talking about your psychiatrist. But when you started to talk about the man in Washington just now, there was no nobody-anybody problem. And when the ring was stolen, it wasn't the lost property that upset you. Lost people lose 'valuables.' You only lost this particular ring." She set her finger on the stone.

How abnormal for two people, one of them young, to have such a mental conversation. Maybe life in New York had forced a girl like Gina to be mental. Clara wondered about that. "Goodbye, Gina."

"Goodbye, Mrs. Velde." Clara was rising, and Gina put her arm about her. They embraced. "With all the disorder, I can't see how you keep track. You do, though. I believe you pretty well know who you are." Gina quickly left the lounge.

Minutes ago (which might have been hours), Clara had entertained mean feelings toward the girl. She intended, even, to give her a hard time, to stroll back with her to her destination, fish for an invitation to the cocktail farewell, talk to her parents, embarrass her with her friends. That was before she understood what Gina had done, how the ring had been returned. But now, when Clara came out of the revolving door, and as soon as she had the pavement under her feet, she started to cry passionately. She hurried, crying, down Madison Avenue, not like a person who belonged there but like one of the homeless, doing grotesque things in public, one of those street people turned loose from an institution. The main source of tears came open. She found a handkerchief and held it to her face in her ringed hand, striding in an awkward hurry. She might have been treading water in New York harbor—it felt that way, more a sea than a pavement, and for all the effort and the motions that she made she wasn't getting anywhere, she was still in the same place. When he described me to myself in Washington, I should have taken Ithiel's word for it, she was thinking. He knows what the big picture is—the big, *big* picture; he doesn't flatter, he's realistic and he's truthful. I do seem to have an idea who it is that's at the middle of me. There may not be more than one in a xillion, more's the pity, that do have. And my own child possibly one of those.

SOMETHING

TO

REMEMBER

ME

BY

_____

When there is too much going on, more than you can bear, you may choose to assume that nothing in particular is happening, that your life is going round and round like a turntable. Then one day you are aware that what you took to be a turntable, smooth, flat, and even, was in fact a whirlpool, a vortex. My first knowledge of the hidden work of uneventful days goes back to February 1933. The exact date won't matter much to you. I like to think, however, that you, my only child, will want to hear about this hidden work as it relates to me. When you were a small boy you were keen on family history. You will quickly understand that I couldn't tell a child what I am about to tell you now. You don't talk about deaths and vortices to a kid, not nowadays. In my time my parents didn't hesitate to speak of death and the dying. What they seldom mentioned was sex. We've got it the other way around.

My mother died when I was an adolescent. I've often told you that. What I didn't tell you was that I knew she was dying and didn't allow myself to think about it—there's your turntable.

The month was February, as I've said, adding that the exact date wouldn't matter to you. I should confess that I myself avoided fixing it.

Chicago in winter, armored in gray ice, the sky low, the going heavy.

I was a high school senior, an indifferent student, generally unpopular, a background figure in the school. It was only as a high jumper that I performed in public. I had no form at all; a curious last-minute spring or convulsion put me over the bar. But this was what the school turned out to see.

Unwilling to study, I was bookish nevertheless. I was secretive about my family life. The truth is that I didn't want to talk about my mother. Besides, I had no language as yet for the oddity of my peculiar interests.

But let me get on with that significant day in the early part of February.

It began like any other winter school day in Chicago—grimly ordinary. The temperature a few degrees above zero, botanical frost shapes on the windowpane, the snow swept up in heaps, the ice gritty and the streets, block after block, bound together by the iron of the sky. A breakfast of porridge, toast, and tea. Late as usual, I stopped for a moment to look into my mother's sickroom. I bent near and said, "It's Louie, going to school." She seemed to nod. Her eyelids were brown; the color of her face was much lighter. I hurried off with my books on a strap over my shoulder.

When I came to the boulevard on the edge of the park, two small men rushed out of a doorway with rifles, wheeled around aiming upward, and fired at pigeons near the rooftop. Several birds fell straight down, and the men scooped up the soft bodies and ran indoors, dark little guys in fluttering white shirts. Depression hunters and their city game. Moments before, the police car had loafed by at ten miles an hour. The men had waited it out.

This had nothing to do with me. I mention it merely because it happened. I stepped around the blood spots and crossed into the park.

To the right of the path, behind the wintry lilac twigs, the crust of the snow was broken. In the dead black night Stephanie and I had necked there, petted, my hands under her raccoon coat, under her sweater, under her skirt, adolescents kissing without restraint. Her coonskin cap had slipped to the back of her head. She opened the musky coat to me to have me closer.

Approaching the school building, I had to run to reach the doors before the last bell. I was on notice from the family—no trouble with teachers, no summons from the principal at a time like this. And I did observe the rules, although I despised classwork. But I spent all the money I could lay hands on at Hammersmark's Bookstore. I read *Manhattan Transfer, The Enormous Room,* and *A Portrait of the Artist.* I belonged to the Cercle Français and the Senior Discussion Club. The club's topic for this afternoon was Von Hindenburg's choice of Hitler to form a new government. But I couldn't go to meetings now; I had an after-school job. My father had insisted that I find one.

After classes, on my way to work, I stopped at home to cut myself a slice of bread and a wedge of Wisconsin cheese, and to see whether my mother might be awake. During her last days she was heavily sedated and rarely said anything. The tall, square-shouldered bottle at her bedside was filled with clear red Nembutal. The color of this fluid was always the same, as if it could tolerate no shadow. Now that she could no longer sit up to have it washed, my mother's hair was cut short. This made her face more slender, and her lips were sober. Her breathing was dry and hard, obstructed. The window shade was halfway up. It was scalloped at the bottom and had white fringes. The street ice was dark gray. Snow was piled against the trees. Their trunks had a mineral-black look. Waiting out the winter in their alligator armor, they gathered coal soot.

Even when she was awake, my mother couldn't find the

breath to speak. She sometimes made signs. Except for the nurse, there was nobody in the house. My father was at business, my sister had a downtown job, my brothers hustled. The eldest, Albert, clerked for a lawyer in the Loop. My brother Len had put me onto a job on the Northwestern commuter trains, and for a while I was a candy butcher, selling chocolate bars and evening papers. When my mother put a stop to this because it kept me too late, I had found other work. Just now I was delivering flowers for a shop on North Avenue and riding the streetcars carrying wreaths and bouquets to all parts of the city. Behrens the florist paid me fifty cents for an afternoon; with tips I could earn as much as a dollar. That gave me time to prepare my trigonometry lesson and, very late at night, after I had seen Stephanie, to read my books. I sat in the kitchen when everyone was sleeping, in deep silence, snowdrifts under the windows, and below, the janitor's shovel rasping on the cement and clanging on the furnace door. I read banned books circulated by my classmates, political pamphlets, read "Prufrock" and "Mauberley." I also studied arcane books, too far out to discuss with anyone.

I read on the streetcars (called trolleys elsewhere). Reading shut out the sights. In fact there *were* no sights—more of the same and then more of the same. Shop fronts, garages, warehouses, narrow brick bungalows.

The city was laid out on a colossal grid, eight blocks to the mile, every fourth street a car line. The days short, the streetlights weak, the soiled snowbanks toward evening became a source of light. I carried my carfare in my mitten, where the coins mixed with lint worn away from the lining. Today I was delivering lilies to an uptown address. They were wrapped and pinned in heavy paper. Behrens, spelling out my errand for me, was pale, a narrow-faced man who wore nose glasses. Amid the flowers, he alone had no color—something like the price he paid for being human.

He wasted no words: "This delivery will take an hour each way in this traffic, so it'll be your only one. I carry these people on the books, but make sure you get a signature on the bill."

I couldn't say why it was such a relief to get out of the shop, the damp, warm-earth smell, the dense mosses, the prickling cactuses, the glass iceboxes with orchids, gardenias, and sickbed roses. I preferred the brick boredom of the street, the paving stones and steel rails. I drew down the three peaks of my racing-skater's cap and hauled the clumsy package to Robey Street. When the car came panting up there was room for me on the long seat next to the door. Passengers didn't undo their buttons. They were chilled, guarded, muffled, miserable. I had reading matter with me—the remains of a book, the cover gone, the pages held together by binder's thread and flakes of glue. I carried these fifty or sixty pages in the pocket of my short sheepskin. With the one hand I had free I couldn't manage this mutilated book. And on the Broadway–Clark car, reading was out of the question. I had to protect my lilies from the balancing straphangers and people pushing toward the front.

I got down at Ainslie Street holding high the package, which had the shape of a padded kite. The apartment house I was looking for had a courtyard with iron palings. The usual lobby: a floor sinking in the middle, kernels of tile, gaps stuffed with dirt, and a panel of brass mailboxes with earpiece-mouthpieces. No voice came down when I pushed the button; instead, the lock buzzed, jarred, rattled, and I went from the cold of the outer lobby to the overheated mustiness of the inner one. On the second floor one of the two doors on the landing was open, and overshoes and galoshes and rubbers were heaped along the wall. At once I found myself in a crowd of drinkers. All the lights in the house were on, although it was a good hour before dark. Coats were piled on chairs and sofas. All whiskey in those days was bootleg, of course. Holding the flowers high, I parted the mourners. I was quasi official. The message went out: "Let the kid through. Go right on, buddy."

The long passageway was full too, but the dining room was entirely empty. There, a dead girl lay in her coffin. Over her a cut-glass luster was hanging from a taped, deformed artery of wire pulled through the broken plaster. I hadn't expected to find myself looking down into a coffin.

You saw her as she was, without undertaker's makeup, a girl older than Stephanie, not so plump, thin, fair, her straight hair arranged on her dead shoulders. All buoyancy gone, a weight that counted totally on support, not so much lying as sunk in this gray rectangle. I saw what I took to be the pressure mark of fingers on her cheek. Whether she had been pretty or not was no consideration.

A stout woman (certainly the mother), wearing black, opened the swing door from the kitchen and saw me standing over the corpse. I thought she was displeased when she made a fist signal to come forward. As I passed her she drew both fists against her bosom. She said to put the flowers on the sink, and then she pulled the pins and crackled the paper. Big arms, thick calves, a bun of hair, her short nose thin and red. It was Behrens's practice to tie the lily stalks to slender green sticks. There was never any damage.

On the drainboard of the sink was a baked ham with sliced bread around the platter, a jar of French's mustard and wooden tongue depressors to spread it. I saw and I saw and I saw.

I was on my most discreet and polite behavior with the woman. I looked at the floor to spare her my commiserating face. But why should she care at all about my discreetness; how did I come into this except as a messenger and menial? If she wouldn't observe my behavior, whom was I behaving for? All she wanted was to settle the bill and send me on my way. She picked up her purse, holding it to her body as she had held her fists. "What do I owe Behrens?" she asked me.

"He said you could sign for this."

However, she wasn't going to deal in kindnesses. She said, "No." She said, "I don't want debts following me later on." She gave me a five-dollar bill, she added a tip of fifty cents, and it was I who signed the receipt, as well as I could on the enameled grooves of the sink. I folded the bill small and felt under the sheepskin coat for my watch pocket, ashamed to take money from her within sight of her dead daughter. I wasn't the object of the woman's severity, but her face somewhat frightened me. She leveled the same look at the walls, the door. I didn't figure here, however; this was no death of mine.

As if to take another reading of the girl's plain face, I looked again into the coffin on my way out. And then on the staircase I began to extract the pages from my sheepskin pocket, and in the lobby I hunted for the sentences I had read the night before. Yes, here they were:

Nature cannot suffer the human form within her system of laws. When given to her charge, the human being before us is reduced to dust. Ours is the most perfect form to be found on earth. The visible world sustains us until life leaves, and then it must utterly destroy us. Where, then, is the world from which the human form comes?

If you swallowed some food and then died, that morsel of food that would have nourished you in life would hasten your disintegration in death.

This meant that nature didn't make life; it only housed it.

In those days I read many such books. But the one I had read the previous night went deeper than the rest. You, my only child, are only too familiar with my lifelong absorption in or craze for further worlds. I used to bore you when I spoke of spirit, or pneuma, and of a continuum of spirit and nature. You were too well educated, respectably rational, to take stock in such terms. I might add, citing a famous scholar, that what is plausible can do without proof. I am not about to pursue this. Still, there would be a gap in what I have to tell if I were to leave out my significant book, and this after all is a narrative, not an argument.

Anyway, I returned my pages to the pocket of my sheepskin, and then I didn't know quite what to do. At four o'clock, with no more errands, I was somehow not ready to go home. So I walked through the snow to Argyle Street, where my brother-in-law practiced dentistry, thinking that we might travel home together. I prepared an explanation for turning up at his office. "I was on the North Side delivering flowers, saw a dead girl laid out, realized how close I was, and came here." Why did I need to account for my innocent behavior when it *was* innocent? Perhaps because I was always contemplating illicit things. Because I was always being accused. Because I ran a little truck farm of deceits—but self-examination, once so fascinating to me, has become tiresome.

My brother-in-law's office was a high, second-floor walk-up: PHILIP HADDIS, D.D.S. Three bay windows at the rounded corner of the building gave you a full view of the street and of the lake, due east—the jagged flats of ice floating. The office door was open, and when I came through the tiny blind (windowless) waiting room and didn't see Philip at the big, back-tilted dentist's chair, I thought that he might have stepped into his lab. He was a good technician and did most of his own work, which was a big saving.

Philip wasn't tall, but he was very big, a burly man. The sleeves of his white coat fitted tightly on his bare, thick forearms. The strength of his arms counted when it came to pulling teeth. Lots of patients were referred to him for extractions.

When he had nothing in particular to do he would sit in the chair himself, studying the *Racing Form* between the bent mantis leg of the drill, the gas flame, and the water spurting round and round in the green glass spit-sink. The cigar smell was always thick. Standing in the center of the dental cabinet was a clock under a glass bell. Four gilt weights rotated at its base. This was a gift from my mother. The view from the middle window was divided by a chain that couldn't have been much smaller than the one that stopped the British fleet on the Hudson. This held the weight of the druggist's sign—a mortar and pestle outlined in electric bulbs. There wasn't much daylight left. At noon it was poured out; by four it had drained away. From one side the banked snow was growing blue, from the other the shops were shining warmth on it.

The dentist's lab was in a closet. Easygoing Philip peed in the sink sometimes. It was a long trek to the toilet at the far end of the building, and the hallway was nothing but two walls—a plaster tunnel and a carpet runner edged with brass tape. Philip hated going to the end of the hall.

There was nobody in the lab, either. Philip might have been taking a cup of coffee at the soda fountain in the drug-store below. It was possible also that he was passing the time with Marchek, the doctor with whom he shared the suite of offices. The connecting door was never locked, and I had occasionally sat in Marchek's swivel chair with a gyne-cology book, studying the colored illustrations and storing up the Latin names.

Marchek's starred glass pane was dark, and I assumed his office to be empty, but when I went in I saw a naked woman lying on the examining table. She wasn't asleep; she seemed to be resting. Becoming aware that I was there, she stirred, and then without haste, disturbing herself as little as pos-sible, she reached for her clothing heaped on Dr. Marchek's desk. Picking out her slip, she put it on her belly—she didn't spread it. Was she dazed, drugged? No, she simply took her sweet time about everything, she behaved with exciting lassitude. Wires connected her nice wrists to a piece of medical apparatus on a wheeled stand.

The right thing would have been to withdraw, but it was already too late for that. Besides, the woman gave no sign that she cared one way or another. She didn't draw the slip over her breasts, she didn't even bring her thighs together. The covering hairs were parted. There were salt, acid, dark, sweet odors. These were immediately effective; I was strongly excited. There was a gloss on her forehead, an exhausted look about the eyes. I believed that I had guessed what she had been doing, but then the room was half dark, and I preferred to avoid any definite thought. Doubt seemed much better, or equivocation.

I remembered that Philip, in his offhand, lazy way, had mentioned a "research project" going on next door. Dr. Marchek was measuring the reactions of partners in the sexual act. "He takes people from the street, he hooks them up and pretends he's collecting graphs. This is for kicks; the science part is horseshit."

The naked woman, then, was an experimental subject.

I had prepared myself to tell Philip about the dead girl on Ainslie Street, but the coffin, the kitchen, the ham, the flowers were as distant from me now as the ice floes on the lake and the killing cold of the water.

"Where did you come from?" the woman said to me.

"From next door—the dentist's office."

"The doctor was about to unstrap me, and I need to get loose. Maybe you can figure out these wires."

If Marchek should be in the inner room, he wouldn't come in now that he heard voices. As the woman raised both her arms so that I could undo the buckles, her breasts swayed, and when I bent over her the odor of her upper body made me think of the frilled brown papers in a box after the chocolates had been eaten—a sweet aftersmell and acrid cardboard mixed. Although I tried hard to stop it, my mother's chest mutilated by cancer surgery passed through my mind. Its gnarled scar tissue. I also called in Stephanie's closed eyes and kissing face—anything to spoil the attraction of this naked young woman. It occurred to me as I undid the clasps that instead of disconnecting her I was hooking myself. We were alone in the darkening office, and I wanted her to reach under the sheepskin and undo my belt for me.

But when her hands were free she wiped the jelly from her wrists and began to dress. She started with her bra, several times lowering her breasts into the cups, and when her arms went backward to fasten the hooks she bent far forward, as if she were passing under a low bough. The cells of my body were like bees, drunker and drunker on sexual honey (I expect that this will change the figure of Grandfather Louie, the old man remembered as this or that but never as a hive of erotic bees).

But I couldn't be blind to the woman's behavior even now. It was very broad; she laid it on. I saw her face in profile, and although it was turned downward, there was no mistaking her smile. To use an expression from the thirties, she was giving me the works. She knew I was about to fall on my face. She buttoned every small button with deliberate slowness, and her blouse had at least twenty such buttons, yet she was still bare from the waist down. Though we were so minor, she and I, a schoolboy and a floozy, we had such major instruments to play. And if we were to go further, whatever happened would never get beyond this room. It would be between the two of us, and nobody would ever hear of it. Still, Marchek, that pseudoexperimenter, was probably biding his time in the next room. An old family doctor, he must have been embarrassed and angry. And at any moment, moreover, my brother-in-law Philip might come back.

When the woman slipped down from the leather table she gripped her leg and said she had pulled a muscle. She lifted one heel onto a chair and rubbed her calf, swearing under her breath and looking everywhere with swimming eyes. And then, after she had put on her skirt and fastened her stockings to the garter belt, she pushed her feet into her pumps and limped around the chair, holding it by the arm. She said, "Will you please reach me my coat? Just put it over my shoulders."

She, too, wore a raccoon. As I took it from the hook I wished it had been something else. But Stephanie's coat was newer than this one and twice as heavy. These pelts had dried out, and the fur was thin. The woman was already on her way out, and stooped as I laid the raccoon over her back. Marchek's office had its own exit to the corridor.

At the top of the staircase, the woman asked me to help her down. I said that I would, of course, but I wanted to look once more for my brother-in-law. As she tied the woolen scarf under her chin she smiled at me, with an Oriental wrinkling of her eyes.

Not to check in with Philip wouldn't have been right. My hope was that he would be returning, coming down the narrow corridor in his burly, sauntering, careless way. You won't remember your Uncle Philip. He had played college football, and he still had the look of a tackle, with his swelling, compact forearms. (At Soldier Field today he'd be physically insignificant; in his time, however, he was something of a strongman.)

But there was the long strip of carpet down the middle of the wall-valley, and no one was coming to rescue me. I turned back to his office. If only a patient were sitting in the chair and I could see Philip looking into his mouth, I'd be on track again, excused from taking the woman's challenge. One alternative was to say that I couldn't go with her, that Philip expected me to ride back with him to the Northwest Side. In the empty office I considered this lie, bending my head so that I wouldn't confront the clock with its soundless measured weights revolving. Then I wrote on Philip's memo pad: "Louie, passing by." I left it on the seat of the chair.

The woman had put her arms through the sleeves of the collegiate, rah-rah raccoon and was resting her fur-bundled rear on the banister. She was passing her compact mirror back and forth, and when I came out she gave the compact a snap and dropped it into her purse.

"Still the charley horse?"

"My lower back too."

We descended, very slow, both feet on each tread. I wondered what she would do if I were to kiss her. Laugh at me, probably. We were no longer between the four walls where anything might have happened. In the street, space was unlimited. I had no idea how far we were going, how far I would be able to go. Although she was the one claiming to be in pain, it was I who felt sick. She asked me to support her lower back with my hand, and there I discovered what an extraordinary action her hips could perform. At a party I had overheard an older woman saying to another lady, "I know how to make them burn." Hearing this was enough for me.

No special art was necessary with a boy of seventeen, not even so much as being invited to support her with my hand—to feel that intricate, erotic working of her back. I had already *seen* the woman on Marchek's examining table and had also felt the full weight of her when she leaned—when she laid her female substance on me. Moreover, she fully knew my mind. She was the thing I was thinking continually, and how often does thought find its object in circumstances like these—the object *knowing* that it has been found? The woman knew my expectations. She *was,* in the flesh, those expectations. I couldn't have sworn that she was a hooker, a tramp. She might have been an ordinary family girl with a taste for trampishness, acting loose, amusing herself with me, doing a comic sex turn as in those days people sometimes did.

"Where are we headed?"

"If you have to go, I can make it on my own," she said. "It's just Winona Street, the other side of Sheridan Road."

"No, no. I'll walk you there."

She asked whether I was still at school, pointing to the printed pages in my coat pocket.

I observed when we were passing a fruit shop (a boy of my own age emptying bushels of oranges into the lighted window) that, despite the woman's thick-cream color, her eyes were Far Eastern, black.

"You should be about seventeen," she said.

"Just."

She was wearing pumps in the snow and placed each step with care.

"What are you going to be—have you picked your profession?"

I had no use for professions. Utterly none. There were accountants and engineers in the soup lines. In the world slump, professions were useless. You were free, therefore, to make something extraordinary of yourself. I might have said, if I hadn't been excited to the point of sickness, that I didn't ride around the city on the cars to make a buck or to be useful to the family, but to take a reading of this boring, depressed, ugly, endless, rotting city. I couldn't have thought it then, but I now understand that my purpose was to interpret this place. Its power was tremendous. But so was mine, potentially. I refused absolutely to believe for a moment that people here were doing what they thought they were doing. Beneath the apparent life of these streets was their real life, beneath each face the real face, beneath each voice and its words the true tone and the real message. Of course, I wasn't about to say such things. It was beyond me at that time to say them. I was, however, a high-toned kid, "La-di-dah," my critical, satirical brother Albert called me. A high purpose in adolescence will expose you to that.

At the moment, a glamorous, sexual girl had me in tow. I couldn't guess where I was being led, nor how far, nor what she would surprise me with, nor the consequences.

"So the dentist is your brother?"

"In-law—my sister's husband. They live with us. You're asking what he's like? He's a good guy. He likes to lock his office on Friday and go to the races. He takes me to the fights. Also, at the back of the drugstore there's a poker game. . . ."

"*He* doesn't go around with books in his pocket."

"Well, no, he doesn't. He says, 'What's the use? There's too much to keep up or catch up with. You could never in a thousand years do it, so why knock yourself out?' My sister wants him to open a Loop office, but that would be too much of a strain. I guess he's for inertia. He's not ready to do more than he's already doing."

"So what are you reading—what's it about?"

I didn't propose to discuss anything with her. I wasn't capable of it. What I had in mind just then was entirely different.

But suppose I had been able to explain. One does have a responsibility to answer genuine questions: "You see, miss, this is the visible world. We live in it, we breathe its air and eat its substance. When we die, however, matter goes to matter, and then we're annihilated. Now, which world do we really belong to, this world of matter or another world, from which matter takes its orders?"

Not many people were willing to talk about such notions. They made even Stephanie impatient. "When you die, that's it. Dead is dead," she would say. She loved a good time. And when I wouldn't take her downtown to the Oriental Theatre she didn't deny herself the company of other boys. She brought back off-color vaudeville jokes. I think the

Oriental was part of a national entertainment circuit. Jimmy Savo, Lou Holtz, and Sophie Tucker played there. I was sometimes too solemn for Stephanie. When she gave imitations of Jimmy Savo singing "River, Stay Away from My Door," bringing her knees together and holding herself tight, she didn't break me up, and she was disappointed.

You would have thought that the book or book fragment in my pocket was a talisman from a fairy tale to open castle gates or carry me to mountaintops. Yet when the woman asked me what it was, I was too scattered to tell her. Remember, I still kept my hand as instructed on her lower back, tormented by that sexual grind of her movements. I was discovering what the lady at the party had meant by saying, "I know how to make them burn." So of course I was in no condition to talk about the Ego and the Will, or about the secrets of the blood. Yes, I believed that higher knowledge was shared out among all human beings. What else was there to hold us together but this force hidden behind daily consciousness? But to be coherent about it now was absolutely out of the question.

"Can't you tell me?" she said.

"I bought this for a nickel from a bargain table."

"That's how you spend your money?"

I assumed her to mean that I didn't spend it on girls.

"And the dentist is a good-natured, lazy guy," she went on. "What has he got to tell you?"

I tried to review the mental record. What did Phil Haddis say? He said that a stiff prick has no conscience. At the moment it was all I could think of. It amused Philip to talk to me. He was a chum. Where Philip was indulgent, my brother Albert, your late uncle, was harsh. Albert might have taught me something if he had trusted me. He was then a night-school law student clerking for Rowland, the racketeer congressman. He was Rowland's bagman, and Rowland hired him not to read law but to make collections.

Philip suspected that Albert was skimming, for he dressed sharply. He wore a derby (called, in those days, a Baltimore heater) and a camel's hair topcoat and pointed, mafioso shoes. Toward me, Albert was scornful. He said, "You don't understand fuck-all. You never will."

We were approaching Winona Street, and when we got to her building she'd have no further use for me and send me away. I'd see no more than the flash of the glass and then stare as she let herself in. She was already feeling in her purse for the keys. I was no longer supporting her back, preparing instead to mutter "bye-bye," when she surprised me with a sideward nod, inviting me to enter. I think I had hoped (with sex-polluted hope) that she would leave me in the street. I followed her through another tile lobby and through the inner door. The staircase was fiercely heated by coal-fueled radiators, the skylight three stories up was wavering, the wallpaper had come unstuck and was curling and bulging. I swallowed my breath. I couldn't draw this heat into my lungs.

This had been a deluxe apartment house once, built for bankers, brokers, and well-to-do professionals. Now it was occupied by transients. In the big front room with its French windows there was a crap game. In the next room people were drinking or drowsing on the old chesterfields. The woman led me through what had once been a private bar— some of the fittings were still in place. Then I followed her through the kitchen—I would have gone anywhere, no questions asked. In the kitchen there were no signs of cooking, neither pots nor dishes. The linoleum was shredding, brown fibers standing like hairs. She led me into a narrower corridor, parallel to the main one. "I have what used to be a maid's room," she said. "It's got a nice view of the alley, but there is a private bathroom."

And here we were—an almost empty space. So this was how whores operated—assuming that she was a whore: a bare floor, a narrow cot, a chair by the window, a lopsided clothespress against the wall. I stopped under the light fixture while she passed behind, as if to observe me. Then from the back she gave me a hug and a small kiss on the cheek, more promissory than actual. Her face powder, or perhaps it was her lipstick, had a sort of green-banana fragrance. My heart had never beaten as hard as this.

She said, "Why don't I go into the bathroom awhile and get ready while you undress and lie down in bed. You look like you were brought up neat, so lay your clothes on the chair. You don't want to drop them on the floor."

Shivering (this seemed the one cold room in the house), I began to pull off my things, beginning with the winter-wrinkled boots. The sheepskin I hung over the back of the chair. I pushed my socks into the boots and then my bare feet recoiled from the grit underfoot. I took off everything, as if to disassociate my shirt, my underthings, from whatever it was that was about to happen, so that only my body could be guilty. The one thing that couldn't be excepted. When I pulled back the cover and got in, I was thinking that the beds in Bridewell prison would be like this. There was no pillowcase; my head lay on the ticking. What I saw of the outside was the utility wires hung between the poles like lines on music paper, only sagging, and the glass insulators like clumps of notes. The woman had said nothing about money. Because she liked me. I couldn't believe my luck—luck with a hint of disaster. I blinded myself to the Bridewell metal cot, not meant for two. I felt also that I couldn't hold out if she kept me waiting long. And what feminine thing was she doing in there—undressing, washing, perfuming, changing?

Abruptly, she came out. She had been waiting, nothing else. She still wore the raccoon coat, even the gloves. Without looking at me she walked very quickly, almost running, and opened the window. As soon as the window shot up, it let in a blast of cold air, and I stood up on the bed but it was too late to stop her. She took my clothes from the back of the chair and heaved them out. They fell into the alley. I shouted, "What are you doing!" She still refused to turn her head. As she ran away, tying the scarf under her chin, she left the door open. I could hear her pumps beating double time in the hallway.

I couldn't run after her, could I, and show myself naked to the people in the flat? She had banked on this. When we came in, she must have given the high sign to the man she worked with, and he had been waiting in the alley. When I ran to look out, my things had already been gathered up. All I saw was the back of somebody with a bundle under his arm hurrying in the walkway between two garages. I might have picked up my boots—those she had left me— and jumped from the first-floor window, but I couldn't chase the man very far, and in a few minutes I would have wound up on Sheridan Road naked and freezing.

I had seen a drunk in his union suit, bleeding from the head after he had been rolled and beaten, staggering and yelling in the street. I didn't even have a shirt and drawers. I was as naked as the woman herself had been in the doctor's office, stripped of everything, including the five dollars I had collected for the flowers. And the sheepskin my mother had bought for me last year. Plus the book, the fragment of an untitled book, author unknown. This may have been the most serious loss of all.

Now I could think on my own about the world I really belonged to, whether it was this one or another.

I pulled down the window, and then I went to shut the door. The room didn't seem lived in, but suppose it had a tenant, and what if he were to storm in now and rough me up? Luckily there was a bolt to the door. I pushed it into its loop and then I ran around the room to see what I could find to wear. In the lopsided clothespress, nothing but wire hangers, and in the bathroom, only a cotton hand towel. I tore the blanket off the bed; if I were to slit it I might pull it over my head like a serape, but it was too thin to do me much good in freezing weather. When I pulled the chair over to the clothespress and stood on it, I found a woman's dress behind the molding, and a quilted bed jacket. In a brown paper bag there was a knitted brown tam. I had to put these things on. I had no choice.

It was now, I reckoned, about five o'clock. Philip had no fixed schedule. He didn't hang around the office on the off chance that somebody might turn up with a toothache. After his last appointment he locked up and left. He didn't necessarily set out for home; he was not too keen to return to the house. If I wanted to catch him I'd have to run. In boots, dress, tam, and jacket, I made my way out of the apartment. Nobody took the slightest interest in me. More people (Philip would have called them transients) had crowded in— it was even likely that the man who had snatched up my clothes in the alley had returned, was among them. The heat in the staircase now was stifling, and the wallpaper smelled scorched, as if it were on the point of catching fire. In the street I was struck by a north wind straight from the Pole, and the dress and sateen jacket counted for nothing. I was running, though, and had no time to feel it.

Philip would say, "Who was this floozy? Where did she pick you up?" Philip was unexcitable, always mild, amused by me. Anna would badger him with the example of her ambitious brothers—they hustled, they read books. You couldn't fault Philip for being pleased. I anticipated what he'd say—"Did you get in? Then at least you're not going to catch the clap." I depended on Philip now, for I had nothing, not even seven cents for carfare. I could be certain, however, that he wouldn't moralize at me, he'd set about dressing me, he'd scrounge a sweater among his neighborhood acquaintances or take me to the Salvation Army shop on Broadway if that was still open. He'd go about this in his slow-moving, thick-necked, deliberate way. Not even dancing would speed him up; he spaced out the music to suit him when he did the fox-trot and pressed his cheek to Anna's. He wore a long, calm grin. My private term for this particular expression was Pussy-Veleerum. I saw Philip as fat but strong, strong but cozy, purring but inserting a joking comment. He gave a little suck at the corner of the mouth when he was about to take a swipe at you, and it was then that he was Pussy-Veleerum. A name it never occurred to me to speak aloud.

I sprinted past the windows of the fruit store, the delicatessen, the tailor's shop. I could count on help from Philip. My father, however, was an intolerant, hasty man. Slighter than his sons, handsome, with muscles of white marble (so they seemed to me), laying down the law. It would put him in a rage to see me like this. And it was true that I had failed to consider: my mother dying, the ground frozen, a funeral coming, the dug grave, the packet of sand from the Holy Land to be scattered on the shroud. If I were to turn up in this filthy dress, the old man, breaking under his burdens, would come down on me in a blind, Old Testament rage. I never thought of this as cruelty but as archaic right everlasting. Even Albert, who was already a Loop lawyer, had to put up with the old man's blows—outraged, his eyes swollen and maddened, but he took it. It never seemed to any of us that my father was cruel. We had gone over the limit, and we were punished.

There were no lights in Philip's D.D.S. office. When I jumped up the stairs, the door with its blank starred glass was locked. Frosted panes were still rare. What we had was this star-marred product for toilets and other private windows. Marchek—whom nowadays we could call a voyeur—was also, angrily, gone. I had screwed up his experiment. I tried the doors, thinking that I could spend the night on the leather examining table where the beautiful nude had lain. From the office I could also make telephone calls. I did have a few friends, although there were none who might help me. I wouldn't have known how to explain my predicament to them. They'd think I was putting them on, that it was a practical joke—"This is Louie. A whore robbed me of my clothes and I'm stuck on the North Side without carfare. I'm wearing a dress. I lost my house keys. I can't get home."

I ran down to the drugstore to look for Philip there. He sometimes played five or six hands of poker in the druggist's back room, trying his luck before getting on the streetcar. I knew Kiyar, the druggist, by sight. He had no recollection of me—why should he have? He said, "What can I do for you, young lady?"

Did he really take me for a girl, or a tramp off the street, or a gypsy from one of the storefront fortune-teller camps? Those were now all over town. But not even a gypsy would wear this blue sateen quilted boudoir jacket instead of a coat.

"I wonder, is Phil Haddis the dentist in the back?"

"What do you want with Dr. Haddis—have you got a toothache, or what?"

"I need to see him."

The druggist was a compact little guy, and his full round bald head was painfully sensitive looking. In its sensitivity it could pick up any degree of disturbance, I thought. Yet there was a canny glitter coming through his specs, and Kiyar had the mark of a man whose mind never would change once he had made it up. Oddly enough, he had a small mouth, baby's lips. He had been on the street—how long? Forty years? In forty years you've seen it all and nobody can tell you a single thing.

"Did Dr. Haddis have an appointment with you? Are you a patient?"

He knew this was a private connection. I was no patient.

"No. But if I was out here he'd want to know it. Can I talk to him one minute?"

"He isn't here."

Kiyar had walked behind the grille of the prescription counter. I mustn't lose him. If he went, what would I do next? I said, "This is important, Mr. Kiyar." He waited for me to declare myself. I wasn't about to embarrass Philip by setting off rumors. Kiyar said nothing. He may have been waiting for me to speak up. Declare myself. I assume he took pride in running a tight operation, giving nothing away. To cut through to the man I said, "I'm in a spot. I left Dr. Haddis a note before, but when I came back I missed him."

At once I recognized my mistake. Druggists were always being appealed to. All those pills, remedy bottles, bright lights, medicine ads, drew wandering screwballs and moochers. They all said they were in bad trouble.

"You can go to the Foster Avenue station."

"The police, you mean."

I had thought of that too. I could always tell them my hard-luck story and they'd keep me until they checked it out and someone would come to fetch me. That would probably be Albert. Albert would love that. He'd say to me, "Well, aren't you the horny little bastard." He'd play up to the cops too, and amuse them.

"I'd freeze before I got to Foster Avenue," was my answer to Kiyar.

"There's always the squad car."

"Well, if Phil Haddis isn't in the back maybe he's still in the neighborhood. He doesn't always go straight home."

"Sometimes he goes over to the fights at Johnny Coulon's. It's a little early for that. You could try the speakeasy down the street, on Kenmore. It's an English basement, side entrance. You'll see a light by the fence. The guy at the slot is called Moose."

He didn't offer so much as a dime from his till. If I had said that I was in a scrape and that Phil was my sister's husband he'd probably have given me carfare. But I hadn't confessed, and there was a penalty for that.

Going out, I crossed my arms over the bed jacket and opened the door with my shoulder. I might as well have been wearing nothing at all. The wind cut at my legs, and I ran. Luckily I didn't have far to go. The iron pipe with the bulb at the end of it was halfway down the block. I saw it as soon as I crossed the street. These illegal drinking parlors were easy to find; they were meant to be. The steps were cement, four or five of them bringing me down to the door. The slot came open even before I knocked, and instead of the doorkeeper's eyes, I saw his teeth.

"You Moose?"

"Yah. Who?"

"Kiyar sent me."

"Come on."

I felt as though I were falling into a big, warm, paved cellar. There was little to see, almost nothing. A sort of bar was set up, a few hanging fixtures, some tables from an ice cream parlor, wire-backed chairs. If you looked through the window of an English basement your eyes were at ground level. Here the glass was tarred over. There would have been nothing to see anyway: a yard, a wooden porch, a clothesline, wires, a back alley with ash heaps.

"Where did you come from, sister?" said Moose.

But Moose was a nobody here. The bartender, the one who counted, called me over and said, "What is it, sweetheart? You got a message for somebody?"

"Not exactly."

"Oh? You needed a drink so bad that you jumped out of bed and ran straight over—you couldn't stop to dress?"

"No, sir. I'm looking for somebody—Phil Haddis? The dentist?"

"There's only one customer. Is that him?"

It wasn't. My heart sank into river mud.

"It's not a drunk you're looking for?"

"No."

The drunk was on a high stool, thin legs hanging down, arms forward, and his head lying sidewise on the bar. Bottles, glasses, a beer barrel. Behind the barkeeper was a sideboard pried from the wall of an apartment. It had a long mirror—an oval laid on its side. Paper streamers curled down from the pipes.

"Do you know the dentist I'm talking about?"

"I might. Might not," said the barkeeper. He was a sloppy, long-faced giant—something of a kangaroo look about him. That was the long face in combination with the belly. He told me, "This is not a busy time. It's dinner, you know, and we're just a neighborhood speak."

It was no more than a cellar, just as the barman was no more than a Greek, huge and bored. Just as I myself, Louie, was no more than a naked male in a woman's dress. When you had named objects in this elementary way, hardly anything remained in them. The barman, on whom everything now depended, held his bare arms out at full reach and braced on his spread hands. The place smelled of yeast sprinkled with booze. He said, "You live around here?"

"No, about an hour on the streetcar."

"Say more."

"Humboldt Park is my neighborhood."

"Then you got to be a Uke, a Polack, a Scandihoof, or a Jew."

"Jew."

"I know my Chicago. And you didn't set out dressed like that. You'da frozen to death inside of ten minutes. It's for the boudoir, not winter wear. You don't have the shape of a woman, neither. The hips aren't there. Are you covering a pair of knockers? I bet not. So what's the story, are you a morphodite? Let me tell you, you got to give this Depression credit. Without it you'd never find out what kind of funny stuff is going on. But one thing I'll never believe is that you're a young girl and still got her cherry."

"You're right as far as that goes, but the rest of it is that I haven't got a cent, and I need carfare."

"Who took you, a woman?"

"Up in her room when I undressed, she grabbed my things and threw them out the window."

"Left you naked so you couldn't chase her . . . I would have grabbed her and threw her on the bed. I bet you didn't even get in."

Not even, I repeated to myself. Why didn't I push her down while she was still in her coat, as soon as we entered the room—pull up her clothes, as he would have done? Because he was born to that. While I was not. I wasn't intended for it.

"So that's what happened. You got taken by a team of pros. She set you up. You were the mark. Jewish fellows aren't supposed to keep company with those bad cunts. But when you get out of your house, into the world, you want action like anybody else. So. And where did you dig up this dress with the fancy big roses? I guess you were standing with your sticker sticking out and were lucky to find anything to put on. Was she a good looker?"

Her breasts, as she lay there, had kept their shape. They didn't slip sideward. The inward lines of her legs, thigh swelling toward thigh. The black crumpled hairs. Yes, a beauty, I would say.

Like the druggist, the barman saw the fun of the thing— an adolescent in a fix, a soiled dress, the rayon or sateen bed jacket. It was a lucky thing for me that business was at a standstill. If he had had customers, the barman wouldn't have given me the time of day. "In short, you got mixed up with a whore and she gave you the works."

For that matter, I had no sympathy for myself. I confessed that I had this coming, a high-minded Jewish schoolboy, too high-and-mighty to be Orthodox and with his eye on a special destiny. At home, inside the house, an archaic rule; outside, the facts of life. The facts of life were having their turn. Their first effect was ridicule. To throw my duds into the alley was the woman's joke on me. The druggist with his pain-sensitive head was all irony. And now the barman was going to get his fun out of my trouble before he, maybe, gave me the seven cents for carfare. Then I could have a full hour of shame on the streetcar. My mother, with whom I might never speak again, used to say that I had a line of pride straight down the bridge of my nose, a foolish stripe that she could see.

I had no way of anticipating what her death would signify.

The barman, having me in place, was giving me the business. And Moose ("Moosey," the Greek called him) had come away from the door so as not to miss the entertainment. The Greek's kangaroo mouth turned up at the corners. Presently his hand went up to his head and he rubbed his scalp under the black, spiky hair. Some said they drank olive oil by the glass, these Greeks, to keep their hair so rich. "Now give it to me again, about the dentist," said the barman.

"I came looking for him, but by now he's well on his way home."

He would by then be on the Broadway–Clark car, reading the Peach edition of the *Evening American,* a broad man with an innocent pout to his face, checking the race results. Anna had him dressed up as a professional man, but he let the fittings—shirt, tie, buttons—go their own way. His instep was fat and swelled inside the narrow shoe she had picked for him. He wore the fedora correctly. Toward the rest he admitted no obligation.

Anna cooked dinner after work, and when Philip came

in, my father would begin to ask, "Where's Louie?" "Oh, he's out delivering flowers," they'd tell him. But the old man was nervous about his children after dark, and if they were late he waited up, walking—no, trotting—up and down the long apartment. When you tried to slip in, he caught you and twisted you tight by the neckband. He was small, neat, slender, a gentleman, but abrupt, not unworldly—he wasn't ignorant of vices; he had lived in Odessa and even longer in St. Petersburg—but he had no patience. The least thing might craze him. Seeing me in this dress, he'd lose his head at once. *I* lost *mine* when that woman showed me her snatch with all the pink layers, when she raised up her arm and asked me to disconnect the wires, when I felt her skin and her fragrance came upward.

"What's your family, what does your dad do?" asked the barman.

"His business is wood fuel for bakers' ovens. It comes by freight car from northern Michigan. Also from Birnamwood, Wisconsin. He has a yard off Lake Street, east of Halsted."

I made an effort to give the particulars. I couldn't afford to be suspected of invention now.

"I know where that is. Now, that's a neighborhood just full of hookers and cathouses. You think you can tell your old man what happened to you, that you got picked up by a cutie and she stole your clothes off you?"

The effect of this question was to make me tight in the face, dim in the ears. The whole cellar grew small and distant, toylike but not for play.

"How's your old man to deal with—tough?"

"Hard," I said.

"Slaps the kids around? This time you've got it coming. What's under the dress, a pair of bloomers?"

I shook my head.

"Your behind is bare? Now you know how it feels to go around like a woman."

The Greek's great muscles were dough-colored. You wouldn't have wanted him to take a headlock on you. That's the kind of man the Organization hired. The Capone people were now in charge. The customers would be like celluloid Kewpie dolls to the Greek. He looked like one of those boxing kangaroos in the movies, and he could do a standing jump over the bar. Yet he enjoyed playing zany. He could curve his long mouth up at the corners like the happy face in a cartoon.

"What were you doing on the North Side?"

"Delivering flowers."

"Hustling after school but with ramming on your brain. You got a lot to learn, buddy boy. Well, enough of that. Now, Moosey, take this flashlight and see if you can scrounge up a sweater or something in the back basement for this down-on-his-luck kid. I'd be surprised if the old janitor hasn't picked the stuff over pretty good. If mice have nested in it, shake out the turds. It'll help on the trip home."

I followed Moose into the hotter half of the cellar. His flashlight picked out the laundry tubs with the hand-operated wringers mounted on them, the padlocked wooden storage bins. "Turn over some of these cardboard boxes. Mostly rags, is my guess. Dump 'em out, that's the easiest."

I emptied a couple of big cartons. Moose passed the light back and forth over the heaps. "Nothing much, like I said."

"Here's a flannel shirt," I said. I wanted to get out. The smell of heated burlap was hard to take. This was the only wearable article. I could have used a pullover or a pair of pants. We returned to the bar. As I was putting on the shirt, which revolted me (I come of finicky people whose fetish is cleanliness), the barman said, "I tell you what, you take this drunk home—this is about time for him, isn't it, Moosey? He gets plastered here every night. See he gets home and it'll be worth half a buck to you."

"I'll do it," I said. "It all depends on how far away he lives. If it's far, I'll be frozen before I get there."

"It isn't far. Winona, west of Sheridan, isn't far. I'll give you the directions. This guy is a city-hall payroller. He has no special job, he works direct for the ward committeeman. He's a lush with two little girls to bring up. If he's sober enough he cooks their dinner. Probably they take more care of him than he does of them."

"First I'll take charge of his money," said the barman. "I don't want my buddy here to be rolled. I don't say you would do it, but I owe this to a customer."

Bristle-faced Moose began to empty the man's pockets—his wallet, some keys, crushed cigarettes, a red bandanna that looked foul, matchbooks, greenbacks, and change. All these were laid out on the bar.

When I look back at past moments, I carry with me an apperceptive mass that ripens and perhaps distorts, mixing what is memorable with what may not be worth mentioning. Thus I see the barman with one big hand gathering in the valuables as if they were his winnings, the pot in a poker game. And then I think that if the kangaroo giant had taken this drunk on his back he might have bounded home with him in less time than it would have taken me to support him as far as the corner. But what the barman actually said was, "I got a nice escort for you, Jim."

Moose led the man back and forth to make sure his feet were operating. His swollen eyes now opened and then closed again. "McKern," Moose said, briefing me. "Southwest corner of Winona and Sheridan, the second building on the south side of the street, and it's the second floor."

"You'll be paid when you get back," said the barman.

The freeze was now so hard that the snow underfoot

sounded like metal foil. Though McKern may have sobered up in the frigid street, he couldn't move very fast. Since I had to hold on to him, I borrowed his gloves. He had a coat with pockets to put his hands in. I tried to keep behind him and get some shelter from the wind. That didn't work. He wasn't up to walking. I had to hold him. Instead of a desirable woman, I had a drunkard in my arms. This disgrace, you see, while my mother was surrendering to death. At about this hour, upstairs neighbors came down and relatives arrived and filled the kitchen and the dining room—a deathwatch. I should have been there, not on the far North Side. When I had earned the carfare, I'd still be an hour from home on a streetcar making four stops to the mile.

Toward the last, I was dragging McKern. I kept the street door open with my back while I pulled him into the dim lobby by the arms.

The little girls had been waiting and came down at once. They held the inner door for me while I brought their daddy upstairs with a fireman's-carry and laid him on his bed. The children had had plenty of practice at this. They undressed him down to the long johns and then stood silent on either side of the room. This, for them, was how things were. They took deep oddities calmly, as children generally will. I had spread his winter coat over him.

I had little sympathy for McKern, in the circumstances. I believe I can tell you why: He had surely passed out many times, and he would pass out again, dozens of times before he died. Drunkenness was common and familiar, and therefore accepted, and drunks could count on acceptance and support and relied on it. Whereas if your troubles were uncommon, unfamiliar, you could count on nothing. There was a convention about drunkenness, established in part by drunkards. The founding proposition was that consciousness is terrible. Its lower, impoverished forms are perhaps the worst. Flesh and blood are poor and weak, susceptible to human shock. Here my descendant will hear the voice of Grandfather Louie giving one of his sermons on higher consciousness and interrupting the story he promised to tell. You will hold him to his word, as you have every right to do.

The older girl now spoke to me. She said, "The fellow phoned and said a man was bringing Daddy home, and you'd help with supper if Daddy couldn't cook it."

"Yes. Well . . . ?"

"Only you're not a man—you've got a dress on."

"It looks like it, doesn't it. Don't you worry; I'll come to the kitchen with you."

"Are you a lady?"

"What do you mean—what does it look like? All right, I'm a lady."

"You can eat with us."

"Then show me where the kitchen is."

I followed them down a corridor narrowed by clutter—boxes of canned groceries, soda biscuits, sardines, pop bottles. When I passed the bathroom, I slipped in for quick relief. The door had neither a hook nor a bolt; the string of the ceiling fixture had snapped off. A tiny night-light was plugged into the baseboard. I thanked God it was so dim. I put up the board while raising my skirt, and when I had begun I heard one of the children behind me. Over my shoulder I saw that it was the younger one, and as I turned my back (*everything* was happening today) I said, "Don't come in here." But she squeezed past and sat on the edge of the tub. She grinned at me. She was expecting her second teeth. Today all females were making sexual fun of me, and even the infants were looking lewd. I stopped, letting the dress fall, and said to her, "What are you laughing about?"

"If you were a girl, you'd of sat down."

The kid wanted me to understand that she knew what

she had seen. She pressed her fingers over her mouth, and I turned and went to the kitchen.

There the older girl was lifting the black cast-iron skillet with both hands. On dripping paper, the pork chops were laid out—nearby, a Mason jar of grease. I was competent enough at the gas range, which shone with old filth. Loath to touch the pork with my fingers, I forked the meat into the spitting fat. The chops turned my stomach. My thought was, "I'm into it now, up to the ears." The drunk in his bed, the dim secret toilet, the glaring tungsten twist over the gas range, the sputtering droplets stinging the hands. The older girl said, "There's plenty for you. Daddy won't be eating dinner."

"No, not me. I'm not hungry," I said.

All that my upbringing held in horror geysered up, my throat filling with it, my guts griping.

The children sat at the table, an enamel rectangle. Thick plates and glasses, a waxed package of sliced white bread, a milk bottle, a stick of butter, the burning fat clouding the room. The girls sat beneath the smoke, slicing their meat. I brought them salt and pepper from the range. They ate without conversation. My chore (my duty) done, there was nothing to keep me. I said, "I have to go."

I looked in at McKern, who had thrown down the coat and taken off his drawers. The parboiled face, the short nose pointed sharply, the life signs in the throat, the broken look of his neck, the black hair of his belly, the short cylinder between his legs ending in a spiral of loose skin, the white shine of the shins, the tragic expression of his feet. There was a stack of pennies on his bedside table. I helped myself to carfare but had no pocket for the coins. I opened the hall closet feeling quickly for a coat I might borrow, a pair of slacks. Whatever I took, Philip could return to the Greek barman tomorrow. I pulled a trench coat from a hanger, and a pair of trousers. For the third time I put on stranger's clothing—this is no time to mention stripes or checks or make exquisite notations. Escaping, desperate, I struggled into the pants on the landing, tucking in the dress, and pulled on the coat as I jumped down the stairs, knotting tight the belt and sticking the pennies, a fistful of them, into my pocket.

But still I went back to the alley under the woman's window to see if her light was on, and also to look for pages. The thief or pimp perhaps had chucked them away, or maybe they had dropped out when he snatched the sheepskin. Her window was dark. I found nothing on the ground. You may think this obsessive crankiness, a crazy dependency on words, on printed matter. But remember, there were no redeemers in the streets, no guides, no confessors, comforters, enlighteners, communicants to turn to. You had to take teaching wherever you could find it. Under the library dome downtown, in mosaic letters, there was a message from Milton, so moving but perhaps of no utility, perhaps aggravating difficulties: A GOOD BOOK, it said, IS THE PRECIOUS LIFE'S BLOOD OF A MASTER SPIRIT.

These are the plain facts, they have to be uttered. This, remember, is the New World, and here one of its mysterious cities. I should have hurried directly, to catch a car. Instead I was in a back alley hunting pages that would in any case have blown away.

I went back to Broadway—it *was* very broad—and waited on a safety island. Then the car came clanging, red, swaying on its trucks, a piece of Iron Age technology, double cane seats framed in brass. Rush hour was long past. I sat by a window, homebound, with flashes of thought like tracer bullets slanting into distant darkness. Like London in wartime. At home, what story would I tell? I wouldn't tell any. I never did. It was assumed anyway that I was lying. While I believed in honor, I did often lie. Is a life without lying conceivable? It was easier to lie than to explain myself. My father had one set of assumptions, I had another. Corresponding premises were not to be found.

I owed five dollars to Behrens. But I knew where my mother secretly hid her savings. Because I looked into all books, I had found the money in her *mahzor,* the prayer book for the High Holidays, the days of awe. As yet I hadn't taken anything. She had hoped until this final illness to buy passage to Europe to see her mother and her sister. When she died I would turn the money over to my father, except for ten dollars, five for the florist and the rest for Von Hügel's *Eternal Life* and *The World as Will and Idea.*

The after-dinner guests and cousins would be gone when I reached home. My father would be on the lookout for me. It was the rear porch door that was locked after dark. The kitchen door was generally off the latch. I could climb over the wooden partition between the stairs and the porch. I often did that. Once you got your foot on the doorknob you could pull yourself over the partition and drop to the porch without noise. Then I could see into the kitchen and slip in as soon as my patrolling father had left it. The bedroom shared by all three brothers was just off the kitchen. I could borrow my brother Len's cast-off winter coat tomorrow. I knew which closet it hung in. If my father should catch me I could expect hard blows on my shoulders, on the top of my head, on my face. But if my mother had, tonight, just died, he wouldn't hit me.

This was when the measured, reassuring, sleep-inducing turntable of days became a whirlpool, a vortex darkening toward the bottom. I had had only the anonymous pages in the pocket of my lost sheepskin to interpret it to me. They told me that the truth of the universe was inscribed into our very bones. That the human skeleton was itself a hieroglyph. That everything we had ever known on earth was shown to us in the first days after death. That our experience of the world was desired by the cosmos, and needed by it for its own renewal.

I do not think that these pages, if I hadn't lost them, would have persuaded me forever or made the life I led a different one.

I am writing this account, or statement, in response to an eccentric urge swelling toward me from the earth itself.

Failed my mother! That may mean, will mean, little or nothing to you, my only child, reading this document.

I myself know the power of nonpathos, in these low, devious days.

On the streetcar, heading home, I braced myself, but all my preparations caved in like sand diggings. I got down at the North Avenue stop, avoiding my reflection in the shop-windows. After a death, mirrors were immediately covered. I can't say what this pious superstition means. Will the soul of your dead be reflected in a looking glass, or is this custom a check to the vanity of the living?

I ran home, approached by the back alley, made no noise on the wooden backstairs, reached for the top of the partition, placed my foot on the white porcelain doorknob, went over the top without noise, and dropped down on our porch. I didn't follow the plan I had laid for avoiding my father. There were people sitting at the kitchen table. I went straight in. My father rose from his chair and hurried toward me. His fist was ready. I took off my tam or woolen beret and when he hit me on the head the blow filled me with gratitude. If my mother had already died, he would have embraced me instead.

Well, they're all gone now, and I have made my preparations. I haven't left a large estate, and this is why I have written this memoir, a sort of addition to your legacy.

ABOUT THE AUTHOR

SAUL BELLOW was awarded the Nobel Prize for Literature in 1976. His novel *Humboldt's Gift* won the Pulitzer Prize the previous year. He is the only novelist to receive three National Book Awards, for *The Adventures of Augie March, Herzog,* and *Mr. Sammler's Planet.*